I0524158

The First Gift of Christmas

A Maple Ridge Romance

For information contact:

Providence Media LLC

http://www.providencemediallc.com

Cover designed by Art by Jules ©

Edited by: Julia Howard & Ryley McCluskey

ISBN: 978-0-9989550-1-8

Library of Congress Control Number: 2019

Published by Providence Media LLC through Ingram Spark

This book is only possible through the great gift that God has given me as a writer. He is the inspiration for everything I do and say.

Chapter One

"5, 6, 7, 8..." Lydia Foster called out as she clapped in time to the music. The dancers twirled and jumped, trying their hardest to be perfectly in sync with the swells of music. They were also trying to keep their anxieties from intensifying under Lydia's scrutinizing gaze.

The mirrored rehearsal room echoed with the sounds of pointe shoes hitting the floor in perfect rhythm to the melody. Occasionally, Lydia tapped her hand against her leg to keep time as she surveyed her second-to-last audition group of the evening. She was tired, as were the auditioning dancers. It had been a long afternoon and evening of running through choreography.

Audition season had begun, which in Maple Ridge, took on a whole new meaning for dancers during the holiday season rush. For most, August began the process of aspiring dancers vying for the role of Clara or the Sugar Plum Fairy in the Nutcracker. However, with Lydia's reputation for her annual holiday celebrations, dancers had begun to step outside of tradition and come to Maple Ridge with a very specific goal in mind. The goal of obtaining a position in her *Magical Holiday Celebration*.

This annual performance was the biggest, most elaborate event west of Boston and people from all around the surrounding area came to see the small town decked out in Christmas grandeur. Showcasing not only dancers, but also singers, musicians, and performers of all ages and backgrounds, the *Magical Holiday Celebration* was a unique festival of the arts. It also supported many of the small businesses in town, which was a huge bonus.

As Lydia observed from her spot at the head of the room, her watchful expression softened as she smiled encouragingly at the dancers. She had to constantly remind herself to smile. A more serious person by nature, Lydia's face didn't always convey what she was thinking. When she did smile though, it was the type of smile that put others at ease, making her green eyes sparkle.

The dancers visibly relaxed at this smile and pushed through the last few steps of the audition choreography. Upon finishing, the dancers curtsied and made space for the final group.

"Ready and, 5, 6, 7, 8…" Lydia counted the final group down as the same music began to play.

Remember to smile at them. Lydia inwardly reminded herself for the millionth time that evening.

The music filled the room, and the echoing footsteps resumed. Lydia tried to force the fatigue away and stifled a yawn behind her hand. *Father, give me the energy I need to continue.* This audition was important, and she just needed to get through one more hour.

Maple Ridge, being a smaller, lesser-known town west of Boston, benefited from the increase in tourism and holiday guests. The theme was the only part of the performance known to the general public until the day before Christmas Eve. Everything else was kept under wraps, building up suspense until the last moment.

This year's performance was expected to be the best event yet, as there was more pressure to succeed. Lydia had received a call from the artistic director of Boston Ballet who had notified her that he was planning on attending the performance and offering Lydia a shot at a job with the company. The job was assistant choreographer for their spring season, and it was a dream come true for Lydia. The artistic director, Anthony Fairfax, was also aware that Lydia's performances attracted some of the best dancers in the surrounding area. He was willing to offer an opportunity for them to audition for scholarships to Boston Ballet, which rarely happened outside the company.

Mr. Fairfax was intrigued by Lydia, and the news of her performances had reached him throughout the past four years. Her unique style of choreography was well-known and many of the dancers at Boston Ballet had been a part of at least one of these performances. More pressure was placed on this year's performance to succeed, which meant better, more elaborate sets, costumes, and decorations. Advertising was more generous for both the event and local businesses, piquing curiosity with the build-up of anticipation surrounding the announcement of the theme in the next day or so.

Lydia took a deep breath to settle some of the anxieties that tightened her chest as she thought about it and scribbled a few notes as she observed. She paid close attention to the dancers who showed potential to be, not just great dancers, but also great performers. Dancers often forgot that acting was an essential part of any excellent ballet performance. As difficult as it was for her, she eliminated those who might not be the best fit despite their dance abilities.

Preliminary eliminations began and Lydia ran through a final group piece that was slightly more complicated than the prior choreography. The remaining dancers, though fatigued, were hopeful that they had an even better chance now at being cast.

This process always made the dancers nervous as Lydia chose to weave through them to get a closer look as they danced. This was when she schooled her features to be less analytical and more relaxed. It helped that she always chose her favorite choreography selection for last. The love she exuded for her job and the choreography showed plainly on her face, watching it come alive.

Lydia had always made it a goal of hers, since opening her own dance studio, to make everyone who entered feel welcome and loved. Even when auditioning for a huge event that required eliminations, dancers didn't feel rejected but thrilled to have been given a chance to show their best. Lydia always made sure to encourage those who had been eliminated to keep pursuing their love of dance and to try again the next year. And most of them did.

As a small-town dance teacher, Lydia realized the importance of cultivating the natural talents of each of her students and the dancers who came to audition. She saw each dancer for their unique gifts and talents which allowed her to build greater complexity into her performances and choreography. As much as the structure of choreography was a joy, Lydia found that spontaneity added a little spice to her shows, highlighting each dancer differently based on their talent in performance and dance. God had blessed her with the opportunity to help her students realize the gifts He created them with. It was the best part of her job.

As the music came to its conclusion, Lydia glanced at the clock on the wall, which showed that it was time to end auditions for the day.

Perfect timing. Lydia smiled to herself as the dancers ended in a beautiful pose, the room suddenly quiet. The dancers immediately curtsied and bowed, clapping as the audition came to a close, taking deep breaths to calm their nerves.

"Wonderful job, everyone! Thank you so much for coming out and auditioning today. It was such a pleasure seeing such beautiful talent represented in all of you. You make my job very difficult."

Everyone laughed softly.

"In the meantime, I will email you with my final decision on the casting this weekend. Now please feel free to take time in here to stretch out a bit before you head home. I know that some of you probably have quite the drive ahead of you. And please don't forget to drink water, catch your breath, and relax. The rehearsal room is yours for the next half hour." Lydia smiled again and the dancers thanked her, some gathering up their belongings to head out, others staying behind to take Lydia up on her offer to stretch or talk with her.

Half an hour later, the last few dancers gathered their belongings and exited the studio. Lydia took some notes on her clipboard full of scribbles, design doodles, and various other holiday planning papers, swatches, and receipts. Tapping her pen a couple times on the table and nodding almost imperceptibly to herself in satisfaction, she gathered up all her papers and began to tidy up a little before flipping the lights off and heading for the main lobby.

Her smile and perky demeanor fell slightly, her eyes tired from a long day of quick observation. She was exhausted. Her smile, though genuine during the auditions, was beginning to cause her cheeks to ache and her throat was dry and voice slightly scratchy from calling out choreography to the large groups. It was time for some rest.

The temptation to curl up in her bed with a cup of tea and a good book was strong. However, it was probably more likely she would end up collapsing and falling asleep right away instead. Entering the lobby, covering a larger yawn than before with the back of her hand, Lydia recognized a familiar face, and a small smile replaced the yawn.

Kate, Lydia's dearest friend and business partner, had arrived an hour earlier to finish up some end-of-month paperwork and was waiting to see how the day's auditions went.

"You had a lot of dancers show up today. I don't know how you do these auditions all on your own. I do think I have a good eye for talent even though dancing is not really my forte. I wish you'd just let me help, or at least one of the other teachers."

Lydia sighed and plopped down into a comfy chair resisting the urge to close her eyes. One of her weaknesses was releasing control, especially of her performances.

"Did you make any cuts today, or did you keep them all?" Kate asked teasingly, knowing her friend's desire to avoid having to disappoint anyone.

"Ha, ha, very funny. I'll have to get someone to help with the auditions next year. I feel like it drains me more and more every year. With the added pressure of Mr. Fairfax coming, it makes auditioning and eliminating even harder. The groups just keep getting bigger and bigger." Lydia stretched her neck and yawned again, not bothering to stifle it this time, before continuing. "To answer your question, *yes*, I did eliminate quite a few dancers today, actually." Lydia stuck her tongue out playfully at Kate. "I have maybe twenty definite choices but that still leaves quite a few spots left to cast. I just don't know how to decide between the couple hundred dancers I've seen the past few days. There are so many talented dancers, it seems a shame to let any of them go."

Kate pat Lydia on the shoulder. "You always have next year. And most of the dancers always come back. So, there's time for each and every dancer to have a shot in one of the performances."

"Yeah, I know, and that's what I tell each of the ones I eliminate. There were so many familiar faces today from last year. I do still have Saturday to get the final casting list out to them so that gives me enough time for more eliminations, I suppose." Lydia paused thoughtfully when she suddenly remembered another reason why she was happy to see Kate.

"By the way, have you chosen a theme from the choices I gave you?"

Kate laughed to herself thinking of the hours going back and forth between the two theme choices Lydia had given her. The theme for the *Magical Holiday Celebration* hinged on Kate. It was her responsibility since Lydia's indecision and overly creative mind couldn't settle on just one. Kate, on the other hand, was creative in her own way but was definitely more decisive.

Her mind went to all the opportunities for business growth and advertising that could come out of the theme they finally chose. As a finance analyst, this was Kate's sweet spot. Every year, Lydia sent Kate two, sometimes three, possible choices. The decision usually required Kate to do a little research and draw out a few designs to see how it would work, logistically. Normally, she had no problem choosing a theme and was ready within a couple days, however, this year, she kept putting it off, unable to make up her mind. Lydia presented her with two excellent choices that provided so much potential for the performance and town that it was a difficult decision to make.

"Yes! I believe I've *finally* chosen a theme!"

"Let me guess…you want to do Peppermint Dreams?" Lydia incorporated sweeping hand motions to add flair to her ideas. "Hot cocoa bar with themed peppermint candies, sweets, and baked goods. Ooohh…and a little peppermint village with a peppermint castle and peppermint king and queen and…"

Kate held up her hands to stop Lydia's creative ramblings, "woah, woah, woah. I can see you haven't given these themes any thought at all." Kate smirked and looked pointedly at Lydia.

Lydia bit her bottom lip and looked guiltily at Kate, holding in laughter. "Nooooo…"

Both friends dissolved into giggles.

"Well, that's not the theme I chose, so you should probably just bank those ideas until another year. Besides, don't you think that having a peppermint kingdom is a little cheesy?"
Lydia gaped in mock offense, hand to chest.

Ignoring her, Kate continued, "I actually decided to give the 12 Days of Christmas a try. At first, I thought it would be too involved and difficult, but then I started sketching it out and thinking about the set designs and everything. How the businesses in town could use the theme in their promotional materials and gifts. I can't even tell you how many times I listened to the song." Kate rolled her eyes making Lydia chuckle. "I really think we could pull it off. It seems like a fantastic choice for a surprise performance because you can do so much with it. Plus, it's not just one theme, technically it's kind of like having twelve different themes wrapped into one. Just think, each day in the song would have dancers in costumes relating to each gift and they can perform on different types of sets. We could even have the sets different heights to create depth. And can you even imagine how cool the Christmas Eve party would be?! I think that it's perfect, and nobody would expect it. Or at least, they wouldn't expect what we would do with it."

Lydia's eyebrows were raised in amusement, a smile playing at her lips. When Kate paused for breath, Lydia responded with humor, "yes, I can imagine all of that. In fact, I think I've rubbed off on you a little. You pretty much have the whole thing worked out; I don't think there's much else for me to do." Lydia shrugged and began gathering her things.

"Well, I take that as a compliment then." Kate tilted her chin up in pride.

"If you're up for the challenge, then I am too."

"Hey, this means that you'll have a lot more spots to fill for the dancing. I guess the elimination process will be a lot easier on you this year." Kate winked at Lydia who was yawning yet again. "Let's get you home." She helped Lydia heave herself out of the chair, her hands full, and headed out to lock up for the evening.

"So, what are your plans for the next couple of weeks?"

"Well, tomorrow we have to audition the musicians. I think we have about eight or nine high school orchestral groups coming so we'll be pretty busy all day." Lydia paused, shifting what she carried into one arm to fish her car keys out of her purse.

"I like auditioning the musicians. Most of them prepare such lovely pieces." Kate crinkled her nose. "I just hope that the band that played those awful rock songs took the hint and won't be coming back this year. I literally thought my ears were bleeding."

Lydia laughed, "I guess that's what we get for choosing a Rock 'n Roll Nutcracker." Lydia found her keys and continued, "For the next couple weeks, I'll be choreographing, depending on how much I procrastinate and then we have our crew meeting on Friday. Our first rehearsal will have to be earlier this year due to all the moving parts of this performance. I'll just plan on having our first dance rehearsal next Monday and choreograph as I go."

"Are you sure it won't be too stressful for you to choreograph like that?"

"Honestly, it probably will be, but I've been through worse, and it seems the best option I have at the moment." Lydia sounded a little unsure. To be honest, she was unsure of whether she could make that work. Normally, she would have a whole month to choreograph everything and make sure it was all sound before getting the dancers involved. But this year was different.

"Maybe next year we should start auditions earlier."

"Yeah, you're probably right. I keep thinking that I'm right on track with deadlines and then we get down to the wire and I'm scrambling. But then again, there is still that added pressure of having to perform for a very prominent gentleman."

Kate blew out a breath. "True…well, if choreographing as you go is okay with you, then I'll help you out as much as I can. I've gathered at least ten more people who are willing to help with the event this year. Ellie and Peter are ready to start rehearsal with the musicians and singers as soon as they're cast, and we'll get a room ready for them."

"Wonderful! All that extra help is going to be amazing! I'll make sure to set aside a rehearsal room for them and shift around some of the regular dance classes to avoid any overlapping in the schedule. They can probably start rehearsing in the next two weeks or so."

Ellie and Peter Miller were the resident vocal coach and musician, respectively. They had met, studied together, and fell in love at Julliard before deciding to move to Maple Ridge once they got married.

Lydia and Kate usually only hired the same eight to ten crew members every year to accomplish everything required to pull off the big event. Having more people added to their crew meant better, more elaborate sets, costumes, and decorations. The crew didn't mind giving up the thrill of surprise for themselves because they loved gifting it to everyone else.

As successful as the previous year was, they all found that a lot was left to the last minute, causing people to rush around, and a couple of near-disastrous occurrences. Thus, Kate fit ten more crew members into the budget to ensure everything was completed quickly and efficiently. Hitches were to be expected, but Kate liked to limit them as much as possible, especially this year.

"We both have a lot of work ahead of us!" Kate took a deep breath and laced her arm in Lydia's.

"Tell me about it! I still have to meet with Ian about preparations for the Christmas Eve party. We'll have to schedule our annual tasting at his place. He will be so excited about the theme! Can you just imagine little hors d'oeuvres and desserts themed as each gift?"

"Oh…that would be so adorable, and fancy." Kate mimed eating a small dessert out of the palm of her hand. They both giggled as they halted by their cars.

"I'll also be working on the countdown to Christmas calendar, planning out the next couple months with as much detail as I can so that we can start checking things off."

"I need to finalize the budget for materials but that probably won't get done until after our meeting on Friday. Thankfully, with your increase in students and my increase in clients, we'll be able to do more this year. I do think that we should continue to use the leftover decorations and things from other performances as much as we can though."

"That won't be a problem. Some things are getting a bit old. I think that the garland is falling apart so I should get some replacements for that. But I'm sure we have plenty of decorations that can be repurposed. Trevor already has all the sets from last year to repurpose. For now, I just want to shower and crawl into bed with some tea." Lydia yawned again.

The sun had begun to dip low in the sky, casting golden rays over the trees and roofs of buildings.

"I don't blame you! It's been a long couple of days." Kate wrapped Lydia in a hug and said goodnight. "I'll see you tomorrow. Get some rest tonight, Lydia. No planning!" Kate pointed an accusatory finger at Lydia and smirked.

Lydia put the hand holding her car keys up in response. "I will rest, I promise. No planning. See you tomorrow."

The friends parted with a wave and got into their cars.

The sun created a beautiful orangey glow above the trees, silhouetted against the horizon. It was starting to get dark sooner. Summer was over, and autumn was beginning to take hold of the little town. It was such a beautiful time of year and one of Lydia's favorites.

As she drove home, Lydia started formulating ideas in her mind about what she wanted the performance to look like. It didn't matter how much she tried to push the planning aside, she was excited to start putting her imaginative efforts into creating yet another amazing holiday season! But, sticking with her promise to Kate, Lydia cuddled up in bed and immediately found herself dozing off, leaving her cup of tea untouched and cooling on the side table.

Chapter Two

Photography prints and canvases were hung on the perfectly white walls of a small, brand-new, local art studio in Boston. The grand opening had gone off without a hitch and the featured artist and photographer, Jordan Williams, was thrilled with the turn-out. As an up-and-coming artist, his manager and old college friend Sarah had jumped at the opportunity to get him involved, especially since Jordan had never been a part of a solo art showcase before. Other showcases featured his travel photography, which is what he was best known for. But since adding other mediums to his art focus, he was not getting as much attention.

It was only by chance that Sarah discovered this adorable art gallery and saw that the owner was looking for artists interested in showcasing their works for their grand opening. She had been able to talk the owner into allowing Jordan a solo showcase, which meant that everyone would see Jordan's art and only his art. It both filled him with excitement and dread.

The thought of parting with his art had seemed a likely prospect but a sad one. They were good "friends" and represented many memories for him. As much as he tried, Jordan always got a little too attached to his works. However, in spite of his attachment, he had sold a couple of his prints during the grand opening to some very enthusiastic buyers. At least he could be happy knowing they went to people who would greatly appreciate them.

There was still an element of insecurity about his art. His photography was well-received and featured in many magazines, books, and advertisements, but he felt that his other art wasn't as polished. At the same time, it made him happy. Jordan loved experimenting with watercolors, acrylics, and charcoal. It was his way of escape which, since his big break up from his high school sweetheart, was something he turned to more and more. It had almost broken him and the only way to deal was through escape.

Adjusting a new print on the wall to replace one sold the night before, Jordan sighed imperceptibly to himself. Instead of thinking of the art that sold, he was thinking that he might run out of pieces to hang in their place. The plan was to allow the showcase to go for the entirety of a week, with the possibility of being the gallery's permanent featured artist depending on how well his art was received. It was highly generous of the owner and Jordan didn't take the opportunity for granted.

"I think it's straight." Sarah had snuck up behind him and was looking up at the print, finger to mouth in thought.

Jordan turned and she winked at him and smiled. He smiled back, eyes crinkling at the corners.

"I was just thinking about how many pieces I'll have to work on to fill empty spots if they keep selling like they did last night." He put his hands on his hips and surveyed the studio. "The artist sure knows what he's doing."

Sarah nodded her head and hummed but didn't say anything. He looked at her again and smiled his charming smile which nobody could resist.

"If you're not careful, you're going to charm your way through Maple Ridge and come back with a line of women following you everywhere."

Jordan blew out a playfully exasperated breath and waved his hand in dismissal.

Sarah chuckled to herself. "I still can't believe you're going to be ducking out of the holiday season completely. What if someone wants to commission a work or another studio calls me up for a show? The holiday season *is* one of the biggest seasons of the year, you know."

"I don't know…I guess we'll figure that out if and when it comes to it. I'm sorry that I won't be here, but I haven't seen my cousin in over a year and it's time that I take a break from the city to clear my head. I trust you to handle everything else just fine. I can't put this off for another week. And I promise that if someone really important wants to host a show, I'll make the trip out for you. I'll be bringing along some supplies, so I can work on commissions while I'm gone, and I'll set aside a time to deliver them to you." Jordan grinned at her as she rolled her eyes in response to his charm.

"Okay, I'll accept it. Not that I have any say in the matter anyway. I just wish you weren't going to be gone for three whole months. Don't you think that's a little overkill? I mean, don't get me wrong, I love my family and everything but that's a long time."

Jordan chuckled as Sarah stuck the title cards to the wall under the new additions.

"You could just go for Thanksgiving and come back after Christmas."

"I know. But to be fair, I did give you plenty of warning that this was happening." Jordan pointed at Sarah teasingly and she swatted his finger away. He became serious again. "A few months with Claire in a town in the middle of nowhere will help me refocus and figure things out. You know how distracted and uninspired I've been lately. And things in the art world haven't exactly been easy. I'm barely making rent."

"You're right, and I know. You haven't quite been yourself lately and I know how hard it's been for you. I still think you should pick up more travel photography." Sarah knew how important family was to Jordan and that travel photography would take him away from them for too long. When he didn't answer, she changed the subject. "Just make sure your phone is on, or at least that you have service so I can contact you in case any surprises come up." She smiled her big, friendly grin.

"Where do you think I'll be? It's a small town, not the middle of a canyon." They both laughed. Jordan checked his watch, "Shoot! I should get going. You're a real gem, you know that?" Jordan kissed Sarah on the cheek before rushing toward the door of the showroom, grabbing his coat on the way.

"What would you do without me?" Sarah smiled and waved her hand nonchalantly like royalty. Jordan shook his head and smiled. Sarah was always a good-humored tease. "Have a wonderful Thanksgiving…and Christmas!"

"Same to you! I'll see you when I drop off new pieces." Waving to Jordan, Sarah smirked and went to take notes in her planner and adjust a few things on the walls.

The chilled air hit Jordan's face as he jogged to his car. Hopefully, Claire wouldn't be upset that he was running late. No chance! His cousin was the sweetest person he knew. But when it came to hot meals, she insisted on punctuality. He knew that she had planned on having a full-blown dinner awaiting his arrival even though he insisted she not go to the trouble.

Jordan smiled to himself as he thought about seeing his cousin again. Every year for the holidays, Jordan got together with his parents for a traditional holiday season together. But this year they had decided to spend a couple of months in Europe instead. It had been his mother's dream to travel to all the countries she'd read about, ending up in Germany for Christmas. Since they were newly retired, they both thought it the perfect opportunity to make her dream a reality. Even though Jordan was invited to join them, he decided to remain at home. He didn't want to be a third wheel during their second honeymoon.

It was a little depressing that he was going to be virtually alone during the holiday season for the first time in his life. That was until his cousin, Claire, invited him to her home in Maple

Ridge for the month of October through Thanksgiving. Jordan's parents felt comforted by the fact that he would have someone to enjoy the season with and left without qualms of leaving their only son behind.

Jordan and Claire had always been close as children. More like siblings than cousins. Now that Jordan lived in Boston, and his job required some amount of travel inside and outside the states, they hadn't seen each other in over a year. This was his chance to spend time catching up with her on everything he had missed, including her new marriage. Claire's invitation came at such an opportune time that he wouldn't turn it down for anything. In fact, she was so excited that he had accepted her offer that she extended the invitation to Christmas as well, seeing as he would be alone for both holidays. How could he say no? She was his favorite cousin, after all.

~

Auditions were over for the season, the crew meeting was a success, and Lydia was relieved. The casting list was finalized, and emails were sent out to either congratulate those who made it in the performance or let them down gently, encouraging them to audition again the next year.

Lydia clicked send on her final email. "Done!" She rubbed her hands together in preparation for her next task. "Now onto the creative process. Where do I begin?"

She shuffled a few papers on her desk and the overwhelming feeling of all the work awaiting her made a flutter of doubt settle around her heart. Lydia thrived on being busy, but this was a feat she didn't really consider until everything was all laid out before her. To add to her regular tasks, she was taking on a more complicated level of choreography that would take her a long time to get right.

Taking a breath to relieve the tension, she started taking notes on some key choreography points she wanted to highlight for each gift in the song. As she continued to sketch and write, inspiration kicked in full force. Lydia built in dance styles that brought the gifts in the song to life using floating movements, suspension, jumps, and lifts. She wanted the dancers to look like birds and toys, not only through movement but also by using face paint and elaborate costuming. During auditions, she had made note of each dancer's various strengths and weaknesses that she could utilize in the choreography.

Two hours later, she had an outline of the performance. She took a deep breath and stretched her neck side to side. "I think that's enough brainstorming for one day." A little sticky note on her calendar attracted her attention. "Oh, shoot!" She snatched the sticky note and frowned in disappointment. She had totally forgotten that their regular set painter had moved into the city a few months ago and wouldn't be available to help them out this year.

It had been hard enough finding a set painter before Lucy, now what was she supposed to do? Having another item added to her to-do list made that knot of anxiety return to her stomach. She'd just have to delegate. There wasn't enough time for her to choreograph, teach, and find an artist who wasn't booked up already for the holidays.

Lydia dialed Kate.

"Hey what's up?" Kate's voice sounded on the line.

"Well, I was just about to call it a day and remembered that Lucy isn't here to paint the sets."

"Yeah, I had forgotten that too." She was quiet for a moment, then she sighed. "We've relied on her for so long that it totally slipped my mind. What do you want to do about it?"

"Would Steve mind taking over the job of finding a replacement? I just don't think I can handle it with everything else I'm juggling."

"I'm sure he'd be happy to help!" Kate's enthusiastic tone released a little of her growing anxiety. Lydia breathed a sigh of relief.

"Thank you! Tell him that I greatly appreciate it."

Kate laughed, "I'll let him know."

"Alright, well that's a great load off my mind! Thanks!"

"No problem! Hey, just remember, Mr. Fairfax isn't coming to see how perfect the sets are. He's coming to see how perfect the dancers are."

"Well, that doesn't put any pressure on me at all."

Kate laughed again, "Sorry. I just don't want you getting your hopes up in case we can't find a seasoned professional."

Lydia sighed. She didn't like compromising on the quality of her performances. But Kate was right. "I'll try to accept it. I guess I should get my dancers perfect then." Lydia infused playful sarcasm into her words.

"You better! Pressure's on!"

Lydia shook her head and laughed at her friend. "Talk to you later, Kate." Lydia hung up the phone and took a deep breath, closing her eyes in relief.

Steve was Kate's boyfriend. Two years ago, Lydia had introduced them. The moment they met, Kate knew that Steve was a guy that she could spend the rest of her life with. He was funny, sweet, and sincere – all the characteristics Kate had trouble finding in most of the guys she had dated in the past.

Lydia loved seeing Kate and Steve so happy together, but there was a slight tinge of disappointment that she had not yet found someone special in her own life. The dance studio demanded a lot of her time, taking the focus off finding love. Or was it that she was choosing to use the dance studio as an excuse? At this point, she couldn't tell the difference. It wasn't exactly easy to meet eligible bachelors in Maple Ridge. Most were either already dating or married.

She had never actually searched for a relationship, and she didn't really travel outside of Maple Ridge often enough to meet anyone new. Her only hope was that someone would dance into her life and sweep her off her feet, as cheesy as that sounded. Maybe a handsome tourist would come to town for the holidays. Was that reaching too far? It hadn't happened so far…

It didn't matter. For now, her focus needed to remain on the *Magical Holiday Celebration*, and she had no intentions of letting anything or anyone distract her from making it the best performance it could be. She couldn't handle any more anxieties clouding her thoughts. Her determination to remain focused on her choreography meant that her heart and mind had to be clear. Distractions almost always led to mistakes, and she wanted everything to be perfect. Even though she knew Kate was teasing, a huge part of Lydia placed pressure on herself to succeed and be as close to perfect as possible. A lot was riding on this performance. The success of their town's tourism and the small businesses depended on how successful the holiday performance was. Even though that responsibility didn't really land on her shoulders, it still weighed her down, making failure not an option. On top of that, her career as a choreographer was now under scrutiny.

Chapter Three

Claire, a beautiful, blonde-haired woman with the most adorable dimples ran out to greet her cousin the moment he pulled into her driveway. He couldn't help but laugh to himself as she bounced on her toes in excitement as he turned his car off and got out.

"You're here! It's so good to see you!" She slammed into him, pulling him into the biggest, and tightest, bear hug.

He shook with genuine laughter at his cousin's enthusiasm as he hugged her back. "You haven't changed a bit, Claire." He managed to pull out of the hug and hold her at arm's length. "There is, however, this new glow about you. Marriage looks beautiful on you." Jordan smiled, his blue-green eyes crinkling at the corners as they did when he was at his happiest.

Claire waved the compliment away and gave him a sly smile. "We saw each other at the wedding a year and a half ago, silly."

"Yeah, but now you've settled into this new phase of life."

"It has been pretty great!" Claire grabbed his arm and began leading him toward the front door.

"Thank you for having me. It's so good to get away from everything back home and breathe in some fresh air for once. Hopefully I won't overstay my welcome."

"Pfft! Nonsense! You could never overstay your welcome. What are the holidays for if not to spend it with those you love most."

As Claire opened the front door and was joined by her husband Kyle, Jordan took in the incredible scent of pot roast and freshly baked bread and his mouth began to water. His cousin was an amazing cook. She always took pleasure in hosting guests and providing them with meals. Admittedly, Jordan was selfishly looking forward to having homemade meals again. Claire even made all his favorite dishes to welcome him, all wholly enjoyed as conversation flowed over the dinner table.

Once everything had been cleaned up and Jordan had taken time to unpack, they gathered by the fireplace with some warmed apple cider.

Jordan sighed in satisfaction, "That was a wonderful meal, Claire! I haven't had food like that in a long time. You're going to spoil me. I might never leave."

Claire beamed, "I figured you hadn't had a proper homemade meal in a while with all the preparing you've been doing for your showcase, the traveling, and late nights. You're not exactly the most stellar chef as I recall."

"I'm getting better." Jordan tried to sound offended but could only smile because he knew she was right. He hid his smile behind a sip of his cider. It had been such a long time since he had felt this comfortable and at peace. It was good that he made this trip. He needed this time to regain his sense of purpose in life and hopefully some confidence in his ability as an artist.

"A lot's changed in Maple Ridge since you've been here last." Claire disturbed the quiet that had settled over the room.

"Mmhmm. The town looks great. There are a lot fewer empty buildings than last time and definitely more tourists meandering around town. I also saw some advertisements for something based on the 12 Days of Christmas. Looks like you have a big event coming up."

Claire looked at him with a mischievous smirk and he knew something was up. "The increase in tourism and business growth has a lot to do with the town dance teacher. She's quite the success, bringing in more business during the holiday season with her annual *Magical Holiday Celebration*. That's what those advertisements are for. They're announcing their theme for the year."

He put his cup down and looked at Claire suspiciously. "Well, that's great for the town."

"I've met her a couple of times but don't know her all that well. She was awfully nice and is well-liked by everyone. Her studio is even a Christian business. She's not afraid of sharing her faith. Maybe you'll have a chance to meet her while you're here." Claire hid a small smile by sipping her cider.

"Very smooth, Claire. I see what you're doing, and you can just stop it right now. I'm not falling into another one of your crazy schemes to get me on a blind date." His eyes narrowed in playful annoyance.

He was the older cousin, but Claire always felt that it was her duty to help Jordan fall in love. During his last visit, she had set him up on a blind date with a woman who, in Claire's words was "pretty, successful, and just his type." Instead, she was just the opposite of his type. She ate right off his plate during dinner while obnoxiously talking about her exes and the worst dates she'd ever been on. It was a nightmarish two hours. To be fair to Claire, however, she hadn't really known the woman for very long.

Claire looked straight at him with the most angelic, innocent expression, "I don't know what you're talking about. I just think that you guys might hit it off. I mean, you're both artists in a sense and love creating for other people."

"Uh-huh, I'm sure."

When he didn't respond with anything more, Claire conceded defeat, "Okay, okay. I just think it's time for you to move on from Kathy. You guys broke up four years ago. I know you took the breakup hard, but I feel like if I don't intervene, you'll never find anyone to share your life with. Your job isn't going to keep you warm at night or greet you when you come home."

The old sting of realization that he was lonely hit his chest. Yes, it had been four years, but he was going to propose to her for goodness' sake. He had his life all mapped out. Propose, marry, spend a year traveling the world and taking photos of the most romantic spots, start a family, yada, yada. It was a good plan until Kathy came to him and told him that the long distance was too hard and that she had met someone else. He felt the familiar pain again. He was terrified of blindly putting his heart on the line again. And it was because of that that he decided to stop traveling so much for work. He couldn't bear to ruin another relationship because he wasn't there to support it.

"Jordan?" Claire had noticed that her words had struck a tender point as his features slowly settled into a thoughtful and somewhat sad expression.

Jordan cleared his throat and shoved all the memories down again, forcing a smile on his face. "I know you want to see me happy, and I love you for that. I'm just begging you to never set me up on a date again." His humor returned.

Claire laughed, "Okay, I promise. But anything could happen in three months." She winked at him.

She might be right. Three months was a long time to spend in an area where everyone knew everyone else. Eventually he'd run into this dance teacher, whether by accident or by Claire's devising. Hopefully the former rather than the latter. The last thing he wanted was for Claire to be interfering in his dating life while on vacation. But truthfully, part of him hoped that he wouldn't run into the town dance teacher. After all, he'd eventually have to go back to Boston and there was no way that he'd get involved in a long-distance relationship again.

~

It had been three weeks since the *Magical Holiday Celebration* committee had begun the search for a set artist, and nothing had come of it. Steve continued to try and find someone who would be available to travel to Maple Ridge for a week to get as much as they could done, but many of the local artists were booked up for the holidays.

In the meantime, Lydia needed to make some progress on the base coats at least. She had taken time to visit the blocked off amphitheater in town, where the sets were transported and completed, to paint what she could the past couple of days. She loved working alone. As much as Lydia appreciated her team, it was nice to get away by herself, especially with all the time the team had been putting in together lately. She saw them every day, not to mention the times she was teaching. It was a lot. Having time to herself felt wonderfully calming.

Trevor had finished ahead of his deadline on some of the larger set pieces, which was fantastic considering how busy he'd been booking holiday jobs, as well as the commission for building the town gazebo. As the town's only carpenter and master builder, he was always in demand. But he always made time to help Lydia out with the holiday performances.

It was a beautiful day! Lydia had some upbeat music playing in the background, making sure it wasn't loud enough to disturb others who might be enjoying the day. It took everything in her not to get up and dance when a favorite song came on. She had to focus.

Lydia was crouched low, meticulously adding a fresh coat of red paint toward the bottom of one of the sets, when she heard the door squeak open. She righted herself and peeked over the top of the set piece.

A man with dark hair was sneaking around the door. She jumped up with only one goal – protecting the secrets that were hidden within. Not that anyone could really tell what those secrets were yet.

"I'm sorry, sir, but you can't be back here." Lydia impulsively ran to him and shoved him out, shutting the door behind them both. She forced herself to ignore the comically shocked expression on his face.

Was he laughing?

"I'm sorry, I didn't know there were government secrets back there."

Lydia looked up at him and flushed in embarrassment under his laughing gaze. She quickly recovered herself and self-consciously tucked a loose strand of hair behind her ear, laughing at her own outburst. At least he had a sense of humor.

"This area is hiding the sets for the holiday performance in December."

"I thought it was construction or some sort of update. I heard the music and saw that the door was slightly ajar, so I gave in to my curiosity." A small dimple showed in his cheek as he smiled at her. A slight flutter in her stomach caught her off-guard.

"I guess I forgot to close the door all the way. Are you just visiting? I haven't seen you around town before."

"I am. Though I've been to Maple Ridge a couple times before." He stuck out his hand, "I'm Jordan, by the way."

"Lydia." She took his hand in hers and shook it.

"Lydia? The dance teacher?"

Her eyebrows knit together in confusion. This guy was a stranger, how did he know who she was? Jordan laughed again, his eyes sparkling with amusement. That little flutter in her stomach returned.

He noticed her confusion and jumped to the rescue. "My cousin, Claire, lives here and has met you a couple of times. She's the one who told me about you and your magical performance thing. The thing with the 12 Days of Christmas."

"Oh, okay." Lydia laughed. "It's the *Magical Holiday Celebration* by the way. The 12 Days of Christmas is our theme this year. No one really does Christmas like Maple Ridge."

"So, I've heard. I've actually never been here during Christmastime so I'm looking forward to it."

They were still holding hands and Lydia felt her cheeks warm as she snatched her hand away. He only smiled as she coughed slightly to gather her composure.

"Well, I'm glad that you could be here this year. Aside from the performance, we also host a Christmas Eve party with food and dancing. Everything you might expect from a good, old fashioned, small-town Christmas, although we like to keep the performance pretty secretive."

"I can tell." Jordan chuckled as he waved his hand over the expanse of the barrier.

Lydia laughed quietly and the old embarrassment from before returned a little as she bit the inside of her lip.

There was an awkward pause between them. Lydia's gaze flitted everywhere but his face to avoid maintaining, what felt like intimate eye contact. Those eyes were so striking! They made her stomach do flips and the crinkles that appeared when he smiled just made them even more tantalizing to look at. She didn't even want to think about that dimple.

She took a deep breath, "I, uh, should probably get back to work."

"Oh, right, yes. I should let you get back to that. Maybe I'll see you around?"

"That's a very real possibility in this town." She turned to head back inside the amphitheater. "It was nice meeting you." Lydia felt flustered and completely forgot common courtesy for a second.

Jordan didn't seem to mind. He just stood there, a small smile playing on his lips. "It was nice meeting you, too. Have a great day!"

"Thank you. You too." She flashed one more smile and waved before disappearing behind the door.

As she knelt back down to paint, she smiled in spite of herself. A little checklist started forming in her mind. Not married…check! She hadn't seen a ring. Charming…check! Sense of humor…check! Incredibly handsome…double check!

What are you doing?! Lydia smacked her palm to her forehead and chided herself. *You can't get distracted right now. There's so much to do.* She groaned.

Who am I kidding, though? He probably has a line of women on his tail. With those eyes and that smile, I'd be surprised if he was still single. No, Lydia, it's not worth wasting the little time you have on thinking about a guy who's probably already spoken for. And, even if he isn't, I don't have time right now.

At least if he were dating, it would make it easier for her to forget him. But as much as she tried to convince herself that he wasn't available, there was a small ray of hope that he wasn't stuck in the back of her mind. Now she couldn't seem to focus on her work, which for painting was fine, but teaching became more difficult as her mind continued to wander. She knew there was no way she could mention this to her mom or Kate. They'd both play matchmaker. *Focus, Lydia.* It was going to be a long day…

~

Jordan turned reluctantly away from the amphitheater and walked back toward Claire's neighborhood. Lydia was not what he'd expected. To be honest, he didn't know what he expected. Claire hadn't been able to help herself. Every chance she got, she'd go into some sort of detail about Lydia, despite his protests against her matchmaking. And yet, a perfect picture of Lydia never formed in his mind.

But now that he'd met her…Jordan let out a breath. He would definitely have trouble focusing on anything else after looking into those beautiful, green eyes. Suddenly, he was thrilled that he was vacationing in a small town. There was no doubt he'd be running into the local dance teacher again.

Jordan frowned. He couldn't get involved. It didn't matter how wonderful Lydia was, he couldn't bring himself to have a long-distance relationship again. Not after what happened with Kathy. He just couldn't risk his heart again like that…but how could he forget those eyes? That smile? He smiled in spite of himself as he remembered the look on her face as she practically shoved him out the door.

Jordan scrubbed a hand over his face and sighed. One thing was for certain. He would *not* be mentioning any of this to Claire.

Chapter Four

Change had always been difficult for Lydia. She thrived on consistency and predictability. In recent years, Kate had played a huge role in helping Lydia step further and further outside of her comfort zone, but she still had a difficult time with change. The only moments Lydia could be unpredictable were in her choreography.

When she was ten years old, Lydia's father was stationed overseas. To maintain stability in Lydia's life, and because it was simply too expensive for all of them to move out of the country, her parents decided it was best for her and her mother to remain in the states. They ended up moving closer to Lydia's grandmother in Maple Ridge but having her father playing such a distant role in her life, made Lydia feel the need to put up barriers to protect her from others leaving her.

As a little girl, Lydia didn't fully understand why her dad was leaving for so long. To make matters worse, she saw the toll it took on her mother no matter how hard she tried to hide it from Lydia. Though she knew her dad loved her, it still felt as if he had abandoned them, and that love didn't make up for the time lost. So, the barriers that she put up around her heart as a child thickened as she continued to be left behind by friends who left for college, left to get married, or moved away. The loneliness she felt was deep and only the most courageous found a way to break down the walls around her heart. Kate, Steve, and Trevor were the precious few who had put in the effort with Lydia.

In the deepest times of sadness, Lydia tried to remember her father's words to her, "Even though I'm not there, sweetheart, you have a Father that will never leave you. He loves you more than your mother or I ever could, and He will comfort you when you feel lonely, sad, or lost, especially when I can't." It *was* comforting to know she was loved by God. And it didn't matter how many people came and went, He was always there.

When they moved to Maple Ridge, the welcoming community surrounded Lydia and her mother. They began helping them with meals and moving into their new home as well as sending event invitations to get them involved in the community. Despite the walls of protection she still had up, Lydia had come such a long way with change. She opened a dance studio with her best friend though she had no clue how far the starter money would go. Then, she decided to start these *Magical Holiday Celebration* performances which was nerve-wracking the first year. With only her, Kate, Steve, Trevor, and a couple of others doing everything on their own, they didn't know how they'd make it. So much went wrong but the people seemed to love it.

So, Lydia threw herself into her work and didn't think too hard about what she was missing. Work was good. It was predictable…mostly. This year was proof that all her hard work was paying off. It had been a dream of hers to work with Boston Ballet in any capacity, but she had given up on it after opening her own studio. Now that her studio was established, and Anthony Fairfax was coming to scout for an assistant choreographer, her dream might actually come true. As long as she continued to stay focused, she could have everything she'd ever dreamed.

~

Knowing that Jordan would be out all-day taking pictures of the town, Claire had set aside some time for them to meet up at the coffee shop. Jordan had found so much inspiration in Maple Ridge that he had never experienced in Boston. Everything was so peaceful, and he found himself getting lost in the secret nooks around town, often not realizing how late it had become until the sun started sinking low on the horizon.

He walked up to the shop and opened the door, taking a deep breath of the wonderful autumn scents. The coffee shop smelled of strong coffee, fresh-baked pumpkin pie, and a hint of cinnamon. Claire had told him earlier that morning that she was heading into town to do some Christmas shopping. Jordan found her sitting at a table by the window, surrounded by bags, sipping a steaming beverage.

"Buy enough gifts?" He teased.

Claire crinkled her nose at him playfully and then smiled. "If you must know, I have officially completed my Christmas shopping."

Jordan chuckled at her as he shifted a bag from the seat across from her.

"Take any good pictures today?"

"I did! It's quite different seeing this place in the fall. Spring is beautiful here, but I don't think anything could top autumn in Maple Ridge."

"Don't speak too soon. I think Christmas might just top fall."

"I guess we'll have to see. I'm going to grab a coffee really quick. Be right back."

As Jordan was heading toward the line, he bumped into an auburn-haired woman, walking toward the door, looking down at her phone.

"I'm so sorry." She apologized, clearly distracted. "I'm not normally glued to my phone like that. It's a busy time of year. But that's not an excuse for being rude."

"It's no problem." Jordan smiled at her good-naturedly.

"I'm Kate." She pocketed her phone and stuck her hand out to him before he could turn to get in line.

Jordan laughed under his breath. "Jordan." He took her hand.

"You just visiting? I don't think I've seen you around town before."

"Yup! Just visiting my cousin." He waved a hand in Claire's direction.

Kate followed his gesture and smiled, waving at Claire who was watching them closely. "Well, welcome to Maple Ridge! We always love having new people visiting our town."

"It's a beautiful town! I've just been out taking photos for my showcase back in Boston. I was thinking about using the lake as a background for a new painting. It's just so beautiful."

"Wait a minute!" Kate put her hands out, grabbing his arms in excitement and exclaimed, "You're a professional artist?"

Jordan's eyes widened in shock at Kate's sudden outburst. "Uh, yes, I am. Why?"

Realization dawned on Kate's face at how crazy she must look to him. She let go, "Oops, sorry again."

Jordan straightened his crumpled shirt sleeves, resisting the urge to laugh at this woman. She was quite the character, but he liked her.

"We, my business partner Lydia, and I, have been looking everywhere for someone to paint the sets for our *Magical Holiday Celebration*. I know you're just visiting, and you probably have no clue what this holiday celebration is, but it's been a nightmare trying to find someone who isn't all booked up for the holidays. Would you ever consider helping us out?"

He didn't know what to say. His head was swimming at the mention of Lydia and the sheer speed of the words coming out of this woman's mouth. The hesitation made her think that he needed more convincing.

"We'll pay you, of course. There are funds set aside for whoever would paint the sets for us."

Jordan gathered his thoughts and took a deep breath. Without thinking of the consequences, he accepted. "I'd love to help you.

I've been running low on activities to keep me occupied lately and this sounds like an interesting challenge. I hope it's okay that I've never painted sets before."

Kate grabbed his arms again in her excitement. "Not at all! As long as you're a professional artist, that's all we need!"

Jordan did laugh this time, "When would you need me?"

"As soon as you're able!"

"I can start on Monday at ten."

"Thank you so much!" On impulse, she pulled him in for a quick hug.

"It's my pleasure." Laughter still rumbling in his chest.

"I gotta go! I'm late already. Lydia will be thrilled! Thank you again. See you Monday at the amphitheater!" Kate waved to him but before she could disappear through the door, she turned, "You know where the amphitheater is, right?"

"I do."

"Great! See you then!" And just like that, Kate disappeared out the door and into the street as quickly as she had appeared.

Jordan resumed his walk toward the line to order his coffee, a humorous smile on his face. He was definitely not in the city anymore. Nothing crazy like that would ever happen to him in a coffee shop in Boston. He'd be lucky if a woman he bumped into didn't glare at him and blame him for not watching where *he* was going. She definitely wouldn't have introduced herself and welcomed him.

As he returned to sit with Claire, she smiled at him, resting her elbows on the table, chin on folded hands. "I see you've met an enthusiastic new friend."

"That's for sure. Apparently, that's Kate and she has been searching everywhere for an artist to paint the sets for the *Magical Holiday Celebration*. I guess I now have a job for the next few weeks."

Claire raised an eyebrow in surprise. "That's great!" She giggled. "Now you'll get the chance to meet Lydia." She waggled her eyebrows at him.

"Ha-ha-ha, very funny. Don't get your hopes up. It's just a job."

"Hmmm." Claire smiled over her sip of coffee.

Jordan changed the subject. "I feel like a horrible cousin, though. Leaving you when you probably have plans."

"Don't be crazy! We will have plenty of time together. Besides, I know that you will do the perfect paint job. When do you start?"

"Monday. I should probably pick up some supplies before then. I didn't even think to ask Kate about what I'd need. I guess I'll find out when I get there. She seemed like she was in a hurry."

What were the odds that he would be pulled into a project that would put him in close proximity with the woman he couldn't stop thinking about? It was a win-win situation. He'd get to spend time with Lydia, *and* he'd get paid for a job that would test his artistic capabilities. This town just kept tossing surprises his way.

~

"Ugh! I'm so sorry I'm late!" Kate joined Lydia in front of Serve It Up, one of the best catering companies outside of Boston.

"It's okay. Ian's just finishing up a few details anyway."

The ladies walked into the newly renovated shop and found Ian setting up his long tasting table for them. The smell of the delectable foods they were about to try made their mouths water.

Ian looked up and smiled at them excitedly, "Hello ladies! Are you ready to try the most amazing foods you've ever tasted?" He gestured toward the two chairs with a flourish.

Kate laughed, "You have no idea how much I've been looking forward to this!"

"If it looks and tastes as good as it smells, then I'm more than ready!" Lydia took a seat.

"I can assure you, everything I bring out will be a ten out of ten on looks, taste, *and* smell." Ian winked and then turned to grab the tray of small bites.

Lydia and Kate "oohed" and "awed" as he set down the tray of twelve, individual, beautiful, mini hors d'oeuvres and desserts themed after the 12 Days of Christmas.

"Wow, Ian, I didn't think it was possible, but you've actually outdone yourself this year!" Lydia's mouth stood agape in wonderment.

Ian smiled proudly and placed his hands on his hips, surveying his handiwork. "I'm just glad you chose this theme. It's been so fun trying to come up with twelve different appetizers and desserts. I was even able to experiment with a couple things I've never tried before."

"Well, I don't know about Lydia, but I'm ready to taste them all." Kate rubbed her hands together excitedly. Ian and Lydia laughed at her in unison.

"I'll just explain what each food item is really quick before you dig in." Ian pointed to each plate as he spoke. "Okay, so the first plate has mini pear tarts with little partridge crisps on top. Homemade caramel turtles with pecans and dark chocolate. Then there are mini drumsticks with crème fraiche-dill dip, mini chicken pot pies, chocolate rings dusted with edible gold luster dust – I figured you'd want your rings to be gold." Lydia smiled at him in approval. He continued down the row. "Deviled eggs with bacon and chives, pavlova swans filled with vanilla bean cream and raspberries, eggnog floats with fresh nutmeg, sugar cookie lords and ladies, parmesan pipes, and finally, mini chocolate drum cakes." Ian took a breath and stood, hands behind his back, beaming with pride in his work.

Lydia didn't know what to say. Everything Ian presented was so exquisitely decorated that they were almost too beautiful to eat. "I have no words, Ian." Lydia stared and shook her head in amazement. "These are so perfect! I couldn't have imagined anything better if I tried."

"I can't believe you actually made something for each day in the song. I honestly didn't think you'd go that far."

Ian laughed and sat down with the ladies, serving them one of everything and then serving himself. "How could I not? Like I said, I'm thrilled that you chose this song as your theme this year. Not to brag, but I think this will be the best party we've had."

"I don't doubt it!" Kate was the first to dig in, her eyes closing with satisfaction. Each dish was more delicious than the last, the room was silent as they all ate.

When the plates were clean, Ian hopped up to start clearing the table. "So, what did you think?"

"That was incredible, Ian! You've gone above and beyond! Those pavlova swans were just fantastic." Lydia handed him her plate.

"Everyone is going to love these dishes! It's a good thing someone will be there to serve, or we'd have people coming back for seconds, thirds, and probably fourths. If you don't have tons of people hiring you for their events after this, then I don't know what's wrong with them." Kate sighed contentedly.

"Well, since there don't seem to be any negatives from you, I'll go forward with the current menu. Kate sent over the final guest estimate so I'm all set to go. I hear the B&B is all booked up for the event already."

Kate's eyebrows went up in surprise. "Wow, I didn't know that. But I guess it's not all that surprising considering the estimate for the party has gone up quite a bit this year."

"I've never been so glad that we limit the number of people to the Christmas Eve party." Lydia had made sure that the guest list was limited for the party to keep costs down for Ian and to avoid overcrowding. With his elaborate menu this year, she was doubly glad she made that decision. Even with the tickets they usually only broke even on the party.

The three friends chatted for a little longer, finalizing a few more details, making sure everything was all set on Ian's end. Even though they still had a couple months to go, Ian and his crew had a lot of prep work ahead of them. They would need all the time they could get if they were going to be ready by Christmas Eve.

The autumn evening had turned chilly and dark when Kate and Lydia said their goodbyes. Stars were beginning to pop out, creating beautiful speckles against the navy sky.

"Oh, by the way, I hired someone to paint sets for us. He'll be meeting us in town on Monday." Kate mentioned as she took a few notes on her phone.

Lydia's brows came together in confusion. "How did you do that? Where on earth did you find an artist? Both Trevor and Steve said that there weren't any in the area that were available."

"I ran into one in the coffee shop today." Lydia laughed at Kate. "I'm serious. He's an artist who is visiting family and happens to have a clear schedule."

"Okay. How fortuitous." Lydia was a little skeptical, but she trusted her friend's judgement.

"I know! Crazy, right? Anyway, I should get going. Steve's waiting for me at the restaurant. Tonight's date night! Though I'm not sure how I'll fit any more food in." Kate pocketed her phone and pulled Lydia into a hug.

"Have fun!" Lydia waved. She laughed to herself as she pulled out of the parking lot. Of course, it was Kate who had just randomly bumped into exactly who they needed, when they needed them.

I guess I'll just have to wait until Monday to see how good this artist actually is. Please, Lord, let him be exactly what we need.

Chapter Five

On Monday, Jordan arrived at the amphitheater exactly at ten o'clock. He caught Kate's eye as she headed toward him, and she waved, a bright smile on her face.

"Good morning! I hope we don't scare you away once you see all the sets that need painted. I can't tell you how much we appreciate this. Lydia will be here any minute."

She led him through the door to the stage and he set down the materials he was carrying. He let out a whistle. This was a bigger job than he'd anticipated. The sets were huge!

"Morning, Kate, what's this surprise you have waiting for me?" He turned at the familiar voice and looked straight into those beautiful, green eyes. A faint blush crept into Lydia's cheeks as she looked at him, making her eyes look even greener. His mouth went dry. Why did she have such a strong influence over him?

"Lydia, this is Jordan. He has graciously accepted the job as our set painter." Kate beamed.

Jordan swallowed and let out a low chuckle. "We've actually met already. Nice to see you again, Lydia."

She smiled at him. It was a smile that made his insides do somersaults. He quickly chided himself for his reaction and tried to relax.

"Nice to see you again, too."

He noticed that Kate's eyes were ping-ponging between them, her smile getting wider as they stood there. She was clearly seeing what he was trying to convince himself wasn't there. Chemistry. An electric chemistry and that drew him to Lydia. Jordan shook his head. He couldn't get involved. But he also couldn't seem to get words to come out of his mouth to break the awkward silence.

Kate clapped her hands together and broke the tension in the air. "Well, we should probably walk Jordan through the sets and give him an idea of our plans so that he can get started."

Thank goodness! Jordan took a deep breath and swallowed.

Lydia opened the bag slung over her shoulder and took out some papers, clearly grateful for her friend's interruption. "We still have two sets that Trevor will be bringing by sometime this week. I brought the drawings with me for you to reference. These are just a basic idea of what we expect them to look like, but you're the professional so you're welcome to take some creative liberty." She handed him the drawings.

They were well drawn, and the designs were so detailed. *This might take a little longer than I thought.*

"If you'll come up on the stage, I'll walk you through what each set is meant to be and how it works." Lydia had made it up the stage while he was looking through the designs and was motioning him to join her.

"I wasn't sure what materials to bring, so I might need to stop by a hardware store for some things."

Kate palmed her forehead, "I'm so sorry. In the moment, I didn't even think of sharing any details with you. Once we go through all the sets, I'll join you and we can pick up what you need. I have a few things in the truck that can be used from previous years, too."

Jordan smiled and nodded. At least he would be going to the store with Kate and not Lydia. Coming to Maple Ridge was supposed to get his mind more focused, not jumbled on feelings he couldn't put words to yet. The chemistry between he and Lydia made him both excited to see what could come of it but also reluctant to spend too much time around her. His thoughts continued to swirl as Lydia explained each set and pointed to her sketched designs.

This is going to be a long few months.

~

Predictability.

There were other times in her life where unpredictability could play a part but right now, Lydia needed predictability to ensure a perfect performance.

Not only was it bad enough that Jordan had scarcely left her thoughts since they first met, now he just *had* to be the one Kate ran into and hired on a whim. This boded ill for predictability for the rest of the holiday season. She couldn't believe her eyes when she saw him on Monday. Since their first meeting, she was slightly disappointed that she hadn't seen him again. And then all of a sudden, he was there. Working for her, no less. She couldn't decide whether it was more distracting before, when she didn't see him at all or now, when she'd be seeing him on a regular basis.

Though she had handled the situation with decorum and professionalism, deep down Lydia knew that working so closely with Jordan could create some issues. She was already thinking about him when she had a moment alone. Now that they were working together, she couldn't think straight when he was near. His blue-green eyes always seemed to make their way back into her thoughts no matter how hard she tried to focus on work. Yesterday, she had done a quick walk-through with some of the dancers, and she could feel his gaze on her. She thought her face would catch fire when her eyes accidentally locked with his.

Unfortunately for her, the need for a set painter overruled her desire to avoid getting too close to him. Maybe she could have Kate meet with him for the approvals. But then again, she'd continue seeing him during rehearsals which took place at least four times a week.

Kate burst through the door with a huge smile on her face. Lydia jerked to her feet, blushing at being caught thinking about Jordan.

"What's going on?"

Kate lifted a finger and bent to catch her breath. "I…think…Steve's planning…something."

Lydia raised an eyebrow in confusion. "What do you mean?"

When had thoroughly caught her breath, Kate responded. "Well, tonight's a special night. It's the anniversary of our first date so he planned this whole evening in the park, which as we all know, is the most romantic part of town."

"Is that it? Doesn't Steve do romantic things like that all the time?"

Kate looked slightly exasperated, "Lydia! He's planning something big!" Her hands went through the air with a flourish.

"Are you saying…"

"That he might propose? Maybe!"

Lydia laughed and pulled her friend into a hug. "If that's the case, I'm so excited for you!" She pulled back and looked Kate in the eyes, "But don't get your hopes up. You know you're impossible to surprise and Steve's adamant that when he proposes, he wants it to be a complete surprise."

Kate sighed, "I know. It just seems like the perfect timing. I'm genuinely not trying to guess what's going on. I just fill in the gaps automatically."

Lydia smiled at her but before she could say anything, someone cleared their throat in the lobby, attracting their attention. Kate frowned when she recognized the tall, slim brunette.

"Sorry to interrupt, but I was shopping across the street when I saw Kate barreling into the studio. I thought for sure that something must be wrong and decided to come and offer my help."

Kate rolled her eyes, "You mean you had hoped that the *Magical Holiday Celebration* had been derailed or cancelled?"

June, a former principal dancer for Boston Ballet and Kate's least favorite person, smiled condescendingly. "Now why would I wish for that?"

Before Kate could snap back a retort, Lydia held up her hand and interceded, "Nothing's wrong. Kate was just excited about something, that's all."

"Yes, I heard. But I'll save my congratulations until the news is official."

Kate rolled her eyes again and sat down behind the front desk. She knew it wouldn't help matters if she got into an argument with June.

"Thank you, June." Lydia hadn't noticed that June was listening to her and Kate's conversation.

"Lydia, I actually do have another reason for being here. Seeing as you had promised me a spot in the performance this year but reneged, I thought I'd offer my help in another capacity."

Lydia suddenly felt extremely uncomfortable and trapped. "June, you know very well that I didn't renege on the offer, you accepted it too late. By then, all the spots were filled."

"Yes, well, that doesn't matter anymore." June waved away Lydia's words. "Anyway, I know how difficult it's been for you, in the past, to keep up with the demands of choreographing, teaching, and all the other jobs you insist on doing yourself. So, I thought I'd offer to be your assistant choreographer."

Lydia couldn't decide whether to be offended or flattered. Kate snorted a sarcastic laugh at June's impertinence which Lydia rewarded with a kick to her foot. June and Kate had never been able to get along. Their two strong personalities always clashed. Ultimately, Lydia had more patience with June…usually.

She started slowly, "I'll admit, it has been difficult juggling all of it." June's smirk grew slightly wider. Lydia took a calming breath. "I suppose having some help with rehearsals might be a good idea. Would you like to come tomorrow and see how everything is going so far? We'll do a trial run."

June gave one curt nod. "I'll be there promptly at two." She raised her nose in the air haughtily, a triumphant smile on her lips.

"See you then." Lydia said as June turned on her heel and walked out the door.

The tension in the room was palpable but Kate cut it with a sarcastic comment, "Thank goodness we get to work with that ray of sunshine for the next couple of months." Lydia snickered. "I just hope you enjoy your time together because I'm staying as far away from June Melvin as humanly possible. I love you Lydia, but you're on your own."

This time Lydia laughed and whacked Kate on the arm, "Hey! I didn't know what to say. And to be honest, it would be nice to have some help. I still have a few details to work on so having someone handling some of that detail work would be nice."

"Then for you, I'll be happy. But I'll save my congratulations until I see the success." Kate mocked June's previous comment, which made Lydia laugh even more. Kate finally smiled, "I should get going and prepare for my date." Her eyebrows wagged.

As soon as Kate left, Lydia slumped over the front desk, her chin in her hands. There goes even more of the predictability she was counting on. First Jordan distracting her and now she was pretty sure she'd be haggling with June over authority. June would likely take the job of assistant choreographer as far as she could, knowing how badly she wanted to return to Boston Ballet. Lydia felt a knot of anxiety settle in her stomach at the realization that this sudden impulse of June's might be due to the fact that Mr. Fairfax was coming to hire an assistant choreographer. If there were two choreographers…Lydia shook her head in an effort to calm her fears. *There's no use entertaining suspicions that are completely unfounded.*

"Ugh! Of all the times to bring a handsome, possibly single man into Maple Ridge and spark possible conflict within the crew, why now?" Lydia looked up in exasperation.

Jordan would be there at rehearsal tomorrow too. How would she get through with him *and* June watching? She barely got through rehearsal yesterday with just him. Without warning, those blue-green eyes popped back into her memory. Those eyes…Lydia rested her chin in her hand as she remembered what they looked like.

"Hey Lydia!" Trevor had walked into the studio disrupting her thought process.

Lydia felt her cheeks turn red. She distractedly shifted some papers on the desk to hide her embarrassment at being caught daydreaming…again.

"Trevor, hey. What's up?"

"I just wanted to stop by and see how the sets were working out for you. I have the last two that I'm about to bring by and set up." He casually sat in one of the lobby chairs and crossed his ankle over his knee.

Lydia, fully recovered, sat in the chair next to him. "That's great! And they're perfect! We just completed our first official rehearsal on them yesterday and all the dancers were thrilled."

"Glad to hear it! It's perfect timing for me to start working on the gazebo project. I've been putting that off for way too long. Before we know it, there could be snow disrupting progress, and we won't have a gazebo until late spring."

"I really appreciate you putting in the time to get them all done so quickly! Don't talk about snow though, I'm not ready to work around that obstacle just yet."

Trevor laughed and placed a reassuring hand on Lydia's shoulder, "Don't worry, snow is far into the future." He heaved himself out of the chair. "I should get going. Gotta get those sets up and ready for you for tomorrow."

Lydia gave him a hug in thanks. "You look tired, Trevor. You'll have to let me buy you a coffee or something to thank you."

"I might just take you up on that. You free tomorrow morning before work?"

"Absolutely!"

"You want to join me over at the amphitheater so I can give you the low-down on all the details of the newest sets? I'm meeting Steve over there now."

"That would be great! I'll just grab my coat and purse and meet you out there."

Trevor headed out to his pick-up truck with a trailer already hitched to the back filled with dismantled set pieces. Lydia joined him a minute later, locking up the studio and hopping into the passenger seat. It was starting to get colder outside. Thankfully, Steve had hooked up some heaters by the amphitheater stage to keep the dancers warm while they rehearsed.

A short drive later, Trevor and Steve met up and started unloading the trailer. With Lydia's help, they all began putting the pieces together. After a thorough walk-through of the area, making sure that all the sets were exactly where they needed to be for the performance, the three of them sat in the front row admiring their work.

"It looks amazing, you guys!" Lydia put one arm on each shoulder of the men on either side of her. "Steve, the snow-globe machine is genius! I can't wait to see how it all looks!"

"Me, too! I think I'll come by on Friday to officially test it out."

As they gazed at their finished work, Kate slipped through the door and walked up to them.

"You guys look cozy." She laughed at them as she looked up at the stage. "It looks great! Now we just need to get them all painted. Jordan's doing an incredible job so far!"

Lydia smiled, "His work rivals Lucy's, that's for sure."

"Maybe we can convince him to help us out again next year?" Trevor poked Lydia in the ribs.

"You guys want to have dinner, on me?" Lydia hopped up, ignoring Trevor's pointed comment. Had she been so transparent? Who was she kidding, Trevor and Kate had known her for ages, they could see right through her.

"We can't. Steve and I have plans tonight, remember? I just came by to pick him up. Rain check?"

"Of course, I completely forgot. Have a lovely time," Lydia winked at Kate. "How about you, Trevor?"

"I can't turn down a meal that I don't have to make…or pay for." Trevor winked at Lydia. He grabbed his tools and led the group toward the exit.

~

It had been a long day! Jordan wiped the sweat off his forehead with the back of his forearm. His shirt was soaked despite the fact that it was a chilly day. Claire's husband, Kyle, was a medical resident at the local hospital and didn't have a lot of time to help Claire prepare for the winter months. She took full advantage of having another man around the house to do the hard labor.

He'd been mowing the lawn, raking leaves, helping Claire get the heavy fall decoration bins from the attic, and chopping and stacking wood. It had been a long time since he'd done manual labor like this, and his muscles were sore already. It was a pleasure to help his cousin out, especially since he was staying with her for free and she was making meals for him every day.

Jordan had made sure to set aside time to help her in between days he was painting sets. Unfortunately, he found out too late that his days off coincided with Lydia's days off which meant he was there for her rehearsals. He'd have to make a mental note to change that soon. It was too distracting. Especially when he found himself staring too long and accidentally making eye contact with her, making his stomach do flips.

Claire's blonde head peeked around the back door. "Hey, you! Would you mind if we ordered dinner to pick up and bring back? I lost track of time and forgot to get dinner ready. Plus, Kyle won't be home until late so he's eating at the hospital tonight."

"Sure, just order me a burger with all the toppings and I'll go pick it up. Let me just grab a quick shower first."

Claire gave him a thumbs up and disappeared inside.

Since accepting the job for the *Magical Holiday Celebration*, Claire had been pestering him for details about what Lydia was like and what it was like working with her. But he didn't give in. She had pointed out yesterday that he was smiling more. It was true. Though he tried hard not to. He felt himself falling headlong into a sticky situation. But watching how Lydia was with others told him a lot about her character, and what he saw was extremely attractive. He was intrigued by her.

Jordan stacked the last couple of logs and stretched his back. He was looking forward to getting to know her better in spite of his better judgement.

The restaurant was crowded, even though it was the middle of the week. Jordan's stomach grumbled as he waited for their meals to be placed in the pick-up lane. All that work had made him hungrier than usual. Just as his name was called, he spotted a familiar face at a table toward the back.

He had seen Lydia yesterday, but he suddenly felt like it had been a week. In that short moment of recognition, Jordan's steps halted as he walked toward the counter. Lydia wasn't alone but with a guy, and they were clearly very close. She laughed at something her date said and it made Jordan's heart drop.

Since they'd met, he couldn't keep his thoughts from drifting to her. Her green eyes…her radiant smile…even her adorable blush of embarrassment whenever she was caught by surprise. He couldn't get her out of his head.

Even so, it was ridiculous that he should be so disappointed that a woman he barely knew was on a date with someone. Of course, she was dating someone. Who wouldn't jump at that opportunity?

His name was called again, and he walked over to the pick-up counter. He thanked the man who handed him the bag of food and headed out to his car. There was no use taking one more look back. Lydia was clearly not available, and he was upset with himself that he was so disappointed in that knowledge.

The whole point of why he came here anyway was because he needed to figure out his purpose. He just felt so insecure about what he was creating. His art just felt a little…bland. Sarah didn't notice, though she did notice his moods were changing. Painting had helped him hide his hurt about his breakup for so long that he didn't necessarily want to continue. But he didn't seem to know how to move forward.

The passion just wasn't there anymore. Jordan had always been confident in where he wanted to end up with respect to his career. Now that his passion for art was waning, he felt a little lost. How was he, as a grown adult, supposed to figure out what to do with his life? Wasn't that supposed to be what you figured out as a teenager? He shook his head, trying to shake away the frustration.

He had hoped that this trip would help rekindle some of the passion he seemed to be losing, or at least that he would find some peace and tranquility around people he loved.

At least now he could refocus on the real reason he came to Maple Ridge, knowing Lydia was clearly off the market.

Chapter Six

Jordan massaged his shoulder as he circled it. He hadn't expected to be so sore. Today would have to be a day for painting the lower levels of the sets. Holding his arms over his head didn't seem possible. His phone buzzed with an incoming text.

"I'm so sorry!" Focusing on the message, Jordan ran directly into a woman, making her teeter and hit her leg hard on a nearby bench.

"Ugh! Ouch!" She reached down to rub her leg.

Jordan grasped her arm to help her regain equilibrium, but she squirmed her way out of his hold. What was it about him and bumping into women? Or was it women bumping into him?

"Watch where you're going!" She looked up at him for the first time. Her eyes shot daggers but then quickly softened as she scanned him from head to toe. A flirtatious grin played on her lips as she tucked a strand of hair behind her ear.

Oh boy! Jordan had a feeling that this woman would be trouble.

"Clumsy and handsome, just like a regular Clark Kent." She smiled and grabbed his hand and shook it. "I'm June. Are you new in town? I think I'd remember a face like that."

He extricated his hand and pasted a friendly smile on his face. "I'm Jordan, and yes, I'm just visiting for the holidays."

"Well, welcome to Maple Ridge, Jordan. I hope this small town isn't too small and cramped for you." Her perfectly straight, white teeth showed as she smiled, a hint of bitterness coloring her statement.

Jordan cleared his throat, "Thank you. Is your leg okay?"

"Oh, yes, it's fine. Don't worry about me." She continued to scan his features which made him uncomfortable. June laid her hand on his arm, moving in a little closer as she spoke. "I hope we'll run into each other again sometime." She turned to leave, flashing another of her flirtatious smiles over her shoulder and waving her fingers.

That was…interesting. He scratched his neck and let out a breath as he continued on toward the amphitheater. Kate would be expecting him to be there any minute now. Part of him hoped that Lydia wouldn't be there, but an even bigger part wished she would. He scrubbed his hand over his face to try and rub away thoughts of Lydia.

Lydia?

He spotted her across the street, coming out of the coffee shop with the guy he saw her with the night before. Jordan let out a sigh, *perfect timing for a reminder.* She didn't look as happy this morning. He couldn't help but wonder why. A hug between Lydia and her date reminded him that it wasn't his business, and he turned away from the scene.

Jordan's phone buzzed again, and he looked at it. Kate was letting him know that she was running late. *Maybe I'll take the long way today.* He pocketed his phone and started walking toward the lake.

~

June Melvin, one of the youngest dancers to be promoted to principal for Boston Ballet, was a force to be reckoned with. She was stubborn, proud, and unbeknownst to most, struggled with deep hurts that made her bitter. When she was at the height of her career, she suffered a severe ankle injury that took her from accomplished ballerina to hobbling homebody.

When the doctor told her that the fracture would heal in time if she stayed off pointe for the foreseeable future, June felt like her life was over. Even after it did heal, it wouldn't be the same.

She had tried other forms of dance, disliking all of them, but ballet was everything to her. Not wanting to give up on dance altogether, she tried her hand at choreography for her senior project and won an award. It was as if she had another chance at making her life a success. Then came Lydia and her silly little Christmas performances.

Lydia was a brilliant choreographer and an excellent dancer to boot. Though she was a little older than June, Lydia was still in her prime. Moving out of the city to a small town was bad enough. June had to figure out how she fit in. Dancing was clearly off the table. It wasn't worth risking another injury and truthfully, the one thing June was truly terrified of was getting hurt again. But once the *Magical Holiday Celebration* picked up, choreography was off the table too. There was no way she could compete with the great and powerful Lydia Foster. Not that she would give Lydia the satisfaction of letting her or anyone else know she admired her abilities.

The hurt of having two huge aspects of her life snatched from her cut deep. So, June held onto the hurt tightly, causing a rift between local dancers, Lydia, and especially Kate. And yet, Lydia was still kind to her. Every year, she offered June a role in the performance or a place on the crew decorating or helping with costumes, which she emphatically turned down. June wouldn't take charity.

When the news spread that Boston Ballet's artistic director was coming to see the performance, June felt it another nail in the coffin of her career. Then again, it could also be her saving grace. Convincing Lydia to accept her as an assistant choreographer was the hard part. Now that she had an in, June could weasel her way into changing the majority of the choreography and claiming it as her own. Then, Mr. Fairfax would have no choice but to choose June for the assistant choreographer position over Lydia. It was brilliant!

June took advantage of Lydia's kindness and was rewarded. Admittedly, she didn't know if her scheme would work. That over opinionated friend of Lydia's was always talking in her ear. But it ended up being as easy as taking candy from a baby. Which meant that June had found her weakness. Lydia would be kind and forgiving, which would allow June to insert herself slowly and carefully into the choreography, so that she wouldn't know what hit her until it was too late. As long as she could get past the trial stage, she'd be golden. It was risky, but worth the risk if it meant regaining a part of her life she had lost and possibly taking Lydia down a few pegs.

~

"Good morning!" Kate was in a peppy mood, but unfortunately, Lydia wasn't. "What's wrong?" Kate put down her clipboard and rushed to Lydia's side, wrapping an arm around her shoulders.

Lydia sighed and set down her things. "My mom got a call from my dad last night. He wanted us to know that he wouldn't make it home for Thanksgiving. Not that I really expected him to, but it's still hard to hear."

"Awe, Lydia, I'm so sorry."

"I shouldn't have got my hopes up so high, but I can't help myself. He did say that there's a good chance he'll have Christmas off, though, so that's a consolation." Lydia smiled sadly.

Kate was a good friend. But she couldn't relate to Lydia in how she felt. Both of Kate's parents were always just a drive away whenever she needed them. The best she could do was support Lydia when she needed it. When words failed, hugs didn't.

"Oh, just to remind you in case you want to leave, June's coming to rehearsal this afternoon."

Kate made a face, "Thanks for letting me know. I'll be sure to finish up all my work and get out of here before she shows up."

Lydia laughed under her breath, "How was your special date in the park?"

"You were right." Kate sighed, "He's still trying to put me off the scent. Either that or he is never going to propose."

"Don't say that! Steve is most definitely going to propose to you."

"Well, it was very romantic. He had everything planned out perfectly and there were even little nods to our first date wrapped up throughout the night." Kate smiled to herself.

Lydia felt a small pang of envy but quickly dismissed it. She was too happy for her friend having someone in her life to love that she didn't want to pollute it with her own envious feelings.

"I'm so glad you had a great time!"

The door clicked shut and Lydia turned to see Jordan sauntering toward the stage. He waved, a small smile on his face despite the fact that he didn't really look thrilled to be there. *Looks like we're both having a blah day.* Lydia waved back a bit unenthusiastically.

"Morning!" Kate beamed at him. Lydia was starting to think that Kate was never in a bad mood. "I'm sorry I was late this morning. Lydia and I are going to help you out today. I figured it would be faster if we finished the base colors on the last two sets while you continued to work on details. Steve will be here around two to start rigging up some of the special effects and lighting, so we'll need at least these two sets dry before he gets here." Kate pointed to two of the smaller sets that needed some detail work toward the base.

They worked and chatted together for about thirty minutes before Kate got an important phone call. She dismissed herself saying that she had some time sensitive paperwork to complete for a client, much to Lydia's chagrin. When she left, silence fell between Jordan and Lydia as they worked side-by-side on two neighboring sets.

Lydia watched as he meticulously painted some details toward the top of the set for the French hens. They had settled on a traditional filigree with some fleur-de-lis sprinkled throughout that perfectly represented French architecture and design. "That's beautiful." Lydia bit her lip. She hadn't meant to speak her thoughts out loud.

Jordan started at the sudden break in the silence and turned to see Lydia flushing, trying to refocus on her own work. She could see him smile to himself in her periphery. Rather than allow an awkward silence to follow her impromptu praise, she continued.

"I have to admit I was a little worried when you started, knowing that you only paint canvases and do photography. But your attention to detail is almost better than our old set designer."

Jordan laughed and smiled wider. "I wasn't quite sure about it myself. I'm glad to have proved both of us wrong. I wanted to make sure I stick as closely to your plans as possible so that takes a little more time."

Lydia relaxed, the embarrassment of breaking the tension gone. "I appreciate that. Feel free to add your own flair though. You are the artist and the whole point of the performance is to allow each artist to be able to show off their own style, whether dance or painting."

"Thank you, I'll remember that. I just hope I can get these all done in time."

"I'm sure you will. You've already made great progress. Even if it's a little close, I'd rather have beautiful detail than a rushed mess, which is what it would look like if I did the details. And don't tell Kate this, but she's not exactly the most talented painter either."

They both laughed and Jordan put his hand up, "I promise I won't tell. It looks like you've done a pretty good job already, though."

Lydia snorted in spite of herself, "Yeah, well, that's a giant surface without any details or lines. That's easy. I gave up on being any type of artist, other than a dancer, a long time ago."

"Oh, come on. You can't be that bad. After all, those sketches you did were really good."

Lydia raised her eyebrow and smirked. "I took an art class that my mom forced me into when I was young and I'm pretty sure that I was only good at collages. The drawing skills came slowly but only if I have a good reference to copy. Base coats, painting walls, and a little drawing are the only artistic skills I possess. Detail work is just…well, let's just say I can't paint a straight line very well."

Jordan stuck out his hand with the tiny paintbrush he was holding and motioned for her to take it. Lydia's hands went up in protest. "No! I'm not ruining that beautiful design." He laughed at her, placed the paintbrush down and shifted to sit beside her where she was painting.

"Okay, then. Try a line here."

One brow came up again as she pressed her mouth into an unsure smile. Jordan laughed at her again and gently held her hand, guiding it in a straight line across the set.

"Drawing lines is one of the first lessons an artist learns. Lines can tell a person how the artist is feeling whether they are curved, diagonal, thick, or straight." He led her hand in each of these movements as he spoke. "They are expressive and form the basis of every piece of art, even if you're not a trained artist."

"I never knew that." Lydia turned her head to look at him, locking eyes briefly. He was far too close. Jordan abruptly released her hand, and she noticed his neck turn a little red as he returned to his side, picking up his own paintbrush.

"I may be good at painting, but I'm a terrible dancer. It always amazes me to see what dancers can do with their bodies. I think I'd break in half."

Lydia laughed at the strange picture that conjured. "Dance is just another way to express emotions whether you're good at it or not."

"Touche." Jordan winked at her. "I actually took lessons for my cousin's wedding, but I don't think the teacher liked me, so I struggled."

"It sounds like your poor dancing ability is more because of a poor teacher and not because you're really bad at dancing."

The silence that settled between them was comfortable this time. Lydia had been so afraid that when Kate left them together, they would sit in awkward and uncomfortable silence until rehearsals finally began. But once they started talking, there was something about Jordan that made her feel like she didn't have to try too hard.

"How long have you been dancing?" Jordan's voice broke the long silence this time.

"It's been about twenty years. I was four when my parents enrolled me in dance. I semi-retired when I started teaching full-time."

"That's a long time! How'd you decide to start teaching?"

"Yeah, it's a huge part of my life. It became my safe haven when we moved to Maple Ridge. It was really the only stability in my life at the time. The teacher at the studio I went to just outside of town was so welcoming. She was firm and strict, but one of the nicest teachers I'd ever had. She challenged me and really inspired me to become a teacher just like her. When she retired, it felt like my green light, and I dragged Kate into the business venture. Mostly, I just wanted to inspire dancers to understand their potential without holding them to an impossible standard of perfection."

"That's really amazing. It seems like you've done a great job at that."

Lydia blushed. "I do my best."

"How did the *Magical Holiday Celebration* come about?"

"I love old movies! My mom introduced them to me when I was little. Musicals are my favorites. Especially the ones with Frank Sinatra, Fred Astaire, Bing Crosby, Ginger Rogers…they're the best. When I started planning my first *Magical Holiday Celebration*, I had just watched White Christmas for the first time. It inspired me to base the whole performance off the movie. Each year since has been based off a favorite Christmas movie or song." Lydia laughed at herself, "Except this year, I gave Kate a wild card of an all-peppermint theme."

"That would've been interesting. Definitely a lot easier to design sets for." Jordan chuckled.

"You can blame Kate for that one."

"*White Christmas* is one of my favorite Christmas movies."

"Really?"

"Yeah, it's a tradition in my family to watch it every Christmas Eve. I'm a little ashamed to say that I haven't seen *It's a Wonderful Life* though." Jordan smiled guiltily.

"It's not a bad movie. It's definitely one that should be enjoyed at least once in your lifetime. I think you'd like it if you like old movies."

"I do."

Lydia smiled at him as they looked at each other for a little too long. Just before she looked away, Lydia thought she saw a flicker of guilt in Jordan's eyes. But he smiled and turned back

to his work too quickly for her to analyze it. She watched him as
he delicately added details to the design. He was so talented.
Every stroke of his paintbrush came so easily to him.

*I'll have to see if Kate thinks we could hire him on
permanently for annual set designs.* Lydia started cleaning up
her space in preparation for rehearsal. It didn't matter that Jordan
lived in Boston. Maple Ridge wasn't too long a drive, especially
if they paid him well and it gave him an excuse to visit his
cousin. It would be nice to have an excuse to see him more
often…maybe he might even decide to stay.

Chapter Seven

Get it together man! Jordan inwardly chided himself as he tried hard not to watch the rehearsal happening on the other side of the stage. *She's clearly dating someone. Stop flirting.*

Their conversation earlier had flowed so easily. He really shouldn't have held her hand the way he did or stare into her eyes for as long as he did. It was just too tempting not to. Beneath Lydia's outward beauty were layers of vulnerability that she kept behind a wall of protection. He knew it would be difficult to break down those walls, but he desperately wanted to accept that challenge head on and try. As soon as the dancers started gathering on the stage, he breathed a sigh of relief knowing that Lydia would be too occupied for him to start any new conversations.

Then he saw June. Jordan's stomach churned a little at the coy smile on her face the moment she caught his eye. Sure, June was beautiful, but her siren eyes and sultry smile made him wary. He'd met women like her before – attractive, confident, and fully aware of their seductive power over men. Thankfully, past experiences taught him to keep his distance. After Kathy, his vulnerability led him into a relationship with a woman that didn't have his best interest at heart. All she wanted was a man who would bend to her will and give her what she wanted, when she wanted it. Fortunately, it hadn't lasted longer than a week.

He wanted more from a relationship. A depth of character that came from a deep and abiding relationship with God. That was something he felt, and saw, Lydia possessed.

"Places please, everyone!" Lydia's voice rang out above the din of chatting and giggling. Her voice commanded authority but remained calm and gentle.

Jordan looked up to see each dancer quietly take their places, Lydia standing at the head with June by her side.

"Before we begin, I just wanted to inform you that June will be my assistant choreographer. If I'm not around, or am busy with another dancer, you can refer to her with any questions regarding choreography." The dancers nodded in unison but didn't exactly look thrilled. Lydia opened her mouth to say something more, but June's sharp voice interrupted her.

"Alright, let's get a move on. We only have two hours to practice!"

Jordan noticed Lydia's jaw tighten in response, but her face remained calm. Somehow her response to June made him proud of her. June clearly didn't respect Lydia, and the dancers didn't seem to respect June.

As rehearsal continued, Jordan felt and heard more than saw the tension that was building on the stage. He hesitated to look up too often as whenever he did, June seemed to notice and flashed a flirtatious smile his way. She was even bold enough to blow him a kiss which Lydia saw clear as day. It had only been an hour and already June had interrupted rehearsal several times to make corrections with her shrill voice. He could sense the frustration in Lydia's voice as she tried to keep the rehearsal running smoothly.

Instinct made Jordan want to jump up and put June in her place. He wanted to help Lydia maintain control, defend her honor, rescue her from frustration. But he knew that it wasn't his place, and he felt that in defending Lydia, he might end up undermining her instead. The best thing he could do for her was pray that she had the strength to stand up for herself and be patient with June.

Be with Lydia, Father. She needs your strength.

~

Lydia's teeth were hurting from the tension in her jaw. She knew that inviting June to be her assistant choreographer might be difficult, but this was borderline impossible, and this was just the trial period. Her forceful comments, most of which were uncalled for, were picking at the smallest things. Lydia massaged her brow in frustration. *It's just her first rehearsal. She hasn't seen the choreography yet. Maybe she'll be easier on the dancers next time.* She tried to give June the benefit of the doubt. If she didn't, she'd snap.

There was another flirtatious smile being directed at Jordan. Lydia felt like she could punch a wall. She couldn't decide whether this constant attention directed at him made her angry because June was not paying close attention or because Lydia was jealous. No! She couldn't be jealous. Why should she be jealous? Jordan didn't seem to be paying much attention to June, and even if he was, he didn't look flattered. He looked uncomfortable. She took a deep breath to try and loosen the knots of tension forming in her neck and shoulders.

Lydia made her way to the middle of the stage as the music wound down. The dancers were getting frustrated too. They could barely get through five minutes of their choreography without June yelling out a correction or pausing the music. It was time for June to back off.

She stopped the music. "The dance looks good so far! Make sure you are using the full length of the stage and don't be shy with spreading out on your sets…those of you who do have sets." Lydia winked and the dancers laughed together at her effort to ease the strain on everyone. June crossed her arms over her chest, clearly not amused. "The drummers and pipers seem to be stumbling over each other, so try and move a little more that way…" Lydia continued to give directions to each group calmly. "Alright, I know you're all tired, but I want to see it from the top one last time *without pauses*." She emphasized the last part for June.

As the music began, Lydia motioned to June to be seated, as kindly as she could without physically shoving her down into the chair. Her frown and firm expression had its intended effect on June, and she sat down without argument. But it was too good to be true. Midway through the dance, June stood and stopped the music. Not expecting the music to abruptly stop, one of the dancers was caught off guard and fell into another dancer, both toppling over one of the smaller sets.

"June! That's enough!" Lydia yelled, running up to check and see if the fallen dancers were okay.

Some of the other dancers whispered to each other. They had never heard Lydia be so short with anyone before. They were used to her calm corrections. The dancers were fine, just a few bruises, but enough was enough.

"Rehearsal's over. Thank you everyone. Please stretch and cool down."

June scowled as Lydia marched to her side. "Continue to interrupt rehearsal and I will be asking you to leave."

"If they were paying attention, that wouldn't have happened." June fired back.

"If you hadn't been yelling at them and stopping the music constantly, these dancers would be confident enough in their routines that they wouldn't need to worry about falling. I asked you to help with choreography, not insult the dancers and disrupt rehearsals. If this happens again, your trial is over, and you won't be returning." Lydia glared at June, inviting further challenge from her.

June finally broke Lydia's gaze and rolled her eyes. Lydia had won. "Go home and get some rest. Rehearsals pick back up on Friday." Lydia's façade crumbled slightly as June stormed out of the amphitheater. She felt her face redden as she realized that she had allowed June to get under her skin. But what else was she supposed to do? Her dancers needed her to be their advocate, or they would never trust her again.

As she turned back toward the few dancers remaining, her gaze caught Jordan's. He had seen the whole thing. She closed her eyes in disappointment and sat down, resting her head in her hands. When she finally looked up, all the dancers had left, and Jordan had packed up all his art supplies.

"Are you okay?" Jordan sat down beside her, a sympathetic look on his face.

Lydia felt like crying but maintained a steady voice. "I will be." She felt his hand on her shoulder; comforting and warm. All at once, the tension in her muscles relaxed.

"Steve is here so I'm going to head out but if you need anything…"

Lydia raised her head and gave him a small smile. "Thank you." Her throat felt thick with frustrated tears.

Jordan rose to leave, but she remembered something important, "Wait, Jordan. I forgot, Kate wanted me to pay you, but I don't have the check here, I left it at the studio."

"I can walk with you. It's on my way home anyway." Jordan's smile helped Lydia put the disastrous rehearsal behind her.

It was a silent walk, but it didn't feel strained at all. Lydia felt content with Jordan's company, silent or not. She went to get the check for Jordan and came back to find him looking at the pictures on the wall of the lobby.

He turned and accepted the check she held out to him. "These are great pictures. Is that you?" Jordan pointed to a picture of Lydia doing a beautiful arabesque en pointe in a flowy costume.

"It is. They're pretty old though. One of my friends was taking a photography course our senior year and I was her model. I keep telling Kate that I need some more professional ones taken."

"If you're interested, I'd be happy to take some new ones for you. I've done action photography, but I haven't tried taking pictures of dancers before."

Lydia started to protest, "I can't ask you to do that. You're already doing so much for us."

"It's no problem at all. Besides, you didn't ask. I offered. I've also been wanting to try out some action shots for my gallery, that is if I can use some of the pictures I take."

This offer meant more time spent with Jordan. More alone time. The thought didn't sound horrible. "As long as you're sure it won't be too much."

"Not at all! Since you don't have rehearsal tomorrow, how about we meet at the park in the morning before the sun gets too harsh?"

"I can meet you at nine. It might be chilly so make sure you bundle up."

Jordan's eyes crinkled at the corners and his dimple showed. "If it gets too cold, we can always go to the amphitheater and take photos on the stage by the heaters."

Lydia laughed. "That sounds like a good plan."

After having such an awful afternoon, Lydia normally would have gone home, had a good cry, and vented to either Kate or her mom. But here was Jordan – calm, positive, and supportive – helping her forget her frustrations by simply being present. He hadn't tried to fix everything or explain away her feelings. He also didn't silently leave her at the theater. He didn't abandon her in her misery.

That meant more to her than flowery words of affirmation. She needed someone to be her strength when she didn't have any left.

Chapter Eight

Jordan awoke the next morning with butterflies in his stomach. He knew when he invited Lydia for a photography session that he was treading on dangerous ground. But the offer just tumbled out before he could reason through it.

He showed up at the park early so that he could scout out the best spots for pictures, ones with flatter surfaces so that Lydia didn't hurt herself. As he was adjusting the settings on his camera, the crunch of dead leaves behind him made the butterflies from earlier return to his stomach.

"Good morning!" Jordan turned to smile and wave.

Lydia returned his smile and tucked a loose strand of hair behind her ear. "Good morning. It's a beautiful day today."

"It really is. I'm glad because I think the park is the perfect backdrop for the photos. But if you get too cold, we'll head for the heaters."

Lydia laughed quietly as she sat down on a bench and started putting on her pointe shoes. Jordan watched as she meticulously wrapped the ribbons around her ankles and adjusted her outfit. Suddenly he felt even more nervous. Not wanting to stare, Jordan walked toward the first spot he had chosen, clearing his throat, and kicking a few leaves away while she finished.

"Now, I have no idea how to direct you since I've never photographed a dancer before, so I guess I'll just let you do your thing and keep up as best I can." His back was to Lydia, but he could feel her approach.

"Sounds good," her voice was next to him now, "I'll try to hold the poses as long as I can. You picked a great spot though. It's nice and flat."

Lydia warmed up a little and then moved gracefully and easily through a couple of her favorite positions, holding them as long as she was able. Jordan kept up with her, capturing everything from different angles and heights. Eventually, as Jordan began to adjust to her pattern of movement, he took her to a different spot and told her to try running through some choreography so he could take some action shots.

After about an hour, Lydia stopped to catch her breath. "With all the rehearsals and teaching, I thought I was in shape." Lydia laughed at herself. "I almost forgot how exhausting this is."

"Well, you did great! These pictures turned out really well." Jordan was looking through the photos on his camera. Lydia joined him, looking over his shoulder. He paused on one of the action shots where he captured Lydia mid-air, legs in a split. "You make this look so easy."

Lydia laughed again, "Thanks. I'm a little out of practice though."

Jordan raised an eyebrow and smirked. "I can't even imagine what you'd look like *with* practice then. This looks amazing."

He noticed a faint blush on her cheeks as she turned back to the bench with her coat and bag. Jordan followed behind her, capping the lens of his camera.

"Depending on what type of dance you're doing or what type of teacher you have, dancing can be easy."

Jordan chuckled to himself, thinking of the uncoordinated attempts he had made during his dance lessons for Claire's wedding. Lydia had put her street shoes back on and stashed her dance shoes away. In an instant, those green eyes came up to meet his, *maybe if you were my teacher*...

As if she had read his thoughts, Lydia smiled and stood up. "Here, I'll show you." There was a flash of indecision in her eyes as she walked up to him, but her smile was still bright. She took his camera and placed it on the bench then returned and took his hands in hers. Lydia stood close enough that he could smell a faint hint of vanilla on her as she took one of his hands and placed it on her back, the other in her right hand.

"I'm going to teach you a basic waltz."

He couldn't focus and his heart began to race. The heady feeling of anxiety and excitement, plus the smell of vanilla filling his nostrils, made him feel a little unsteady.

The dance instructions began slowly as Lydia allowed him enough time to follow along. "Now, it's important to count as you step. We're going to try a simple box step. You want to count 'one, two, three.'" Jordan nodded when she paused to make sure he understood. "Step forward with the left foot." She waited for him to move, "Good! Now step to the side and together. Great! That's your first three-count step for a waltz."

Jordan stared down at his feet as Lydia led him through the dance, one step at a time. Eventually, he was confident enough to look up. She allowed him to pick up the lead as he learned the steps. They were actually very simple. The space between them slowly closed as the dance picked up speed. Lydia's beautiful green eyes took his breath away. They had little flecks of gold in them that you couldn't see unless you were up close. As much as winning this woman's heart would be a wonderful challenge, he didn't want to dig himself too deep.

Without warning or direction, Lydia pulled away and turned under the arm of the hand she held, taking him slightly off-guard. Just as he was about to pull her back in to dance some more, Lydia lowered her eyes and backed away, releasing his hand.

"You're not a bad dancer." A faint blush colored her cheeks as she tucked that loose strand behind her ear again.

That must be what she does when she's nervous. It's kind of cute. Jordan smiled to himself. "I guess I just didn't have the right teacher." He said out loud. Her eyes raised to his again but only for an instant.

"I'm getting a little hungry." Lydia picked up her bag and put her coat back on.

"Yeah, I completely forgot about breakfast."

"You're doing me a huge favor by taking these pictures, the least I can do is treat you to breakfast."

"You don't have to do that."

"No, I insist. I'd like to take you to breakfast." Lydia gave him the teacher face that challenged an argument. Straight face, single eyebrow raised. He'd seen her give it only a couple times. It could be intimidating if she wanted it to be, especially if anger bubbled below the surface as it did with June yesterday. Today, it was softened by humor.

Jordan chuckled, "Well, okay then."

Lydia's lips curled into a smile, and they started toward town.

~

It was a quiet walk to the coffee shop. Lydia battled with conflicting emotions the entire way. She was shocked at her impulsive decision to teach Jordan to dance. It wasn't like her to be so unguarded around someone she barely knew. And yet it didn't feel wrong. Standing so close to him earlier felt good…right. Like that's exactly where she belonged.

But she also felt too vulnerable. At such an important time in her career, vulnerability could end up being a weakness. Especially since June was now working so closely with Lydia and seemed to be sabotaging things for her. Lydia knew that if she allowed him to be, Jordan could be a great source of strength to her. However, she also knew that if she allowed him to get too close, he could be her greatest distraction as well.

Lydia sighed as she tried to shove all those thoughts down. Jordan didn't seem to notice, or chose not to notice, her silence.

He seemed content to quietly walk to the coffee shop, order breakfast, and take a seat by a window. They made some small talk to keep the silence from becoming embarrassing. After they had made a sufficient dent in their breakfasts to keep their stomachs from rumbling, Jordan relaxed back into his seat and smiled.

Lydia's eyes met his shyly and she smiled back, "Thank you for the pictures. I can't wait to see how they all look."

"It's my pleasure! Thank you for the breakfast." His smile grew slightly wider. "And the dance lesson."

Her heart fluttered slightly under his gaze. *Best to change the subject before this breakfast gets too cozy.* Lydia looked back down at her food, avoiding eye contact. "Have you always been a photographer, or do you like painting better?"

She could see his smile falter a little in her periphery. "Painting has always been something I dabbled in but never really got into. My manager, Sarah, convinced me to experiment with different mediums so I picked it up more seriously the last few years. Photography…I don't know…it just seems…more me, I guess." He stared out the window as he tried to find the words. Their eyes met again, "I especially love travel photography." Jordan's eyes lit up with enthusiasm.

"That sounds adventurous. Where have you traveled?"

"All over the place! Costa Rica, Florence, Paris, the Grand Canyon, Iceland…lots of places."

Lydia could almost feel the passion radiating off him. "That's amazing. I wish I could travel more. Being a small business owner doesn't really afford me much vacation time."

"Traveling is great, but it's nice to have stability. That's something I didn't really have for a while. But the thing about travel photography is you get to share the beauty of the world with people who might never get to visit those places. I also always thought that it was more meaningful for people to look at pictures taken by someone who loved the places they went to, instead of those taken by someone just wanting to get paid.

"Makes sense."

Lydia continued to listen as Jordan told her some stories of his favorite places. The people he'd met, the food he ate and tried to replicate at home, the cultures. His passion for his artform was obvious and exciting.

"Why don't you do as much travel photography anymore if it makes you so happy?" Lydia asked.

Jordan's smile faded, "I wanted to be near my family. I took all those travel jobs during a time I was in a serious relationship, and it ruined things between us. I decided to give up the whirlwind career and painting came as a way of escape after the really bad break up that followed. But that didn't really help me heal…just put off the healing. I realized how important being around people who love you was for healing a broken heart." Jordan laughed softly.

"And how's the broken heart now?"

"It's mending. Being here with Claire is good for me."

Lydia bit her lip. He was opening up to her and about something so personal. *Time for another subject change.* But before she could say anything, Jordan broke the silence.

"So, I know why you chose to be a dance teacher, but what made you decide to go into business with Kate? She doesn't strike me as the dance teacher type. Not that…I mean…that sounded bad." Jordan shook his head in embarrassment. "I really put my foot in my mouth there."

Lydia let out a belly laugh. "That's because she isn't. And I won't tell her you said that. She emphatically refuses to take any dance classes. Says it's not her calling or her passion. But she's my best friend and I trust with her my life…and my business."

"It's quite a blessing to have a friend that you trust that much."

"It really is. I thank God every day for her. She had moved from Boston a couple years after I graduated high school, and we immediately hit it off when we met. Kate's a contract finance analyst for small businesses. In Boston, she worked for big, corporate ones, but it burnt her out too quickly. Since I'm not entirely the fondest of juggling the finance portion of the business, we fit together perfectly."

As if their conversation had summoned her, Lydia recognized Kate's auburn hair as she ordered coffee. Another laugh bubbled from Lydia as she pictured Kate's face if she had heard what Jordan had said about her. She knew Kate wouldn't be offended, only amused, but she'd keep her promise not to tell.

"Hello! I never expected to find you two here, together, during my morning coffee run." Kate joined them and winked at Lydia. "I thought you weren't heading to the amphitheater today, Lydia."

"I'm not. We were actually taking pictures in the park for the studio wall." Jordan had stood to greet Kate and offered her a seat at their table. She took the offered seat while Lydia spoke.

"I see…That sounds fun. I can't wait to see them. We've been needing some updated photos. I hear the park is one of the most romantic spots in town." Kate covertly nudged Lydia in the side with her elbow. Lydia felt her face grow warm.

"Kate, I thought you had something important to finish up at the studio this morning." Lydia gave Kate her best *"back off"* look without being too obvious. However, she could tell that Jordan had seen it despite her efforts as he hid a smile behind a sip of coffee.

Kate had apparently understood the meaning behind Lydia's look as she quickly changed the subject. "Jordan, the sets look amazing! I was just over there to drop off some extra supplies for you."

"Thanks. I've been trying to speed things up a bit. I think I'm actually going to get some work done today since time's running a bit short." He took one final sip of his coffee and gathered his dishes. "I'll see you both later. Thanks for breakfast Lydia." Jordan said his goodbyes, giving Lydia a lingering glance and smile before leaving.

Kate sighed and slowly turned to face Lydia, a guilty look on her face. "I'm sorry. I took that too far."

"Really?" Lydia pursed her lips and raised her eyebrows.

"Oh, come on. You were thinking the exact same thing about the park. But I *am* sorry that I teased you in front of him."

Lydia shook her head, eyes narrowed in playful annoyance. Then she started giggling. She could never keep a straight face with Kate.

"You two just looked so cozy and cute together." Kate poked Lydia in the ribs. "Do you like him?" The smile that slowly spread over Lydia's face gave her answer. Kate laughed at her and placed a hand on Lydia's. "Well, I'm pretty positive he likes you too."

"I should get going." Lydia stood up to leave and Kate followed.

"You know, I've never seen you like this."

"Like what?"

Kate waggled her eyebrows. "In love." She said in a sing-song-y tone.

Lydia wacked her arm. "I'm not in love."

Kate laughed and wrapped her arm around Lydia's shoulders as they walked. "Okay, maybe it's just a crush. But I don't really know how else to describe it except that you look like how I felt when Steve and I started getting to know each other. How I still feel every time I see him."

Lydia didn't respond. She didn't exactly know what to say. The thoughts she was battling earlier came flooding back, sending a shot of fear through her.

"Just please don't let this guy get away from you." Kate interrupted her thoughts and unknowingly created more knots of anxiety in Lydia's stomach. "Believe me, you'll regret it if you do."

Kate meant well, of course. When they parted ways, Lydia tried to take deep breaths to settle her stomach. It was starting to feel like her and Jordan were connected by some invisible force that kept pushing them together. Even though they hadn't known each other for very long, they were opening up to each other without hesitation. She felt safe with Jordan.

Though Lydia was more reserved and quieter than her bubbly friend, she was never shy. Kate was always the one to attract all the guys. They loved her positivity and fun-loving personality. Lydia often felt that she was labeled as shy because she didn't purposefully insert herself into conversations or groups. Recently, she had been surprising herself with her confidence when she was with Jordan. It was a nice thought for her to encourage a romantic relationship, but the timing wasn't right. Kate was right that she would be crazy to let him go. But she needed space right now. No distractions.

She had plenty of time after the *Magical Holiday Celebration* was over to pursue something more. Lydia chewed her lip. It was a simple decision. Create space between them until the performance was over. Then why did it feel anything but simple?

Chapter Nine

Kate loved surprises, but she was almost never surprised. She was the master at recognizing tells. Lydia always joked that Kate would be an excellent poker player. It wasn't that she purposefully tried to figure out surprises, it just so happened that she could tell when something was up.

The funny part was that she was dating someone who loved organizing surprises for others. Steve joined the team for the *Magical Holiday Celebration* because of his love for surprises. He took so much joy out of seeing everyone's faces during the whole event. She and Lydia joked that he was probably the most excited of all of them during the holidays.

Even though Kate was good at sniffing out surprises and guessing them correctly, there had been at least two occasions on which she had been completely unaware of Steve's intentions. The first was when he asked her on their first date and the second was when he surprised her and her family with a trip to a New Hampshire ski resort last winter.

Kate had hoped that Steve was going to propose during their romantic date in the park. It was the perfect opportunity. He had laid out a picnic under the stars with personal heaters and cozy pillows to curl up on. He had even brought her favorite movie along to watch in the bed of his truck afterward. But the night ended without a proposal.

Oh well! At least she was secure enough in their relationship to know he wasn't just stringing her along. They both had an understanding that they wanted to get married someday soon. They'd only known each other for a year, but that year felt like a lifetime.

Then again, he *was* stringing her along in a way. Planning romantic dates one after another so that he *would* surprise her and throw her off with false guesses. Kate's heart began to flutter in anticipation and a smile grew on her face at the thought.

No, Kate! Stop trying to figure it out. If that is the case, you'll definitely ruin the surprise. She turned her attention back to the financial papers in front of her. This particular client needed to have them analyzed before November, which was quickly approaching. The small businesses she worked with had limited resources and tight timetables, so she tried her best to get the work done promptly.

A knock on the door drew her attention away again. "Come in." Kate called. Her office was at the dance studio which made it easier to get the work done for her business as well as others.

Steve opened the door and relaxed against the door jam, smiling at Kate. Her heart began to flip-flop again. That smile of his would forever melt her heart. "Hey, you. What's up?"

"I was just wondering if you were up for a little break?" He sauntered over to her desk and propped his hip against the edge.

Kate smirked, "Break? I've barely begun working on this." She hesitated, "What did you have in mind?"

Steve laughed, "So you're interested, then?"

"Maybe a little."

"Well, I was thinking about taking Trevor's boat out and having lunch on the water. The sun's out and it's a little warmer than yesterday."

"Hmm…that sounds nice." Kate battled with her strong desire to go with him and the necessity of finishing up her paperwork.

"I promise I'll have you back by two and I won't bother you again for the rest of the day. Lydia doesn't need you this afternoon, right?"

"Not that I know of. She's working with June all afternoon on choreography, so I'll be keeping my distance."

Steve winced, "How's that going?"

Kate sighed, "Not the greatest. I think Lydia marked her territory well, but June's still pushing back hard. Lydia looked exhausted this morning and the dancers aren't looking so happy anymore. I just hope June doesn't ostracize everyone from auditioning again next year with this whole situation."

"They trust Lydia. I don't think everyone would just give up on the performance because of June's inability to be nice."

"Yeah, well, even though I don't want to be within ten feet of June, I told Lydia that if she needed someone to stick it to her, I'd be more than happy to give her a what-for." There was no way that Kate would allow June to bully her friend. If Lydia didn't stick to her word and kick June out if she continued to be a bully, Kate would do it herself.

Steve helped her on with her coat. "I don't doubt that at all. But maybe it's best that you don't make things worse with June. She's been through a lot, and she needs friends more than she needs enemies."

Kate turned and grabbed onto Steve's coat lapels. He was always choosing to make peace. That was one of the biggest things she loved about him. "You're right. Just because June rubs me the wrong way, doesn't mean *I* should be ostracizing her. She's just so…frustrating and impossible to get along with."

Steve kissed her forehead. "You both have strong personalities. It makes sense that you'd butt heads a little. Plus, you're protective of Lydia and seeing her struggle makes you want to step in and help."

"I love that you know me so well. But it's also so annoying that I can't hide anything from you."

Steve laughed again and bent to kiss her. "But you wouldn't have it any other way."

Her eyes narrowed in mock annoyance. "No, I wouldn't."

They both headed out of the studio and to the lake where a beautiful boat picnic was awaiting them. Maybe this would be the moment he would propose. Or maybe this was just another one of his distractions to keep her from guessing when it *would* happen. Kate took a deep breath and calmed her nerves. Either way, she'd fully enjoy the time they spent together.

~

June had kept her distance most of the afternoon. In fact, she'd been a bit easier to deal with the past couple of weeks. However, Lydia knew by the way she scribbled in her notebook that June was going to have a lot of notes to go over at the end of rehearsal. She tried to keep her thoughts on the dancers rather than anticipate the drudgery of that discussion. Once the final run-through was finished with minimal correction, Lydia thanked everyone as they gathered their belongings.

"What did you think? I think they're doing an excellent job, even with the changes we implemented." Lydia tried to be enthusiastic with June in spite of the rigid superiority she emanated.

"Excellent? Did you see the flexed, sickled feet? The fingers poking straight up into the air? The pas de deux where Alex almost dropped Lisa? The dancer...what's her name...who almost fell out of the hoop onto the floor?" June crossed her arms and narrowed her eyes at Lydia.

The last dancer she had referred to was the one portraying the partridge in a suspended hoop. It was a very challenging dance, but she was doing such a fantastic job picking up the choreography so quickly. Today she didn't grasp the hoop on time and fell out of the position she was trying to hold. Thankfully she wasn't injured, only a little embarrassed.

"Yes, I did notice those things…"

"And yet you didn't correct them?" June interrupted.

Lydia's façade of calm disappeared entirely. "No, June, I didn't address those issues because they weren't pertinent. There were bigger issues to deal with today like timing, placement, and making sure each dancer was confident in their roles. Those minor details will come once the rest of the choreography is solid. It's still the beginning of November."

"They may be small details, but they are important."

"I didn't say they weren't important, I said they weren't pertinent right now." Lydia forced herself not to yell in June's face. She needed to maintain some amount of calm this time. It wouldn't do to blow up in her face like she did during their first rehearsal together.

"Well, I disagree and will certainly be addressing these issues in our next rehearsal. On another note, I have some thoughts on a few changes."

Lydia huffed a frustrated sigh and pinched the bridge of her nose. "June, we can't change things now. It's too far into rehearsal to be switching up the choreography on the dancers."

"They're professionals…or at least they're supposed to be professionals. They can handle a few changes thrown their way."

It wasn't worth the fight, so Lydia consented to at least take a look at June's notes. They were ridiculous and unnecessary. June had made notes on major changes that wouldn't go over well with the dancers. One thing that was abundantly clear was that June didn't care that Lydia had to maintain a good repour with these dancers in order to have them return the next year.

The last thing she wanted to do was frustrate the dancers to the point of having them cut all ties with the studio. Not to mention the risk of word spreading about the overbearing assistant choreographer. What would that end up doing to her prospects with Boston Ballet? After about half an hour of going back and forth about which changes to institute and which ones to disregard, Lydia finally consented to allowing one of June's major changes to the pas de deux. It was better than nothing. This close to Thanksgiving, it was a huge risk to be changing anything.

Once that was finalized, June grudgingly gathered her things and left, head held high. Lydia stretched her neck back and forth, a headache beginning to spread at the base of her head. Closing her eyes, she took a deep breath to try and release the tension.

"Hi." A voice came from the auditorium and startled her. Lydia's eyes flew open and focused on Jordan. There was a look of concern on his face as he walked toward her. "I'm sorry if I startled you. Everything okay?"

After the photography session in the park, Lydia was trying to maintain distance between her and Jordan. She showed up right when rehearsals were to take place and left before he could pull her into conversation. With her conversation with June and trying to ward off a tension headache, Lydia had dropped the ball. It had slipped her mind that Jordan might be coming by with Steve for something. She greeted him with a half-smile as she began gathering her things.

"I'm fine, just tired. Did you need something?"

Jordan's smile faltered and she immediately felt a pang of regret at her bluntness. "Um…no. I was just seeing if Steve was here to help me finish the snow globe."

"He said he'd be here by two." Lydia glanced at her watch. "I guess he's running a little late today."

Jordan made a slight humming sound in response as he sidled up the stairs to the stage. "Sounds like June's still a handful."

Lydia turned; her brow furrowed. She didn't want to talk about it, but she also didn't want to be rude. "Loitering around the amphitheater, are we?" She managed to smirk.

"Maybe a little. I got here a little early and saw a little of your…conversation."

"Conversation is putting it mildly." Jordan smiled but didn't respond. "June and I don't get along very well, as you saw. She's always seen me as competition. But at least she wasn't as bad as she was the first week."

"I'm guessing that with the artistic director coming, the competition is fiercer than ever for this assistant choreographer position?"

"Unfortunately, I think that does play into this. I'm coming to a point where I think I'll have to let June go in order to keep the peace."

"Well, if there's anything I can do, let me know."

Lydia couldn't think of any way that Jordan could help her out of this. But it was a thoughtful gesture, so she thanked him and smiled, their eyes meeting. "I should get home. I haven't eaten yet and I'm starved."

Jordan broke eye contact and rubbed the back of his neck, stepping aside to let her down the steps. "Of course. I'll see you later."

She needed to get home. To rest and figure out her next move with June. If anything, Lydia knew her mom could help her decide how to handle things. The past week had been so stressful that she wasn't sure how much more she could take, especially with time running out so quickly. Lydia's career depended on how well this performance turned out and if June was determined to ruin things…she shook her head to dispel the negative thoughts. No. Before she started thinking the worst, she needed to talk to her mom.

Chapter Ten

Lydia loved her mother's garden. It was a sanctuary where she could relax, clear her mind, and smell the beautiful flowers blooming. There was even a bench under a beautiful arbor, thickly wrapped in clematis and morning glory, where she loved to sit and sketch out ideas or read a book.

When she had returned to the house, Lydia found her mother in the garden, covering her more delicate plants with burlap and mulch to keep them warm in preparation for the first frost. Lydia was deep in thought, brow knit, as she absent-mindedly pulled out little weeds from one of the flower beds.

"Lydia? What are you thinking about?" Her mother, Allison, gently laid her hand on Lydia's shoulder, pulling her out of her thoughts and into the present.

"Oh…I was just thinking about June. I've been struggling to maintain my composure with her. She fights me on everything, and I just don't know why or how to control the situation. Unfortunately, the dancers are now just as frustrated with her, and we are falling so behind with the progress of the performance." She shivered slightly as a cool wind began to blow through the trees overhead. The sun had been covered by a thin layer of clouds all day and the usual warmth of the afternoon was gone along with the sunshine. *The weather seems to fit my mood.* Lydia thought to herself.

"I had a feeling that's what's been bothering you." Allison's mouth pressed into a concerned line. "Let's go in for some tea and warm up."

They gathered the gardening tools, storing them in the shed and headed into the kitchen where Allison prepared tea with her fresh mint from the garden. It filled the room with a wonderfully fresh scent that reminded Lydia of summer and she smiled. With her hands wrapped around her mug, Allison looked thoughtfully at her daughter, "So, June?"

Lydia sighed deeply, "She's making things so…impossible. For me and the dancers. Every little mistake means pausing the music, disrupting practice, and berating the dancers with corrections. She keeps changing up parts of the choreography and I've snapped at her more than once in front of everyone."

"I'm sorry that's happening. I know that June's always felt that you and she were in competition with each other. Maybe it would be best if you let her go?"

"I thought the same thing, until I got a call on the way home saying that Mr. Fairfax would like me to come and do an interview in Boston the weekend after Thanksgiving. If I fire June, I won't have anyone to lead rehearsal while I'm gone. And we can't afford to miss even one rehearsal at this point. I am also afraid that if I do fire her, she'll find another way to make this performance fail. If she can't compete for the job as assistant choreographer, she won't want me to have it either."

"Isn't that jumping to conclusions a bit? How do you know she'd try to ruin the performance?"

"I don't know. I guess based on what she's been doing so far, that's all that makes sense."

"Making assumptions about somebody isn't going to fix ill will. It's going to make you trust her even less than you already do, especially if you're expecting the worst out of her." Lydia opened her mouth to respond but her mom stopped her short. "I know she's a difficult person to trust. *But* she deserves respect as much as the next person. That might mean that you need to talk to her, dancer to dancer, and let her know that if it continues, you'll have to release her from her position as assistant choreographer. As far as finding someone to handle rehearsal while you're gone, it might mean having the dancers rehearse on their own."

"I've tried talking to her."

"But you lost your temper, right?"

Lydia gave an exasperated look. "I started out calm and respectful but she just…ugh!"

"Pushed too many buttons?"

Lydia nodded. "It just seems like we've reached an impasse. Anytime I'm nice to her, she fires back. It feels pointless."

Allison took a deep breath to gather her thoughts. "I know it can feel that way sometimes, but you never know what a difference you are making just by being kind. Continue to be kind to her and earn her trust. Lashing out at her isn't going to do that. It's going to do the opposite. She wants to get under your skin. Tell her that, by the end of the week, if she can't find a way to respect your position, you won't be needing her help anymore. As much as you should be kind to her, you can't be subjecting yourself and those dancers to toxic behavior. That might make her think about her attitude."

"Or it might make things worse." Lydia grumbled.

Allison reached across the table and placed a reassuring hand on Lydia's. "Have faith that she'll come around. Have you prayed about this situation?"

Lydia bit her lip, "Not really." Why hadn't she thought to pray about it? She'd even prayed a little about the situation with Jordan. For some reason, when it came to June, Lydia felt that she hadn't ever truly cared about her. Suddenly, Lydia felt guilty about her behavior. She wasn't being kind; she was just tolerating June.

"Maybe that's the best way to move forward. God will know better than the both of us how to handle June."

It felt as though a small weight had been lifted from her shoulders. Relying on God's wisdom, strength, and patience had never failed her in the past and she knew it wouldn't fail her now. June was loved by God just as she was.

"Is that all that's bothering you?"

Thoughts of Jordan began forming in her mind. She'd told her mom about hiring him, their photography session together, and the fact that she thought they were getting too close. Allison had given her the same advice that Kate had. Don't let a great guy slip through your fingers. Lydia hadn't exactly told her mom that she'd made the decision to create space between them, and she didn't really want to open that can of worms with her now. Instead, she turned to the subject that always weighed on her. "The closer we get to Thanksgiving, the more I dread it. I'm just tired of spending the holidays without dad."

Allison squeezed the hand she still held and smiled sadly. "I know, sweetheart. He doesn't like it any more than we do. But he did say that he's coming to see your performance and spend Christmas with us, so that's something to look forward to. And just think, next year he's retiring, and he will be ours again. No traveling, no missed holidays."

"It just seems like such a long time from now." Lydia tried to smile.

Her mom pulled her in for a side hug and kissed her head. "We'll get through this together. He'll be here before you know it."

Lydia admired her mother's bravery throughout her father's deployment. As hard as it was for her to be missing her dad, Lydia knew it was even harder for her mom to be missing her husband. Her mom was right. They would get through this time together just like they had since Lydia was ten years old. It was one final Thanksgiving without him. He'd be back soon, and their family would be whole again.

~

"That looks incredible!"

Jordan turned to see June watching him from the front row of the amphitheater. He decided to stay behind after Steve helped him finish the final electrical details on the last set. How long had she been there watching him paint? He didn't even hear the door click shut.

"Thanks, June." Jordan wiped his hands on his painting pants and stood to begin rinsing out his paintbrushes. It was getting late, and chilly. The set was finished, which meant that he only had three more left. A good, homecooked meal was waiting for him at Claire's and he was eager to get home. Plus, June always made him nervous.

"You're welcome. You headed out?"

"Yeah, my cousin's expecting me for dinner in a few. Were you looking for Lydia?" In an effort to keep the conversation casual, Jordan tried to keep his gaze focused everywhere except on June.

June scrunched her nose in response to his question and shook her head, donning a flirtatious smile. "No. Just thought I'd left something here earlier."

Jordan smiled politely but didn't say anything. He continued to clean up his workspace, his back toward June.

"You're an amazing artist, you know. We're lucky to have you in our crew." June had walked up to the stage and was standing close to him. Too close for comfort. He took a step back and almost trampled over her foot in the process. She took the opportunity to place her hand on his back to not only stop him from crushing her toes, but also to close the distance between them.

"I'm so sorry!" He side-stepped to restore the space between them.

"It's okay. It seems like you have a knack for trampling over women." Her lips parted in a flirtatious grin. She was taller than Lydia and those chocolatey-brown eyes met his without him having to dip his head. Before he knew what was happening, June had closed the distance again. Placing a hand on his forearm, June was so close he could feel her breath on his face. His heart pounded as he felt danger was in sight, but he was trapped between June and a set, unable to move. Before he could do anything to stop her, the click of the door sounded and Jordan finally broke free of June's eye contact finding Lydia's green eyes staring up at him, mouth agape.

He cleared his throat and gently pushed June away, immediately feeling as though he'd been caught cheating or something. Lydia's eyes widened slightly at seeing them in such an intimate position and a faint blush crept into her cheeks. Jordan nervously rubbed the back of his neck.

"I'm…sorry…" Lydia's voice faltered. She looked like she wanted to disappear through a hole in the ground.

"Hi Lydia." June turned toward her slowly, her head cocked to the side, the flirtatious grin still playing on her lips. "I was just stopping by to see if I had left my choreography notes here. Turns out I didn't." She let out a low chuckle.

Jordan didn't know how to defend himself. Lydia wouldn't make eye contact with him. June was watching them, probably realizing the tension now created between Lydia and himself. The last thing he wanted to do was give June more ammunition to make Lydia's life even harder. After their time together in the park, Jordan had hoped he had a chance at competing for Lydia's affections. As bad as it made him feel at times to try and win another guy's girl from him, Jordan couldn't deny his obvious feelings for her and the chemistry that sparked whenever they were together.

"I just…uh…stopped by to see if Kate was here. She wasn't at the studio, and I needed to tell her something." The awkwardness of the situation was making Lydia flustered.

"She told me she was working at home tonight, and I could text her if I needed anything." Jordan finally found his voice.

Lydia looked at him for the first time since she entered, "Thank you."

Her soft-spoken words cut to his heart. She looked at him with such disappointment in her eyes. As soon as the door clicked closed behind Lydia, June took advantage of Jordan's distraction, placed her hand on his shoulder and kissed him on the cheek. "See you on Monday." She flashed her most alluring smile and hurried away.

What in the world just happened? He was in a daze. Everything had happened so fast that he couldn't keep up. This was new territory. New territory that he had tried so hard to avoid. It was his fault for watching rehearsals so intently. June must have got the wrong idea. Jordan knew from the moment he met June that she needed to be kept at arm's length.

How could you be so stupid? He frowned at himself and finished gathering his things. He didn't know how, but Jordan needed to let June down quickly and quietly, and he needed to do it soon. The last thing he wanted was to hurt Lydia or send her mixed signals.

Chapter Eleven

June was being…pleasant. After the whole incident at the amphitheater last week, she figured that she could give Lydia a little break. Besides, she had Jordan where she wanted him, and Lydia clearly had a thing for him which could be a great distraction. June just needed to keep her assistant position long enough to implement a few changes while Lydia was in Boston. Kate was such a blabbermouth that she'd heard the news of Lydia's trip over the weekend.

A small amount of guilt hovered around June's heart, as she considered that changing things up this close to performance day might ruin the chances for some of these dancers to earn a scholarship. However, it was a small price to pay for Lydia losing the position of assistant choreographer. The bottom line was that June wanted the job and if she couldn't have it, Lydia couldn't either.

Jordan was a plus. If she could flirt her way into his good graces, he might end up actually liking her. June's confidence faltered when she thought of that. As always, Lydia had gained ground first. Then again, Lydia wasn't even taking any action toward gaining Jordan's attentions, so he was fair game.

The music stopped and June began to give corrections. As Lydia predicted, the dancers were annoyed by the significant change to the pas de deux. June had noticed that the dancers were beginning to push back and ignore her, so she knew she needed to change tactics. That's why she was being pleasant. Her corrections were less sharp and more relaxed. *These dancers are so petty and weak. They can't even handle constructive criticism.* June thought to herself as she sat down to watch them run through the dance again.

Lydia was very quiet today. June glanced over at her without being too obvious. She noticed a small smile on Lydia's lips, but her eyes looked distracted and tired. June had never seen Lydia so gloomy before. She shook her head. It didn't matter to her. Why should it?

As the music wound down to its last few notes, June stood to address the dancers before they left. "That was passable, I guess. Be here bright and early Friday. We'll have to make up time on Monday since Thanksgiving limits the time we have." She nodded once and the dancers left.

"June, can we talk?"

June rolled her eyes at Lydia's oh-so-sweet voice. "Sure, Lydia." She matched the sweetness of Lydia's voice with her own, mocking tone.

Lydia frowned. "As you can probably tell, the dancers are burning out. They're tired and trying their hardest to incorporate the changes. While I'm gone, I want to make sure that you're not pushing them too hard."

"It's not my problem they can't keep up."

"No. It's mine if they fall behind. I'm the one with the reputation on the line. If you continue to push these dancers too hard, you're inviting ill will between the dancers and this studio. On top of that, how do you think burning them out will affect their prospects with Boston Ballet?"

How dare Lydia throw that responsibility on her shoulders? It wasn't her problem if they failed to impress the artistic director. That tiny whisper of guilt gnawed at June again, but she shoved it down. "If these dancers are going to be so soft as to crumple under the pressure, they don't deserve to be with Boston Ballet!" June lashed out. "Boston Ballet is for the very best. The ones who can take constructive criticism. Dancers who dedicate their whole lives to ballet." Her voice faltered a little as sudden emotion clogged her throat.

Lydia didn't know how to respond. June invoked pity instead of anger in Lydia. There was a deep sadness behind the anger in her eyes and a bitterness to her words that made Lydia's heart hurt for her. She hadn't realized that June was still so angry about having to drop out of the company. And why shouldn't she be? As far as she knew, June had dedicated her whole life to the company and when she got injured, that life was ripped from her.

"June, I trust you to take care of the dancers while I'm gone. I'm just asking that you treat them with the same respect you would want others to pay you."

It looked like June was going to say something, but she clenched her jaw and stormed off the stage and out the door. Lydia took a deep breath and closed her eyes in prayer. *Thank you, Lord, for patience and mercy. Be with June. Help her come to peace with her past. Soften her heart and help her see your love for her.* She took another deep breath and smiled.

This was no longer about being the best choreographer or even getting the job with Boston Ballet. God had worked on her heart all week. It was about protecting the minds and hearts of the dancers under her care. That included June. Lydia didn't care as much about the job as she did winning over June's trust. For the first time in a month, Lydia felt a weight had been lifted from her shoulders. Her mom was right, prayer and patience had worked.

Lydia felt a joy radiating from her. *God is so good!* She felt peaceful about leaving her performance in June's hands for one rehearsal. Everything would be just fine.

Chapter Twelve

It was the day before Thanksgiving and Lydia hadn't even begun to prepare their meal. It would just be her and her mom with Kate and Steve this year, so it had fallen to the bottom of her to-do list. Her grandmother usually took care of Thanksgiving preparations but had decided to go on a cruise this year with some friends. Lydia thought that she'd have enough time with no rehearsals all week, but other details came up such as finalizing costumes and the music arrangement.

Her and her mom hadn't even found time to get their turkey, which was a risky thing to leave to the last minute. Nonetheless, they decided to check the grocery store and see if there were any left. Before they could leave the parking lot, Lydia spotted Jordan exiting the store. He noticed her, a sheepish grin on his face. Next to him, a blonde woman followed with a rosy smile on her face, showing off the most adorable dimples.

That must be his cousin. Dimples must run in the family.

"Good morning." Lydia smiled courteously, trying to avoid eye contact with Jordan.

"Morning…this is my cousin, Claire." He turned to Claire, "Claire, Lydia."

Claire stuck her hand out and shook Lydia's. "Nice to meet you, officially. Jordan's told me a lot about you."

Lydia returned Claire's beaming smile with one of her own. "Nice to meet you, too. This is my mom."

Jordan and Claire greeted Allison.

"Are you ready for Thanksgiving?" Claire asked.

"Not really." Allison laughed, "We're actually hoping that there is a turkey left to cook up tomorrow."

"Good luck with that! I didn't notice any while we were in there, but you never know."

Lydia scuffed her toe into the ground and Jordan shoved his hands into his pockets, allowing Allison and Claire to take charge of the conversation. Claire was wonderful! It was no wonder her and Jordan were so close. After the usual small talk, Lydia noticed Claire nudging Jordan in the side, which brought his gaze up from the ground.

"Jordan and I were just talking about how giant our turkey is and that we might have leftovers coming out our ears." Claire laughed and Jordan smiled. Her face brightened even more, which Lydia didn't think was possible. "Would you like to join us for Thanksgiving dinner?"

Jordan's eyes widened slightly, and they locked with Lydia's. Lydia broke eye contact and was about to politely refuse when her mom answered.

"Really?"

"Absolutely! The more the merrier! It's just me, my husband, and Jordan. We'd love to have you!"

Lydia tried to think of some excuse to make, but nothing came to mind. She was supposed to be creating distance between her and Jordan, not getting closer. Spending a holiday with him and his family would most definitely bring them closer. An idea popped into her head. "I forgot! We have already invited Kate and Steve to join us for dinner. I wouldn't want to put you in the position of having four extra mouths to feed."

"Not a problem at all! Like I said, there's plenty of turkey and we just picked up extra supplies for the side dishes. They are more than welcome to come as well." Claire was so excited that Lydia couldn't help but be amused by her generosity and bubbly personality.

"I don't think they'd be opposed to a change of scenery, do you, Lydia?" Allison laid her hand on Lydia's shoulder.

She bit her lip. "No, I suppose not. Thank you, Claire!"

"Perfect! Oh, this is so exciting! It's been such a long time since we've hosted a dinner party." Claire was almost jumping up and down as she grabbed Jordan's arm in her excitement. Jordan laughed at her.

"Is there anything I can bring?" Allison offered.

"We could always use some extra mashed potatoes and rolls."

Lydia's eyes darted between Claire and Jordan as the details were ironed out for dinner the next day. Her heart fluttered when her eyes accidentally met Jordan's and he smiled at her.

"It was wonderful meeting you! See you tomorrow!" Allison was waving at Claire as they started to walk toward their car. She turned to Lydia, "Well that's a weight off my shoulders. I guess we don't have to go to the store after all."

They returned to their car in silence. As they were pulling out, Allison smiled. "Jordan seems very nice." She glanced over at Lydia.

"He is." Lydia replied nonchalantly.

"I look forward to getting to know him and his cousin better. For such a small town, I'm surprised we haven't seen more of Claire."

Lydia stared ahead, frowning. This was not going to be the simple, laid-back holiday she'd expected. Claire was wonderful and she did look forward to getting to know her better. But Jordan? What was she going to do about him?

~

Claire wrapped her arm in Jordan's and giggled to herself as they walked back to the car.

"What are you laughing at?" Jordan turned to look at her.

"You."

"What did I do?"

"Jordan. You didn't tell me you liked Lydia." She accused, continuing to giggle. He stopped to look at her, confused. "I mean, I guessed it since you've been in a cheerier mood lately, but I didn't think it was *this* serious."

"What are you talking about?"

Claire laughed at his comical expression. "I'm pretty sure everyone would have noticed the tension between you two. In fact, I'm almost positive her mom noticed too."

Jordan blushed at the mention of Lydia's mother. Had she really noticed? It didn't even seem like Lydia was glad to be there. After the incident at the theater with June, and the space Lydia seemed to place between them, he didn't expect anything less. He cleared his throat. "I don't know what you're talking about. Besides, Lydia's too busy with the performance for anything outside of it. And I'm pretty sure she's dating someone."

"Hmm…well, I think there's more there than you think. On both sides. This will definitely be an interesting Thanksgiving." Claire laughed again and Jordan shook his head.

Interesting or terribly awkward. He almost wished he'd made some sort of excuse for Lydia and her mom not to come. Lydia had seemed to be fishing for an excuse too. At least Kate and Steve would be there to break up the awkwardness a bit.

Chapter Thirteen

The smell of fresh baked pie, turkey, and garlicky mashed potatoes wafted through the house as Claire rushed around, getting things ready for their guests. She, with the help of Jordan and Kyle, had been cooking all day and the smells were starting to make their stomachs growl. One of Claire's greatest joys in life was hosting people. She absolutely loved cooking for them and opening her home to anyone who needed a hot meal and friendship.

About ten minutes before the expected arrival of their guests, Claire had shooed both men to their rooms to change into something "more respectable." A knock on the front door made Jordan's heart skip a beat. Right on time. His fingers suddenly felt like sausages, and they fumbled with the buttons on his shirt as he tried to calm the mix of anxiety and eagerness swirling around in his stomach. When Lydia's voice trailed up the stairs as she talked to Claire, he smiled in anticipation.

Jordan headed down the stairs and found his cousin "oohing" and "awing" over a delicious-looking sweet potato casserole Lydia's mother was carrying. Claire led the way to the kitchen. Lydia was removing her coat and he noticed that her red dress brought out the golden highlights of her hair and flattered her figure beautifully. As he was admiring her, Lydia's eyes met his and he felt his cheeks go warm.

"Happy Thanksgiving!" Jordan walked forward and grabbed her coat from her and turned to hang it on a coat hook by the door.

"Happy Thanksgiving." Her reply was so quiet, he almost didn't hear it at all.

Before he could say anything else, another knock echoed in the hall. Kate and Steve joined the party and everyone's voices mingled together in excitement.

"Oh, good! Everyone's here!" Claire came into the hall, greeted her guests, and clapped her hands together. "I'm so glad that you could all come and spend Thanksgiving with us. Now, I don't know about you, but I'm ready to dig into this delicious-smelling meal."

They all followed her into the dining room chatting comfortably as they went. Jordan hung back a little from the group, not quite sure how to proceed with Lydia. She seemed happy to be there, but there was still the unpleasantness from the whole June situation they had to get past. He thoughtfully watched her as she interacted with everyone, and he found himself a little envious of everyone she smiled at. Lydia hadn't smiled at him with that genuine, joyful smile in a while. About a week and a half actually. Not that he was keeping track.

Gathered around the table, Kyle said a prayer over their meal and the people who were gathered together. As dishes were served and passed, light conversation and laughter filled the room. Jordan had been quietly observing and listening to everything when Allison dragged his attention away from his meal.

"So, Jordan, do you like living in Boston?"

"I do. It's vibrant and exciting, especially for a photographer. But sometimes it can be a little overwhelming and loud. I think Maple Ridge has ruined me a little. It's so peaceful and laid back here. It almost makes me want to relocate somewhere quieter." Jordan glanced in Lydia's direction, but she seemed to be entranced with her mashed potatoes.

"Maple Ridge is a beautiful place. I'm sure Claire would be thrilled to have you move closer considering what she was telling me about how close you both were as kids."

"I've been trying to get him to move here for years. If you can find the secret to getting him to stay, please share." Claire teased.

Jordan looked over at Lydia again, knowing full well that she would play a part in his decision to stay or return to Boston. He hadn't exactly thought too hard about staying in Maple Ridge, but the past few weeks of getting to know Lydia and spending time with his cousin, made him consider it. Before he could look away, Lydia glanced up and looked straight at him, but only for a second. She probably didn't expect him to be staring at her because he could see color suffuse her cheeks before he turned his attention back to Allison.

The look on Allison's face told him that the split second of eye contact between him and Lydia hadn't escaped her notice. It was his turn to feel his cheeks go warm with embarrassment and he looked down at his food again.

"Claire," Allison redirected the conversation, "what is it that you do?"

"Well, I'm kind of in between jobs at the moment. I used to work for a business in Boston as their accountant until I realized that I actually hate accounting." She chuckled to herself. "Right now, I'm thinking about opening my own bakery."

"That's amazing! It would be such a relief to have a bakery around here. The coffee shop is great and all, but their baked goods aren't the best." Lydia finally joined in on the conversation.

"Yeah, I noticed that food isn't really their priority there which is too bad. Who doesn't want a pastry *with* their coffee? But I figured since I love to bake, I might as well share it with the rest of the town." Claire beamed.

"It would also be better for us if she were to sell all the extras, or I won't be able to fit through the door anymore." Kyle teased his wife.

Lydia snickered. "What is it that you do, Kyle?"

"I'm finishing up my last year of residency at the hospital. Next year, I'll be a full-fledged doctor. If all goes well, I'm planning on starting a practice closer to town as a GP."

"That's really great. Congratulations."

"Thank you. It's been a huge help having Jordan here to help Claire out, preparing for winter and the holidays. I will definitely not miss the long hours of residency."

As conversations continued, Jordan's mind couldn't focus. Lydia was clearly avoiding his gaze, but he could still see those green eyes lighting up with amusement and laughter at the others at the table. The food was wonderful, but it felt like he'd swallowed a rock. After dinner, he needed to talk to Lydia about what she saw between him and June. Getting her alone would be a challenge but he couldn't put it off any longer.

~

Lydia couldn't help but glance in Jordan's direction every now and then during dinner. His warm, friendly smile showed that tempting dimple. She could tell that Kate and her mom were catching each glance. Kate had even nudged her playfully when Lydia's mom talked to Jordan about moving to Maple Ridge.

Once dinner was over, Claire started to clear plates. "Let me help." Lydia stood and gathered the dishes around her, following Claire into the kitchen. "That was an amazing dinner, Claire. Thank you so much."

"It was my pleasure! I'm so glad you enjoyed it. Thank you for the help."

"It's the least I can do."

Allison joined them with more dishes. "Claire, I hope you don't mind, but it's a tradition of ours to watch *It's a Wonderful*

Life after Thanksgiving dinner with some cocoa. I brought the movie and some cocoa mix if you're up for it."

"That sounds wonderful! I can start the cocoa if you would like to put the movie in. Jordan can show you where the DVD player is."

"Lydia, I'll help Claire with some of these dishes if you can go get the movie ready."

Lydia gave her mom a look as she took the DVD that she held out and went to find Jordan. He was sitting next to Steve, laughing about something. She took a deep breath to calm her nerves.

"Excuse me, Jordan. Claire said you could help me set up the DVD player for a movie."

Jordan's eyes met hers and he smiled. "Of course. Right in here." He led her into the living room and got the movie all set up. In the quiet, Lydia looked around at some of the pictures on Claire's wall.

"All set!"

Lydia turned back toward him. "Great, I'll go let everyone know."

Before she could leave, Jordan reached out and laid a hand on her arm to stop her. "Wait, Lydia. Can I talk to you for a second?"

She wanted to escape but she couldn't get her feet to move. Lydia nodded, unable to form any words with her heart fluttering so irritatingly.

"Lydia, at the amphitheater…when you walked in…I…" He looked up at the ceiling as if the words he was looking for were pasted there.

"Jordan, look, it's none of my business."

"I still want you to know that there's nothing going on between me and June." Lydia didn't respond, just pressed her mouth into an unsure smile. "In fact, since meeting you, I had hoped that you and I could…but that's crazy because you're already dating, and I shouldn't have even said anything." Jordan scrubbed his face in frustration with himself.

Lydia was completely confused. Dating? Her? Where on earth did he get that idea? Her face must have shown her thoughts because he looked at her funny.

"I should explain. I saw you with your boyfriend a couple of times. Once in a restaurant and the next day at the coffee shop."

Lydia stared. Who would he have seen her with that would give him the idea that she was dating? In a moment, the pieces started coming together and she laughed. "Do you mean Trevor? He's the set builder. You must have seen us out to dinner after he'd finished building all the sets. The next day, I invited him for coffee." She continued to laugh. Jordan's look of confusion was comical. "I'm sorry. Now *I* need to explain. Trevor is like my brother. We're really close, but not in that way. I had invited him to dinner and coffee to thank him."

A look of relief passed over Jordan's face as he comprehended everything. "So, you're not dating?"

"I'm not." Her laughter ceased as Jordan's look of relief became one of complete hope and desire. It took her breath away. All at once, she felt the walls around her heart crumble into dust. Creating space between them would be impossible now with him looking at her like that. Especially when that look made her heart feel like it was going to escape her body with its thumping.

"Hey you guys!" Kate came in, cutting the tension in the room with her cheerful greeting.

Jordan smiled at Kate and excused himself from the room to gather everyone together. Lydia tried to get her heart under control.

"Did I interrupt something? You look like someone's just punched you in the stomach."

Lydia tried to smile but her nerves were preventing it from reaching her eyes. She was still trying to figure out her feelings about Jordan and the fact that he had practically admitted that he wanted to date her. "I'm fine. Just getting the movie started."

Kate's brows went up, "That's not all there is. Putting a movie in a DVD player doesn't make you blush to your eyeballs. Has your flirting paid off?" A teasing smile played on Kate's lips as she wrapped her arm around Lydia's shoulders.

"Flirting?"

"Girl, you may not realize it, but you bat your eyes at that man constantly. It's a wonder it's taken him this long to make a move."

"Bat my eyes? I do no such thing. I've been trying to maintain space, not get closer."

"How's that working out for you?" Lydia looked at Kate with a helpless look that revealed everything. Kate laughed at her. "I was right! I can see double-dates in our future, just no double-wedding. I want that day all to myself."

~

As he left the room, Jordan felt like his feet weren't even touching the floor. Lydia wasn't dating anyone! The smile on his face felt silly but he couldn't help it. Claire even looked at him quizzically when he called everyone to the living room to start the movie. It didn't even matter. He had struggled with guilt over flirting with someone already spoken for, but now there were no barriers to keep him from pursuing Lydia. Even the idea of a possible long-distance relationship didn't scare him. Maple Ridge was too special to him now to leave. How he'd break the news to Sarah, he didn't know, but he knew deep down that Boston was no longer his home. Getting to know Lydia, even at a distance, had changed his mind about a lot of things.

Jordan had a hard time focusing on the movie. Halfway through, Claire paused it and nudged him where he was seated on the floor with her foot.

"Jordan, I think it's about time for some dessert. Could you slice up the pie and bring it in on the large tray? I'll set up the coffee table."

He looked up at her and gave her a regal smile. "I'd be happy to my lady." Jordan stood and bowed to his cousin as he picked up the tray of empty mugs. He caught Claire rolling her eyes and chuckling at him. Allison was also asking Lydia if she'd help.

In the kitchen, Jordan got the pies out and started slicing them. Lydia joined him and he smiled at her. "You were right. The movie is pretty good. Not as good as *White Christmas* but still good."

"I'm glad." She returned his smile with one that made her eyes sparkle. Here he was envying everyone who was on the receiving end of that smile all night and now it was directed at him. He laughed softly to himself. "What?"

"Oh, nothing. I was just thinking about something. Here…" Jordan handed Lydia a plate with a slice of pie on it. "This is Claire's famous recipe. She says it's better plain, but I like mine with just a dollop of whipped cream on top. I'll let you be the judge of which way tastes better." Giving her a fork, he looked at her expectantly.

Lydia looked at him curiously and took a bite. "Wow! This is amazing!"

"Okay, now try it with some cream." Jordan plopped some fresh whipped cream on part of the pie.

She giggled and took another bite. "I don't know. Both ways are delicious."

He raised his eyebrows in question, "But…?"

"But if I were to pick one…I'd go without the cream." She pulled in her bottom lip and smiled guiltily.

Jordan sighed and hung his head in playful defeat. "I guess I'm not able to win anyone over to my side. None of my family members like it that way either. I'm the only one." He gave her puppy dog eyes which made her laugh.

"Well, if it makes you feel any better, my dad is a huge whipped cream fan so he'd probably side with you." Lydia's eyes sparkled from their shared amusement. Any tension that had hung between them earlier in the night was completely gone.

"Speaking of, I don't want to pry but…" he hesitated.

"Where is my dad?"

"Yeah." Jordan replied cautiously.

"He's stationed overseas and won't be home until Christmas. My parents thought it would be best for my mom to have the support of my grandmother while I was growing up, so my mom and I moved here." Lydia looked down as she absently poked at her pie. He felt horrible for bringing up such a delicate and tender subject. Without thinking, Jordan placed a hand on her shoulder and placed gentle pressure reassuringly.

"I'm sorry that you don't have your dad here with you. I can't imagine how hard that must be for you and your mom."

Lydia smiled up at him sadly. "Thank you. It's difficult, especially during the holidays, but I'm used to it."

"That doesn't make it any easier." Jordan could see the pain in her eyes. He suspected some of the distance she had been creating between them was probably because she was afraid of losing someone close to her. Knowing that he'd return to Boston after the holidays, it all made sense that she'd keep her distance.

"No, it doesn't. But he'll be retiring in the new year so that's something to look forward to." Lydia's answer brought his mind back to their conversation.

"That's exciting!"

"It is!" Lydia's smile returned, lighting her eyes.

Jordan's eyes instinctively dropped to her mouth and then up again. He was close enough to notice the flecks of gold in her eyes.

"We should probably get these pies in to everyone." Lydia broke the silence.

"They're probably wondering what's taking so long." Before he could pick up his tray, Lydia grabbed Jordan's arm.

"Jordan, I'm sorry if I've been a little distant lately. I just…I…" She bit her lip, struggling to find the right words.

"It's okay." His smile seemed to reassure her.

"It's just that, my dad always left. I know he loves me, but he was never there. Getting close to people it's…"

"Scary?"

Lydia nodded.

"I can't promise I won't leave, but I can promise to try my best to be available. That is, if you are interested."

She smiled again and his heart leapt at the possibilities that smile opened to him. Her hand slid down to his hand and rested there for a second before she snatched it away, picked up her own tray, and headed back to the living room, flashing a slightly flirtatious smile over her shoulder.

The music ended and Claire flicked the light on.

"I'm going to have to join one of your dance classes, Lydia, to work this pie off." Kate laughed.

"I didn't realize how late it was." Steve checked his watch.

"It's been a wonderful evening!" Allison hugged Claire.

Claire made sure that everyone had the dishes they had brought with them. Goodbyes were said as everyone filed out the door, starting with Kate and Steve. Jordan followed closely behind so he didn't miss his chance to say a final goodbye to Lydia. Just when he thought he'd miss his chance, Allison remembered she had left her keys inside, leaving Lydia and Jordan alone on the front step.

"Thank you for introducing me to Claire's amazing pie."

Jordan smiled. "Thank you for introducing me to a new Christmas movie."

The silence that fell between them was comfortable. It had been the perfect night. They'd cleared up some misunderstandings and Lydia had even opened up to him about something very personal. He took that very seriously. Lydia didn't strike him as the type of person to confide in just anyone. It made him feel like he was welcomed into her inner circle of trust, which had to be a difficult thing to achieve. Jordan wanted to know everything there was to know about Lydia.

She looked so beautiful tonight. The dress, her hair, those perfectly glossed lips. What would it feel like to kiss those lips? As he thought about it, they parted slightly, as if she was thinking the same thing. Without any thought, he felt himself leaning toward her, getting closer and closer. Her head tilted up in response instead of turning away and just as he was about to have his question answered, the door swung open and he jumped back, a blush suffusing his cheeks and neck.

Allison and Claire were chatting and laughing, not seeming to notice what had almost happened between him and Lydia. Lydia smiled shyly at him and almost imperceptibly shrugged a shoulder as if to say, "maybe next time." That look made his heart soar. *Yes, maybe next time.*

Out loud, Lydia simply said, "goodnight, Jordan," and flashed those beautiful green eyes at him over her shoulder as she walked with her mom to the car.

Chapter Fourteen

Preparations for Christmas had begun on Monday, and the town was almost completely decked out in holiday adornments. New menus were posted in the restaurants and the coffee shop, the bed and breakfast was fully booked for the holidays, and the amphitheater was slowly receiving a holiday makeover.

All at once, Lydia felt the pressure. Time was flying by, and she still had so much to do before performance day. In the back of her mind, she knew she had plenty of time to get everything perfect. The trick was trying to convince herself there was nothing to worry about. Having the added pressure of relinquishing control over an entire day of rehearsal to June didn't help though.

Her trip to Boston was still four days away, and she was only going to be gone for three days, but Lydia felt that her leaving was imprudent. Never had she ever left during the final stages of performance preparations. Sure, June was capable of handling rehearsals well and even Kate could perfectly handle everything else, but she couldn't let go. Then again, this interview with Mr. Fairfax was important and strategically planned so that she wouldn't be running around like a chicken with its head cut off the day of the performance. Since he'd be conducting individual auditions with the dancers the day of, he wouldn't have time for her. It was a really considerate gesture on his part.

Lydia took a deep breath to calm her nerves. It wasn't worth worrying over something that was out of her control. She thought about the fact that the town would probably be all decked out by the time she got back. The Christmas tree in town center would be going up and decorated on Saturday.

She touched up her makeup in the mirror while she went over her mental checklist. Her hotel was booked for Friday and

Saturday night, her interview would be Friday afternoon, Saturday she would be touring the company, and she could spend her extra time exploring the city a little. Kate had insisted that Lydia make this weekend trip a vacation and spend Sunday in the city to decompress. Lydia's mom had agreed saying, "it's only three days. What could go wrong in that short amount of time?"

If Lydia were honest, the thing that made her most nervous was the interview itself. Lydia had never been interviewed for a job before. She was blessed to have started her own business early in life, so she'd never had to look outside the studio for work. Her apprehension returned.

You'll do great! You've been a choreographer for years. Just because you are interviewing for a position at a prestigious company, doesn't mean that the job will drastically change. Lydia tried to give herself a pep talk. It wasn't working. The anxious tumble of knots in her stomach tightened. *Let's think of something else...*

Her thoughts veered to Thanksgiving. It had been better than she'd ever expected. Lydia barely slept that night thinking about her and Jordan's "almost kiss."

He was about to kiss her, right?

It certainly seemed like he was. She'd given him an opening and she noticed him leaning in. Lydia sighed. If only her mom and Claire had stayed inside for a few more minutes, then she'd have found out for sure what his intentions were.

But even if he hadn't planned on kissing her, just the way he looked at her throughout the night would have given her sleep troubles. They definitely had chemistry pulling them together. She smiled at her reflection, noticing the natural blush that suffused her cheeks, and bit her lip as if trying to hold in all these new feelings.

It had been three days, and she already missed seeing Jordan. He'd probably be there at the amphitheater today, finishing up the final details on the last set. The anticipation made it feel like her heart would pound right out of her chest and she hurried with her hair.

Lydia met the dancers at the studio for a quick warm-up before heading to the amphitheater. With the weather cooling down so quickly, they needed to start limiting their time outdoors, especially the musicians. When they arrived at the stage, Steve had the space heaters going.

Everyone took their places and Peter tapped his conductor's wand on the music stand. As the music began, Lydia's heart fluttered, but this time in excitement at watching her hard work come to fruition. A proud smile remained on her face the entire time as the dancers "flew" and leaped. It was beautiful! All their collective hard work was visible. When the music ended, all that could be heard over the heavy breathing of the dancers was Lydia's clapping.

"That was amazing! The pas de deux looks great! Just make sure you continue to support one another. We don't need anyone falling this close to performance. I don't want our musicians and singers to freeze so let's run through it one more time with them." Lydia gave some additional corrections and then the performance began again.

Lydia could feel rather than hear Jordan's entrance. It was as if his presence alone had the power to alter her heart palpitations and make her warm enough to endure the chill of the air. She chanced a glance over at him and she met his ready smile with one of her own. As she turned to face the dancers again, she locked eyes with June. She watched as June's features darkened and her eyes snapped in the opposite direction. Lydia's smile faded, *is it possible that June has real feelings for Jordan?*

When the final corrections were made and the musicians dismissed, June stormed off the stage, brushing past Jordan on her way. This wasn't a good sign so close to Lydia's trip to Boston. The last thing they all needed was conflict, creating tension while she was gone. Jordan watched June leave; confusion etched on his face.

"Is she okay?" Jordan asked when he and Lydia were alone, as the dancers took a short break at the back of the stage.

"I'm not sure."

Jordan's expression changed from confusion and concern to genuine warmth. "The performance looks amazing!"

"It does, doesn't it!" Lydia couldn't contain her excitement. She was so proud of her dancers.

A chuckle shook Jordan's shoulders. "So, umm…" his face slowly flushed which made Lydia feel a little shy. "…Claire and I were planning on going to look at Christmas trees this weekend. Would you like to join us?"

"I would love to, but I'm actually taking a trip into the city this weekend for my interview with Boston Ballet." Jordan's face fell slightly in disappointment. "But my mom wanted to get one before I left because once I get back, it's all-hands-on-deck until performance day. You can join us if you don't mind moving your tree shopping up to Thursday instead."

Relief replaced disappointment and Jordan smiled, that tantalizing dimple making its appearance. "I think I could convince Claire."

"Great! I should get back to rehearsal." They organized their meeting time before Lydia turned back to the waiting dancers. For the first time since she was a little girl, Lydia was excited to shop for their family Christmas tree for reasons completely unrelated to the holidays.

On Thursday, the sun was making an appearance, but it didn't hide the fact that there was a bitterly cold chill in the air. It was early in the season to be choosing a Christmas tree, but Allison knew there wouldn't be any time later with Lydia working so hard on the *Magical Holiday Celebration*. Nonetheless, there were still customers milling about the lot, looking for their perfect tree. Lydia and her mom had dressed warmly and stopped for some hot tea on their way into town to keep the chill off. They sipped their steaming drinks as they waited for Jordan and Claire to join them.

"It's nice that Jordan and Claire were able to join us for tree shopping."

"Mmhmm…" Lydia shivered and wrapped her hands more tightly around her cup.

Allison looked over at her daughter, a knowing smile on her face. Before she could say anything, Claire was practically skipping toward them. "Good morning!" Claire gave them each a bear hug. "Isn't this just the most exciting time of the year?" Claire's enthusiasm for life made everyone smile.

Lydia's eyes met Jordan's, and they exchanged smiles. She instantly felt warmer under his gaze.

"I'm so glad you both could join us!" Allison pulled her coat a little tighter as a chill breeze blew by them.

"Me too! I only wish it were just a tiny bit warmer." Claire giggled.

"Would you like me to get you some hot tea?" Jordan offered, tearing his eyes away from Lydia.

"Please!" Claire hugged his arm. Jordan chuckled at his cousin as he headed toward the little drink station the lot had set up. "How's everything going with the performance?" Claire asked.

"Great! Our costume fitting was yesterday so we'll have costumes to rehearse in soon. I don't know what we would've done without Jordan. Thank you for lending him to us. He's done such a wonderful job with the sets. I can't wait for you to see them." Lydia stamped her feet a little to warm up her legs.

Claire smirked, "He puts his heart into his art. I know he's really enjoyed his time working with you." She winked at Lydia, making her blush and Claire bubbled over with laughter again.

"What's so funny? You didn't tell them any embarrassing stories did you, Claire?" Jordan handed her a steaming cup of tea.

Claire took her cup and started walking toward the middle of the tree lot, flashing a conspiratorial smile over her shoulder. "Maybe…" Allison followed, snickering, and discreetly waving Lydia toward Jordan.

Jordan rolled his eyes and shook his head. Lydia laughed at him. "She didn't reveal anything, I promise. Although, one of these days I'm counting on her telling me just a couple embarrassing stories."

"Maybe there aren't any."

Lydia narrowed her eyes at him and smirked. "I doubt that."

"I think I saw a really great balsam fir over here on our way in." He led the way, the smell of pine heavy in the air around them.

"Changing the subject, huh?" They laughed together, their breaths fogging the air. "Mmm…I love the smell of Christmas trees."

"Me too." Jordan leaned in and took a sniff but one of the branches poked him in the nose which made him jerk back. He rubbed his nose. Lydia snorted and quickly covered her mouth with her hands.

"Did you just snort?" He chuckled.

Lydia's shoulders shook with laughter but instead of controlled giggles, she snorted again which only made her laugh even more. "That's so embarrassing." She tried to gain control of her mirth.

Jordan brushed her hair over her shoulder, "I think it's actually kinda cute."

"Well, hello. What are the odds that I'd run into you two here?"

Lydia froze and her giggling stopped. Jordan removed his hand from her shoulder and turned. "Hi, June." She greeted, though not very enthusiastically.

June didn't even acknowledge Lydia but went straight up to Jordan. "Have you found anything you like yet?"

Jordan glanced at Lydia, a small smile twitched on his lips, and his eyes sparkled still from their shared moment. "Not yet. We haven't actually been able to look around a whole lot yet."

Without warning, June wrapped her arm in Jordan's and led him further into the trees. "Maybe you could help me then. I found this incredible tree over here. Do you believe in love at first sight? Like, when you meet someone…um, find a tree, you can immediately fall in love with them…I mean, it?"

He looked over his shoulder at Lydia and mouthed "sorry" as he was dragged away.

Lydia shrugged her shoulders and pressed her lips together in a small smile. She watched them disappear into the trees. It felt colder than before. "Well. So much for one-on-one time. What do you think? Should I follow?" Lydia talked to the tree that poked Jordan in the face, brushing its branches gently with her gloved hand. June's laughter caught her attention and she saw her pulling Jordan closer, making him laugh with her. A sigh escaped, fogging the air around her. "I should probably find Claire and mom."

Not too long after she had found the ladies, they were paying for their trees. Jordan was helping June carry hers to the counter as she continued to pause to caress his arm as encouragement. Lydia was tired. Her nose felt chapped, and her legs were cold. She was disappointed that she didn't get to spend more time with

Jordan. A large part of her knew that Jordan liked her, but June's constant attentions didn't make her feel very confident in herself.

While June paid for her tree, Jordan rejoined Lydia sheepishly. His puppy eyes made her laugh. How could she ever be jealous of June?

"Sorry about that. I couldn't get away." He reached for Lydia's hand and held it as they walked toward their cars. It was the first time they'd held hands. Even through their gloves, Lydia felt the pressure and warmth of his hand and it made her shiver with delight.

"Don't be. It looked like you enjoyed yourself anyway."

Jordan paused to look over at Lydia, his blue-green eyes a little darker than usual. "I would've enjoyed myself more if we had had more time alone." Lydia felt her breath catch. The space between them crackled with mutual attraction.

Before either of them could continue their conversation, June walked past them, leading the employee holding her tree toward her car. She glanced down at their joined hands and smirked. "It's been fun, Jordan. But clearly, I've taken you away from the one person you *do* have eyes for."

"June, I..." Jordan started but June held her hand up to stop him.

"There's no need to explain. I'm used to losing to her." Without another word, or allowing a response from Jordan, June breezed away and got into her car, her tree already strapped to the top while they were talking.

Lydia felt a stab of pain to her heart at June's words. June was hurting so badly and there was nothing she could do about it. Jordan simply stared after her. How did one respond to something like that? After a long moment, June was gone, and Lydia released Jordan's hand. He finally looked at her and she could see a sadness in his eyes.

"I didn't expect that type of response." He scrubbed a hand over his face and sighed. "I didn't realize she actually liked me, I just thought she was trying to…" he paused and looked down at Lydia again.

"Trying to get at me?" Lydia offered. He nodded. "That's possible. It's hard to read her intentions. June's never been able to let go of past hurts. Only recently did I find out that she was still hurting so badly. It has nothing to do with either of us though. I really think she just needs a friend more than anything. But she won't let anyone in."

"You know, you're a very generous person. Not many would treat June with as much patience as you do."

"Believe me, there have been times that I've lost my temper. But I'd rather maintain the possibility that there is still a chance that June can change than burn the bridge altogether. Besides, God has been showing me that June might just be in my life for a reason. I just keep praying for patience."

Jordan smiled thoughtfully. "I'll be praying too." He reclaimed her hand and led her toward a bench. "So, are you ready for your interview tomorrow?"

Lydia felt some of the anxiety from the day before returning. Christmas tree shopping, and being in such close proximity to Jordan, had thoroughly distracted her. "I think so. I'm a little nervous. I'm not exactly looking forward to taking public transportation. Driving in the city scares me."

"You know, if you need a chauffeur, I'd be happy to lend my services. My manager, Sarah, has been bugging me about coming into the city to bring more canvases for some empty spots at the gallery. I've been working on some for her in my spare time and was considering going next week, but she'd be thrilled to have me sooner."

"Are you sure?" A faint fluttering replaced the knots of anxiety.

"Absolutely! Like I said, I need to go anyway, and the set painting is finished, so I don't have anything to keep me here. It would give me some time to meet with someone about a commission Sarah has lined up for me as well."

"Okay! Thank you! I have the hotel already booked and I was planning on leaving tomorrow morning, so I could get checked in and ready before my interview. Since I don't get to the city very often, I thought it would be fun to spend my extra time and all of Sunday exploring."

Jordan's face lit up. "Well, as a Boston native, I'd be happy to show you some of the best spots. I can pick you up at nine tomorrow morning."

The anticipation of three whole days with Jordan was almost too much for Lydia to bear. Three whole days! Suddenly the lost time together in the tree lot seemed trivial. Now this trip would feel a little more like a true vacation. Wait until Kate hears about this. She'd never let Lydia live it down. She could hear her now giving the "I told you so" speech. But it didn't matter. Lydia was thrilled and couldn't wait to have time to get to know Jordan better. It was all too good to be true.

Chapter Fifteen

Lydia waited anxiously for Jordan the next morning. She hadn't slept particularly well, knowing what was awaiting her the next day. Her nose was pink from the cold, and she shivered. Whether the shiver was from nervousness or simply the biting wind, she wasn't sure. Jordan's dimpled grin greeted her, easing her mind a little, as if by magic.

"Good morning!" Jordan's bright and cheery mood reminded Lydia of Claire. They were so much alike.

"Good morning."

He put her bag in the trunk and helped her into the passenger seat.

"I saw that there might be a little bit of traffic, but we should definitely get you there with time to spare."

Jordan kept up a steady thread of conversation going during the trip to help Lydia relax. As they drove into the city, the buildings of Boston rose around them. Could she actually picture herself living here? It was a far cry from her small-town life. They arrived at the hotel with just enough time for Lydia to check in and fix her makeup and hair before heading to Boston Ballet.

"Here we go." She stared out the car window at the company entrance for a beat, trying to convince herself to get out.

"You'll be great! I'll pick you up when you're done. Just send me a text." Jordan placed a reassuring hand on her shoulder. His comforting presence gave Lydia the confidence she needed. Having him come with her was the best idea she'd had…he'd had. Whose idea was it again? Her head was swimming with too many things. Hopefully she'd be able to focus during her interview.

"Thank you." She tried to smile as she got out of the car.

Lydia walked into the building looking more confident than she felt. Though her posture was straight and tall, her knees were a little wobbly. This was the opportunity of a lifetime and one that she'd been dreaming about since she was a teenager. Knowing that she was finally here made her feel a jumbled mix of emotions. Excited, nervous, capable, terrified. She'd have to rely on being excited and capable if she were going to get through this interview, shoving nervous and terrified to the side.

"You must be Lydia." Anthony Fairfax welcomed her into his office and shook her hand firmly. He was shorter than she'd expected and sported a closely trimmed Van Dyke beard that added to his charm. His sparkling brown eyes and reassuring smile made Lydia feel more at ease. "I'm very glad to meet you. I've heard such wonderful things about your business and choreography." He gestured for her to take a seat opposite him.

Lydia sat, folding her hands in her lap to keep them from trembling. "Thank you. I can't tell you how surprised I was to hear from you. It's always been a dream of mine to work with Boston Ballet in any capacity."

"Well, I hope we'll be able to make that dream a reality for you. However, you know that there are other choreographers vying for the position as well." Lydia smiled nervously. "Today I just wanted to get a better sense of who you are and how you think you would fit in with the company. Even though this would be a seasonal position, there is still a possibility that it could become permanent. We've been trying to expand our performance palette, so to speak. We're looking for choreographers who are out-of-the-box thinkers. I think you have what it takes. And that's why I'll also be coming to see your performance. So I can see for myself the wonderful work you do."

It hadn't occurred to her that the position could become a permanent one. That meant the stakes were even higher. She could quite possibly move to Boston permanently. Was she ready for that type of commitment? What about the studio? Kate? Lydia shook her head and refocused on what Mr. Fairfax was saying. *Stop worrying about future events that might or might not happen. Father, give me strength and help me focus.*

An hour passed as Mr. Fairfax asked her questions about her job, her vision as a choreographer and role model, and her aspirations. He loved her readiness to answer his questions and her love of dance, and her students, was apparent. It was an exciting process, and she felt a little silly for being so scared before. The more they talked, the more Lydia relaxed and felt she belonged. And the more she felt at home, the less she thought about the repercussions of moving to Boston.

"Thank you for coming out here to meet me. I know you have been busy preparing for your holiday performance, but it's been an absolute pleasure. I look forward to showing you around the company tomorrow. The dancers will be rehearsing for their Nutcracker performances, so you'll be able to sit in on a couple of those." He stood to shake Lydia's hand again.

"Thank you so much for your time, Mr. Fairfax. I look forward to tomorrow as well."

Anthony smiled and Lydia left the office feeling much lighter than when she had entered. She sent a text to Jordan to let him know the interview was over and not long after, he was waiting outside for her.

Since Lydia hadn't eaten lunch yet, or really had any breakfast for that matter, Jordan took her to one of his favorite lunch spots. Once they'd ordered their food and had settled in, Jordan asked about her interview.

"It was a lot easier than I expected. I think he was really impressed."

"That's awesome! How could he not be impressed by you?" Jordan smiled at her, and she felt her cheeks flush.

"How did *your* meeting go?" Jordan had scheduled time to meet with Sarah to discuss a high-profile commission work she had lined up for him while Lydia was at the ballet company.

"Very well! I met with the client, and we discussed some ideas for his commission. He wants something special for his wife, so that was fun to work out. Sarah even has a guy coming to the showcase tomorrow night who is interested in hosting me at his gallery in New York."

"That's incredible, Jordan!"

"It is." He replied nonchalantly as he fiddled with the silverware on the table.

"You don't seem too excited about the prospect."

"It's not that I'm not excited, it's just that I'd hoped to stay local. That sounds stupid now that I think about it though. It's not like I'd be there long-term or anything. I wouldn't even have to be there at all if I didn't want to. But…I don't know, it just feels like I'm being trapped into a career I'm not sure about anymore."

"What kind of changes would you make to your career if you could?"

"That's just it. I have no idea. All I know is that I'm no longer content with living in Boston or with painting. Photography makes me so much happier, but I don't necessarily want to travel as much as I did before. Then again, I love traveling and seeing different cultures and people. I don't know…" Jordan sighed. Their food was served, and some time passed before the conversation resumed.

"I know exactly what you're going through by the way." He looked up at Lydia. "For the longest time, I couldn't decide what I wanted to do. I just knew I couldn't do all the jobs required to run a studio *and* successful, annual holiday performances. Kate was actually the one who helped me figure out how I could do what I loved while figuring out how I needed to compromise in other areas. I don't know if that's possible for you, but maybe sitting down and mapping it all out for yourself might work."

"Maybe you're right. That's the part I've been procrastinating. It's just hard to figure out where to start. Maybe I should hire Kate. She seems to be quite brilliant."

They both laughed. "She'd love to hear that. She really is amazing. I'm sure if you're serious about it, she'd be more than happy to help. Organizing businesses and getting them up and running is what she's best at."

"I might just do that."

Silence fell between them as they continued to eat. Jordan seemed to have forgotten something and excitedly pulled an envelope from his jacket pocket. "I almost forgot! Have you ever seen a performance by Boston Ballet?"

"I never had the chance with my whirlwind career." Lydia waved her hand in the air majestically. He handed her the envelope, and her eyes went wide as she pulled out two tickets.

"How would you like to see The Nutcracker with me tomorrow night?"

She gaped. "When did you get these?"

"I picked them up at the office not too long after you'd gone in for your interview. I thought it might be a fun little outing. Especially since you'll be there for rehearsals earlier in the day."

"You really didn't have to do that." She held the tickets in a reverential way.

"I've never seen a ballet before, so it's just as much for me as it is for you. It seems fitting to see a performance by the company that you might possibly end up working with, right? And, I'll admit, I've been wracking my brain trying to think of how I'd plan a unique first date."

Lydia flushed at the mention of a date and suddenly became shy, handing the tickets back to him. "I don't know what to say."

Jordan laughed and placed the tickets back in his pocket. "I'll drop you off at the hotel to get ready after your tour and will be back to pick you up about thirty minutes before the performance."

There were no words to express how Lydia felt at that moment. She was about to experience her first professional ballet performance with the man she was…

Lydia's mouth went dry as she thought.

Was she falling in love with Jordan? She looked up at him and knew the instant his eyes met hers. Yes. She was definitely falling in love. When did that happen?

Chapter Sixteen

Kate found that Friday rehearsals weren't going as badly as she'd expected. Though she hadn't exactly stuck around too long to watch the whole thing, it seemed like June was treating the dancers with a modicum of respect. Plus, her quick run-in with her earlier showed that her mood wasn't totally horrible.

This was the first year Lydia hadn't been around twenty-four, seven for performance preparation so Kate tried her best to fill her shoes whenever she could. Besides, she wanted Lydia to fully enjoy her time away without worrying about what was happening back home.

They had already set up the giant Christmas tree in the center of town, with the help of pretty much everyone they could gather. It was a little sad that Lydia wasn't there to be a part of it. It was one of her favorite parts of the town decorating. What hit Kate even harder was the thought that there was a small chance that Lydia wouldn't be around for other future events. She doubted that Lydia had even considered the possibility that if she were good enough, Boston Ballet might hire her full-time; that is, if she got the seasonal position. Then again, Kate was more of a big-picture thinker, whereas Lydia tried to focus on what she could control in the here-and-now.

Kate shook the thoughts away with a swish of her ponytail. Lydia was right to focus on only what she could control. Thinking too hard and dwelling on future events outside of her control was pointless. She was confident that everything for *this* year was falling into place perfectly. The next year could take care of itself. The sets were completed before Jordan left, which had allowed Steve to continue to finalize the details of all the special effects and lighting. The costumes would be ready by the end of the weekend, in time for rehearsal when Lydia returned. If everything continued to go well, Lydia wouldn't have anything to worry about.

Speaking of Lydia, Kate smiled as she thought back to their earlier conversation on the phone. Lydia had told her all about her interview and her date with Jordan. Kate had silently done a happy dance when Lydia mentioned the date. *It's finally happening!* Kate gushed to herself. And then she gushed to Lydia about how romantic it was. They'd talked for a while, trying to figure out what Lydia would wear to the ballet.

Kate was so happy for her friend. So happy that she'd completely forgotten about her upcoming date that weekend with Steve. She'd totally forgotten to mention it to Lydia. Then again, it was probably going to be just one of Steve's typical, romantic, well-thought-out dates that she'd grown accustomed to being treated to. For the first time, Kate didn't overthink the date. It could have been that Steve had spoiled her so much with a succession of special dates that she didn't think anything of this one. Or it could have been that she was too busy with the *Magical Holiday Celebration* to think of anything else.

She hated to admit it, but she was beginning to feel a little frazzled. A new respect grew for Lydia and the work she put in for these performances alongside everything else she did at the studio. Then her thoughts turned back to the idea of Lydia leaving. They'd have to figure out the logistics of how the studio would run without her. Panic had clenched Kate's heart as Lydia talked so glowingly about Mr. Fairfax and the company.

What if she did get the job?

Would she decide to stay when the season was over?

As much as she tried to shove the thoughts deep down, they continued to resurface. Steve had even noticed that she'd seemed a little edgy when he'd come to drop off her lunch. Kate had always been so stable. Fear and worry weren't part of her vocabulary. Sure, she regularly had to think about the future, but she'd never gone into it thinking about all the negatives. Kate was a leap before you look type of person and always plunged ahead with her career, friendships, and dating.

But the thought of losing her friend to the city she'd left behind was too much. Her and Lydia had shared such a precious bond.

Kate's ponytail swished again, and she let a deep breath out.

"I'm not going to dwell on things that haven't even happened yet!" Her stubbornness allowed the anxieties to ease a little. "Father, I just pray that you help Lydia find her clear path in life. Help me to be at peace about whatever changes come and lend me comfort. Most of all, continue to grow our friendship in the midst of whatever happens."

This simple prayer removed the last bit of panic that still held a grip on her heart. She took another deep breath, closing her eyes. Kate had never been one to pray or even trust in God about her future. But Lydia had shown her time and time again that God was good, and that faith brought blessings and peace. She'd even convinced Kate that their studio and business was a blessing and gift from God.

Then she met Steve, and he encouraged Kate in her budding faith. Taking her to church, teaching her about the Bible, being patient with her many questions. In more ways than one, Steve was one of the best things to ever happen to her. All because of Lydia's introduction. Because of him, she'd begun to pray more in times of uncertainty, and it had brought serenity to her life. A peace that passes all understanding.

No, it wouldn't matter if Lydia moved to Boston for a season, or even permanently, because Kate knew their friendship would endure. It wasn't that far away. They could easily visit each other. God had been good to the both of them throughout their friendship. She also knew deep down that He wouldn't let that friendship be severed by a short distance. Whatever happened in the next couple weeks, Kate knew that it was going to be exciting!

A smile lit her face as she returned to work, her head and heart clear.

Chapter Seventeen

This was her moment.

June had to take advantage of every minute she had with the dancers to ensure she had effectually injured Lydia's chances at getting the job with Boston Ballet. It would be difficult since she was most likely nailing her interview. Everyone seemed to adore Lydia, so it would be no surprise if she charmed her way through the interview with Mr. Fairfax.

That meant that the second part of her interview – the performance – would have to change his mind about her competency. Sure, that could mean that none of the dancers would secure a spot with the company either, but it was a risk June was willing to take. Her only disappointment was that Lydia would have plenty of time to fix whatever June did to the choreography.

She had to bank on the fact that they only had a couple weeks to get everything finished and Lydia would probably be rushing around, distracted, trying to juggle it all. However, if she annoyed the dancers enough, forced them to rehearse every day instead of taking the weekend off, and altered the choreography just enough that Lydia might not notice, mistakes could be made which could ruin the perfection of the performance. It wasn't a perfect plan, she'd admit, but it was a plan.

In June's eyes, she felt that Lydia got everything she wanted. She had a thriving business, a loyal and loving best friend, the community's support and admiration, the handsome hero who was head-over-heels for her, and now the prospect of working with one of the best ballet companies on the East Coast.

It simply wasn't fair.

June's eyes burned a little with frustrated tears, but she blinked them away. She couldn't let any of the dancers see her crying. She wouldn't allow herself to be weak.

Being more nonchalant than usual was working to help the dancers feel a little more at ease. If they were to put their guards up right away, they wouldn't listen to any corrections or changes and probably wouldn't even show up for rehearsal until Lydia returned. They were already upset that June wanted them to come tomorrow and Sunday too.

She could tell they were getting tired. The little voice of guilt at the back of her mind told her that running these dancers ragged could endanger them. If she exhausted them, they could end up like her; with a broken ankle and terminated career. She shoved it down. June wasn't going to allow anyone to physically hurt themselves permanently, but she could hurt their immediate chances.

There were many other opportunities for excellent dancers, like these ones, to earn a spot with the company. If they were lucky, Mr. Fairfax would see through the disjointed choreography and realize that the dancers themselves weren't the problem. Besides, he'd be coming in to do individual interviews and auditions the day of the performance. That would tell him everything he needed to know about their true talent. June breathed a small sigh of relief. At least they had some chance.

After the whole incident at the tree lot, however, June felt more dejected. Lydia had been nice to her despite her bad attitude. Why? The thought of Lydia being nice, even though June didn't deserve it, made her angry. Why did she have to be so nice? The more she thought about Lydia's kindness, the more she considered abandoning her plan, which only made June angrier.

She couldn't back down now! *You deserve to be at Boston Ballet, not Lydia!* June tried to talk herself back into sticking with her plan. Then another thought occurred to her.

What if she just changed things enough to claim ownership of the whole performance?

Why hadn't she just thought of that before?

Mr. Fairfax was interviewing other choreographers, why couldn't she interview for the position alongside Lydia? June rolled her eyes and smiled to herself. That's exactly what she'd do.

Confident that there wouldn't be any risk to the dancers, June could simply undermine Lydia with Mr. Fairfax, effectively destroying her reputation with the company and placing herself as superior. It was perfect!

The music wound down and stopped. The dancers, breathing heavy and staring at June, awaited her comments. With her plan all organized in her mind, June snapped her attention back to the dancers.

"Alright everyone, I have a few changes to implement." The dancers groaned which made her scowl. "Oh, please. They're not that big."

The next hour, June made changes to the choreography, big enough to be able to claim it as her own but small enough to avoid wasting too much time learning. Three days would be sufficient to make this work properly.

Chapter Eighteen

Lydia was adding the final touches to her makeup when a knock sounded at her hotel room door. The moment the door opened, Jordan's eyes came up from his feet to meet her eyes, a smile spreading over his face that made her stomach do flips.

"You look amazing!" His eyebrows were raised in admiration.

"Thank you." Lydia bit her lip. He looked so handsome in his suit and tie. "You don't look so bad yourself."

"Really? I wasn't sure what to wear to a ballet. I figured it was probably similar to something I would wear to an orchestral performance or something." Jordan was fidgeting with his jacket lapel as he spoke. Lydia could see that he was a little nervous, which made her smile.

"You look perfect." She placed her hand on his hand to stop his fidgeting. He looked up at her again, the connection between them so strong, Lydia doubted she could ever pull her eyes away.

Jordan was the first to break the sudden tension. He cleared his throat. "We should probably get going."

"Right! Yes!" Lydia pulled her hand away from his and tucked a strand of hair behind her ear, grabbing her purse and following him out.

The performance was impeccable! Lydia couldn't take her eyes off the stage the entire time. She was enthralled with the intricacies of the choreography, the costumes, and the music. It was beyond perfect for her first time at a professional ballet. She didn't notice how Jordan would occasionally glance at her and smile, seeing the joy on her face as she watched. It was almost as if he derived more pleasure from watching her watch the ballet than he did from seeing the ballet for himself.

After the final bows, Jordan led Lydia to the lobby filled with excited audience members chatting about what they had just seen. She still couldn't believe that she'd been able to be a part of both rehearsal and performance for the full backstage experience.

"That was beautiful! The dancers, the choreography…everything!" Lydia beamed. "I don't think I've seen such beautiful choreography. At least not in-person like that."

"Does it make you wish you were up there, too?"

Lydia thought for a minute. "Maybe a little. Who wouldn't?"

"I think you'd make a beautiful Sugar Plum Fairy. You'd steal the show for sure."

"That would be a dream. But I'd miss my students and studio. And choreographing my own performances." Jordan hummed thoughtfully in response. "Throughout the year, I get to watch my students grow and discover their passions. I love being a part of that! I love seeing their joy when they accomplish a really difficult technique. I'd miss all that if I were the one on stage all the time."

"Do you think that experience might change if you were to get the job here?" Jordan asked.

"Maybe a little. But I'd still be working behind the scenes, watching dancers evolve and learn. And even if I did get a little homesick for my own students, it's a seasonal position anyway."

Jordan nodded. He didn't need to respond. She could feel his understanding support without words. A comfortable silence fell between them as they walked into the chilly, winter night air.

"This might seem really strange, but…" she hesitated and felt her cheeks flush "…this is the first time I've ever been on a date."

Jordan turned to her; eyebrows raised in surprise. "Really?" Lydia nodded a little shyly, not quite able to meet his eyes.

"Well, I don't know how that's possible, but I don't think it's strange. I actually feel quite honored."

It looked as though Jordan was puffing out his chest in pride and his stride seemed more deliberate which made Lydia giggle. "I never had any time. With dancing in high school and then opening the dance studio after graduation, I never found the time to go on dates. Besides, I was never interested in any of the guys my age. Trevor was really the only one but he's like a brother to me. Plus, he was dating someone at the time we first got to Maple Ridge, so he wasn't really on my radar. He helped me and Kate with the studio and performances, and he even helped me and my mom move in."

"Explains why you're so close."

"Yeah, I can see why you would've thought we were an item." Lydia laughed and playfully elbowed Jordan in the ribs.

"Hey!" He joined in the laughter at his expense. Grabbing Lydia's hand, Jordan pulled her closer to his side. He smelled so good. "But seriously, I feel honored to be the first one to take you on a proper date. In fact, I made a reservation for dinner if you're hungry."

"I'm starving!"

~

Dinner was just as wonderful as the ballet. They'd been shown to a cozy little corner table, and they talked as if they'd known each other for years, instead of only a couple of months. They discussed their individual dreams and ambitions, and they laughed over family stories. He even shared some embarrassing moments with her. Better him than Claire. She'd probably overdramatize certain points anyway. Lost in conversation, neither one realized how late it had become. Jordan wished the night would never end. Being with Lydia made him feel like anything was possible.

"Jordan?" A woman's voice called from behind him.

On hearing his name, Jordan turned to see who it was. A brunette with clear, blue eyes and a slinky black dress walked toward their table. He stood the moment he saw her, and he felt his throat tighten.

"Kathy?" The woman instantly wrapped him in a hug that showed more intimacy than simple acquaintanceship. Jordan was careful to make sure it didn't last too long.

"It's been so long! I saw Sarah at the gallery yesterday and she told me you were taking some sort of extended vacation. I never expected to see you here in Boston."

His old flame was here, standing in front of him, unchanged and as beautiful as ever. He tried to clear his throat. "Uh…yeah, I've been visiting Claire. What are you doing in Boston? I thought you and your family had moved south."

Kathy flipped her hair over her shoulder and the smell of her perfume filled the air. "We did. But my cousin still lives here and is getting married tomorrow. What are the odds that we'd be in the same place at the same time?" Kathy laughed and rested her hand on Jordan's arm. His pulse picked up. She was still able to make him so nervous and all his insecurities from when they were dating flared up in his mind. His eyes drifted down to her hand. "Jordan, are you okay?"

Jordan's eyes snapped back up to hers and he cleared his throat again. "I'm fine. You just caught me off guard." He tried to smile. Kathy glanced at the table with her charming smile. He followed her gaze and remembered that Lydia was sitting there patiently watching them. "Oh! Sorry! Kathy, this is Lydia. Lydia, Kathy, my…" Jordan stammered and flushed.

How was he supposed to introduce his old girlfriend – the one he had almost proposed to – to the woman he was falling in love with? Lydia knew about Kathy from brief conversations they'd had, and Claire had filled in some of the details, much to his chagrin at the time. But this situation was just awkward.

Before he could finish his sentence, Kathy chimed in, sticking her hand out for Lydia to shake. "I'm his old girlfriend from college."

Lydia smiled in response and replied with a good humored "Nice to meet you," but Jordan could tell when she glanced at him that she was uncomfortable. He had to think of a way to ease the situation.

"Would you mind if I sat for a minute?" Kathy asked.

"Sure." The word tumbled out before he could think. Here he was on a date, and he was allowing his old girlfriend to join them. Stupid! He bit back a groan of annoyance toward himself. Meanwhile, Kathy took one of the empty chairs nearby and moved it to their table.

"So, what have you been up to lately?" Kathy asked as they took their seats.

Since when was Kathy so inconsiderate? Jordan thought as he anxiously looked over at Lydia again. Boy, this woman was amazing! She was trying so hard to be respectful and kind to Kathy, even though the latter had been the intruder on such a special night. He really felt like an idiot now. *God, please help me gently escape this situation without hurting either woman.*

He took a deep breath to calm his racing heart and tried to steer conversation into neutral territory. A half-an-hour passed as they both discussed their current careers and reminisced about old times. Their conversation began to flow easily, and Jordan felt the pull of Kathy's charms. He suddenly felt comfortable with her, like no time had passed. After a while, Kathy changed the subject and addressed Lydia for the first time since their introduction.

"Lydia, I'm so sorry. We're completely leaving you out of the conversation and ruining your evening."

Lydia forced a smile that didn't quite reach her eyes and spun her wine glass on the table absentmindedly. "Oh, no, it's okay. You must have a lot to catch up on." Her eyes met Jordan's and the happiness from earlier had effectively died.

That was it. Lydia's smile, or non-smile more like, broke the spell. He'd set out to get Kathy to leave but ended up being pulled in instead. Jordan felt his heart ache for Lydia. She didn't deserve this.

Kathy must have seen the exchange between them and stood. "I'm sorry for being so inconsiderate. I've ruined your dinner. I didn't realize how long I'd been here. I just couldn't believe my eyes when I saw you." Jordan stood with her out of respect and relief at seeing her take her leave. "It was wonderful seeing you again and catching up." She gave him a lingering hug before pulling back and kissing him on the cheek.

"It was nice seeing you, too." It *was* good to see her, even though he'd have preferred the reunion under very different circumstances. Kathy had changed a lot since he'd last seen her. She wasn't the same person he'd wanted to marry years before. At least now he had closure.

"It was nice meeting you, Lydia." She gave Lydia a friendly smile, waving as she turned to leave.

Jordan watched Kathy leave, a small smile on his face at the realization that Kathy's kiss hadn't inspired anything romantic at all. He was finally over their breakup. All because of Lydia. Lydia! He turned to find her watching him, her eyes glazed over with disappointment. She looked miserable but was trying her best to hide it. It was funny how easily he could read her now.

"It's getting late." Jordan waved to the waitress for the check. "I'm so sorry that our date was interrupted like that." He timidly glanced up at her, but she was avoiding his gaze.

"It's okay, You guys had a lot to talk about."

"Still…"

"Thank you for dinner." Lydia interrupted. Her voice sounded a little choked now.

"It was my pleasure." Jordan placed his hand over hers, but she gently extricated it and placed it in her lap. "I almost forgot! I was planning on visiting the gallery tomorrow to meet the gallery owner from New York and I was wondering if you'd like to join me."

Lydia forced a small smile and finally met his eyes. "Sure."

Her coldness made his heart squeeze with anxiety. Was she mad at him? Of course she was! Why wouldn't she be? He was irritated with himself. "It starts at seven. There's something I'd really love to show you. We can just drop in, I'll show you around, and we can leave whenever you want."

"That sounds nice."

Jordan paid for the meal and helped Lydia on with her coat. The cold air felt even colder now that there was a rift between them. Instead of allowing any misunderstandings and conflict between them to fester, Jordan decided to get them all out in the open. He laid a hand on Lydia's arm to stop her from walking. "Lydia, I really am sorry about Kathy."

"It's okay."

"No, Lydia, it's not. I shouldn't have allowed her to stay."

She shook her head, "It's not that. I just…you guys seemed to be comfortable with each other."

Did she think he was still pining over Kathy? Jordan furrowed his brow in frustration. "Kathy and I have known each other for years." He held both her arms and turned her to face him. Those mossy green eyes met his and his breath caught. Lydia looked so vulnerable. "But that doesn't mean that I still want to be with her. You're the one I want to be with. I'm so sorry I didn't make that clear with Kathy tonight." Lydia's cheeks flushed faintly, and he could see a small smile form on her lips. A real smile this time. "I had a wonderful time with you tonight."

Lydia didn't say anything, she simply pulled free of his grip and slipped her arm into the crook of his elbow and began walking toward the car again. Jordan took a deep breath. He knew how much Lydia struggled with the idea of people leaving her. The last thing he wanted to do was be the reason for fear of abandonment to flare up.

As he helped her into the car, Lydia looked up at him, her eyes darker in the dim light but still just as beautiful green. "This has been one of the best first dates a girl could ask for."

Jordan smiled at her in response and realized…he was completely, unequivocally in love with Lydia Foster.

Chapter Nineteen

The gallery had a steady flow of people coming and going when they arrived. Sarah quietly excused herself from the people she was mingling with when she saw Jordan. As she walked up to him, her mischievous smile made him wary. He knew from experience that that smile meant she had something big to tell him.

Lydia must have sensed some of the anxiety that suddenly gripped him and gave his hand a squeeze. Since talking to her about trying to figure out the next step in his career, the thought of a big project or even the possibility of showing his art in New York made him feel restless and a little cornered.

He'd made up his mind to set aside some time with Kate, probably after the holidays, to discuss a business idea that intrigued him. If this idea panned out, he would have even more of an excuse to stay in Maple Ridge. Not that he really needed one…other than Lydia that is. Once he had a good foundation for his idea, he'd discuss it with Sarah. But not before. He didn't want to cause her any more anxiety than he probably already did.

"You made it!" Sarah grabbed his arm and leaned in to peck Jordan's cheek. He saw Lydia's eyebrows go up and her lips quirk in amusement.

"Of course I made it. You didn't think I'd stand you up, did you?" Turning to Lydia, who still had an amused smirk on her face, he introduced them. "Lydia, this is my amazing manager, Sarah. Sarah, this is Lydia."

Sarah rolled her eyes at him at his introduction of her but smiled and enthusiastically shook Lydia's hand. "It's such a pleasure to meet you, Lydia. I've heard a lot about you."

"You as well. Jordan says he wouldn't have gone very far in his career without you."

"Pfft!" Sarah batted her hand through the air. "That's not true. He's extremely talented, my job is fairly easy."

Jordan laughed and shrugged his shoulders, "Maybe so, but you are still irreplaceable."

"Stop. You're making me blush. To change the subject, I want to show you something." Sarah's mischievous smile returned as she led them toward the back of the studio. When they got to the little desk where transactions were made, Sarah picked up a piece of paper and shoved it at Jordan.

"What's this?" His pulse quickened as he looked at a series of numbers that seemed too good to be true. He met Sarah's gaze questioningly.

Her smile was even bigger than before and purposefully kept him in suspense a little longer. When he felt that he couldn't handle waiting anymore, she finally answered. "You sold the entire photography collection!" Sarah's hands clapped together in excitement.

Jordan's eyebrows shot up, mouth agape.

"That's amazing, Jordan!" Lydia grabbed his arm and shook him slightly to encourage him to respond.

"I…you're kidding." He finally stammered.

Sarah simply shook her head in response. "Why don't you go ahead and check it out for yourself and show Lydia around. I bet she'd like to see that last-minute addition to your impressions collection." She winked and shoved him toward his own art.

Jordan felt his face warm as he pocketed the paper. He'd been looking forward to showing Lydia his newest addition to the gallery, but now that he was doing it, he felt a little nervous. Averting his gaze from Lydia, he led her toward his photography collection. He could feel her watching him, which made him even more nervous.

They walked together through the entire showcase as Jordan explained each piece to Lydia. He saw the little "sold" stickers beside each piece in his main photography collection. Sarah hadn't been joking. As they continued through the gallery, Jordan explained a little behind where he was when he found the inspiration for each piece and what was happening at the time. Then he led her toward the newest addition Sarah had mentioned. Jordan now watched her closely as her eyes widened in recognition. Even though it was an impressionist piece, the inspiration behind it was unmistakable. All at once, he felt shy and awkward.

"Is that me?"

Jordan cleared his throat and rubbed the back of his neck. He forced a light laugh to ease his awkwardness. "Uh…yeah. I used one of the photos I took of you in the park as my inspiration."

"It's beautiful." She hadn't even looked away from the painting, but he was watching her.

"I had a beautiful subject."

Lydia finally turned and locked eyes with him. His mouth went dry, and he felt he couldn't breathe. She smiled up at him, the green in her eyes accentuated by the pink on her cheeks. Everything around them dimmed as his senses were focused solely on Lydia. Just then, Sarah tapped him on the shoulder and broke the connection. Lydia's gaze immediately flicked back to the painting, but he couldn't take his eyes off her.

"I'm so sorry to do this, but since you're here, would you mind if I introduced you to a few people? I have the owner of the New York gallery as well as some potential buyers over there who'd like to know the artist."

Without turning away quite yet, Jordan answered in the affirmative. "I'll be right back, Lydia." She smiled and nodded, and he turned to follow Sarah.

He couldn't focus on much knowing that Lydia was just a few feet away. The fluttery dress she wore kept tugging at his periphery, but he knew that making connections was an important part of these showcases. Plus, Sarah wouldn't allow him to ignore his duty for long. So, he tried to focus on the people in front of him. Lydia would be there when he was finished.

~

"So, what do you think?" Sarah had sidled up to Lydia.

"Jordan's done such an amazing job! He's an incredible artist." Lydia tried to keep herself from gushing. Watching him interact with these important people who could launch his career made her so proud.

"He certainly is." Sarah looked at Lydia for a moment, a knowing smile on her lips. "I guess he showed you his favorite painting?" Lydia couldn't help but smile. "Apparently, he was really inspired. It's the most popular piece of his entire collection. I can't tell you how many buyers have asked after it as well as whether he will be adding any more dance-themed works to his repertoire. He refuses to allow me to sell it. Says he has a special purpose for it."

Lydia's brow creased in confusion as she turned to face Sarah.

"Shoot! I probably shouldn't have said anything. Honestly, I don't know anything other than that."

Lydia glanced in Jordan's direction, where he was laughing and chatting up a couple of flirtatious women.

"You've made quite an impression on him, you know. I haven't seen him this happy or this inspired in a very long time. He thinks I don't notice, but he's been distracted lately and confused about where his life is headed."

"He seems in his element right now."

"Yes, but I can tell he's happier in Maple Ridge. When I talked to him last week, I could hear the change in his voice."

Sarah turned to face Lydia again, who's gaze was still admiringly fixed on Jordan. "He couldn't stop talking about the community and the people. Especially you."

Lydia returned her full attention to Sarah, hopefulness filling her heart at Sarah's words. She knew how Jordan felt based on how he treated her and talked to her, but hearing the announcement of his admiration from someone so close to him made it more real. "Thank you."

Sarah didn't ask why Lydia was thanking her. It was as if she instinctively knew what Lydia meant. No wonder Jordan trusted her with his career. She was loyal and discerning. Lydia felt they'd get along really well in the future.

The ladies continued to chat some more until Jordan sauntered over, a huge smile on his face. As he approached, his hand came to rest on Lydia's lower back. The light touch made her skin tingle with awareness.

"What have you ladies been talking about?"

Sarah flashed a teasing smile at him and quirked her eyebrow. "Just some girl stuff."

Jordan narrowed his eyes at her playfully. The exchange between the two friends made Lydia giggle. Sarah had explained that they were close. Like brother and sister. They teased each other and told each other secrets. Jordan and Claire were also very close since they'd grown up together and she knew Jordan better than anyone, but there was something different about Sarah.

If Lydia wasn't so sure about his feelings for her, and Sarah's insistence about them being only friends, she'd suspect romantic chemistry between Jordan and Sarah. It was good to see how well Jordan gelled with his friends and family. And even though Sarah said otherwise, Lydia could tell he was in his element here with these art aficionados. If only he could find a way to feasibly combine his two loves into one – his love for Maple Ridge and its serenity, and his love for the constant stimulation of the city and traveling. Lydia sighed to herself as Jordan and Sarah talked about upcoming projects.

"I'm sorry, Lydia. I didn't mean to bore you." He glanced at his watch. "I also didn't realize how late it was getting."

"You're not boring me at all. I'm having a great time. I was just thinking."

"Well, we should probably head out anyway. I told Claire I'd be back for dinner tonight and I can only imagine that she has a full-blown smorgasbord planned. Thank you, Sarah, for everything. I'll be back in a couple weeks to fill in the gaps from the missing photography prints." He leaned forward and kissed her cheek.

"It was wonderful meeting you Lydia. I'm so glad I am finally able to put a face to the name. I will definitely be there to see your performance and, of course, this Maple Ridge Jordan's been raving about."

"That would be wonderful! I'll reserve a seat for you up front." Lydia hugged Sarah.

After their goodbyes, Jordan led Lydia to the car. This trip to Boston had been better than she could have imagined. Their first date was pretty nearly perfect. The only thing that could have made it better was…well…a kiss. Lydia's cheeks suffused with color as she thought back to their "almost kiss" at Thanksgiving. They'd missed the moment once; she didn't want to miss another. The next time the opportunity arose, she was determined to make the thought a reality.

Chapter Twenty

Kate tapped her foot on the floor eagerly. Meeting Lydia at the coffee shop was the best way she could imagine breaking the news. When they'd talked on the phone, Lydia was just bubbling over with excitement over her tour with the ballet and all the possibilities presented to her with this potential job. It had taken everything in Kate to keep from announcing her own news right then and there. But she thought better of it. This was something best done in person. Besides, she wanted to see her friend's full reaction.

Finally, Lydia walked into the coffee shop and instantly caught Kate's eye. As if she were sitting on a spring, Kate popped up out of her seat and practically pulled Lydia off balance in an attempt to make her move faster. Lydia was laughing as she was shoved into a seat across from Kate.

"What in the world?!"

"I have something to tell you!" Kate bit her lips to keep her excitement in check but her voice sounded a lot louder than she had intended.

Lydia's brows went up in surprise and amusement. "Okay. It must be pretty big. You can barely sit still." She laughed again.

Instead of saying anything, Kate simply shoved her left hand in Lydia's face, her cheeks aching from her huge smile. Lydia's eyes widened and her mouth was agape. After a few seconds of trying to comprehend everything, Lydia grabbed Kate's hand, looked into her face, and squealed. Both friends immediately jumped out of their chairs and embraced, bouncing up and down. They probably looked like crazy people, but neither one of them seemed to care or notice.

When they finally settled down, Lydia laughed, "So, he finally did it, huh?"

"Oh, Lydia, it was so perfect! I was so busy trying to keep things in order that I didn't even go into the date thinking about an engagement. I guarantee that was his plan." Kate giggled as she looked down at her sparkling ring. "Apparently, Steve roped Ian and Trevor into stringing lights up in that new greenhouse outside Ian's place. Ian provided the food, and your mom even supplied some of her best flowers. It was so perfect." Kate sighed happily.

Lydia's smile was radiant. Kate could see the happiness radiating off her friend, which made her heart swell with gratitude.

"Steve made your mom promise she wouldn't say anything to you because he knew I had to see your face when I told you."

"Well, I can't imagine getting the news any other way. I'm so happy for you two!" Kate and Lydia continued to chat away about wedding preparations and the bachelorette party. Finally, a break in conversation allowed Kate to direct the focus onto Lydia.

"So, how was the trip?" Kate smirked. "I already know about your date and how magical that was. I also know that Jordan didn't even bother to kiss you goodnight, which just makes no sense whatsoever." Lydia shook her head and rolled her eyes. "But what about the showcase?"

"It was nice." A wistful look passed over Lydia's face.

"Just nice?"

Lydia's cheeks flushed as she shifted her weight in her chair. "Okay, it was wonderful. Jordan was completely in his element. I finally got to meet Sarah, his manager. She's really sweet and even told me how Jordan's been talking non-stop about Maple Ridge and me." Lydia paused, the smile on her face fading a little and a little crease appeared between her brows.

"You're worried about him going back to Boston, aren't you?" Kate prodded.

"Maybe a little. He seems so comfortable with the bustle of the city. But then, I keep thinking that if I did get the job with Boston Ballet, I'd be there too."

"And if you don't get the job?"

Lydia took a deep breath and blew it out slowly. "I don't know."

"Maybe that's a conversation you should have with him. The hallmark of a strong relationship is good communication." She winked at Lydia.

Kate knew how difficult it was for Lydia to open up to someone like Jordan who could vastly change her life's trajectory. Though the timing couldn't be better for it. However, she could see the confusion and fear in her friend's expressions when they discussed Jordan's plans after the holidays. He didn't even know where he would end up after Christmas. That was proven at Thanksgiving. It was clear that Lydia worried that he'd get bored in this small town, if he *did* decide to stay.

In an effort to redirect Lydia's thoughts on the present, she expertly changed the subject. Besides, it was important that they focus as much of their efforts as they could on getting everything ready for the upcoming performance.

"Well, as for right now, June's been doing a pretty decent job with the rehearsals. I haven't stuck around to watch the whole thing, but no dancers have run to me crying so…"

Lydia shook her head and laughed. "I'm looking forward to seeing what they've been working on. Although they must be tired with the extra rehearsal June decided to add to the schedule while my back was turned."

"Yeah, well, you had to see that one coming."

"Speaking of rehearsal, I should get going. I need to prepare for tomorrow and I still have to make sure the countdown calendar is updated. Thank you so much for holding down the fort while I was gone."

"No problem! I don't know how you do it all though. I'm glad you're back."

Kate wrapped her arm around Lydia's waist as they walked out of the coffee shop together. The next couple of weeks would be crazy busy. This moment was simply the calm before the storm.

~

Getting back into the swing of things had been more difficult than she thought it would. Lydia rarely saw Jordan, as she was too busy fixing the choreography June altered while she was away. It wasn't bad, but the dancers were struggling to keep up with the demands. Keeping Jordan at a distance was good, as his presence always distracted her, which right now could be detrimental.

Unfortunately, things got a little more complicated when the head dance instructor called in sick, meaning that Lydia had to fill in for her classes. The added workload forced Lydia to place June in charge more often than she preferred. It also meant that June took advantage of Lydia's distractions by calling for additional rehearsals. Everything now felt like it was falling apart.

Then again, the dancing was the only thing not panning out perfectly. Everything else was pretty much under control and almost ready. Steve had placed the finishing touches on the very last set: the snow globe, and it worked like a dream. Kate was meeting with Ian to finalize the details of the menu. The costumes were perfect, decorations were up and only a few were waiting until the last minute, tables and chairs were rented, all the businesses had their flyers and advertisements hanging in windows and on doors. To the outside observer, this whole event was running smoothly, and all the details seemed to be accounted for. Nothing to worry over. But to Lydia, the dancing was the most crucial part of the whole event. Having that fall behind made her gut twist with anxiety.

Lydia let a deep sigh escape her as she wiped down the barre for the next class.

"I thought you might be hungry." She turned to see Jordan standing in his socks, holding a basket. "Kate said you had about forty-five minutes before your next class, so I wanted to stop by and share some of Claire's amazing cooking with you." He looked down at his feet where Lydia's gaze and smile were directed. "I saw the sign for no shoes in the dance room." Lydia laughed at him.

"I appreciate that. And I really appreciate the meal. I've been here pretty much all day and haven't eaten since breakfast."

He set his basket down on the floor and laid out a blanket for them to sit on. Lydia just stared in awe of this man who had such a big heart. His generosity astounded her. When he was finished, Lydia joined him on the floor.

"We haven't seen much of each other the past week, so I wanted to make sure I take advantage of any spare moment you have."

"You've been busy too, I hear. Have you been working on some new art?"

Jordan smirked and looked down to serve her some salad. "Sort of."

Lydia cocked her head in question, but he didn't elaborate. Instead, he changed the subject.

"I'll be heading back into Boston on Friday to drop off new prints to Sarah."

Clearly Jordan was hiding something. He seemed to have a hidden amusement that Lydia wasn't allowed in on. *Maybe it's a Christmas present! Oh, I should go shopping for a Christmas present. I'll have to rope Kate in on a little shopping trip sometime this week.* Lydia smiled to herself. She sounded a little like Kate. Whatever it was that Jordan was hiding was probably a secret for a reason and guessing could only ruin the surprise.

Once the meal was finished, Jordan stood to clean up and repack the basket. "I better get myself out of here before your students show up."

"Yeah, that's probably not a conversation I want to have with meddlesome teenagers. My students make a point of ensuring that my private life isn't quite private." They both laughed. "Thank you so much. This was lovely." Lydia's eyes met Jordan's. His eyes were so blue. She moved closer and placed her hand in his. Her thoughts immediately went to Kate and her irritation at him for not kissing Lydia after their date. A little chuckle bubbled to the surface.

"What?" Jordan smiled at her mirth.

"Oh, nothing. It's just something Kate said a couple days ago."

She glanced at the clock on the wall. Ten minutes until class started. That was plenty of time. She felt Jordan inch closer to her. The door was closed, right? Lydia double-checked past his shoulder. It was still open a little, but that was okay. It still allowed some privacy.

They had missed their opportunity once before; she didn't want to miss it again. They were close enough now that Lydia could feel Jordan's breath on her face when he exhaled. Tilting her chin up, her eyes flicked to his mouth, hoping he'd take the hint. Clearly, his thoughts were veering in the same direction, as he closed the distance between them completely, his lips finally meeting hers.

Jordan's hand rested at the small of her back, pulling her to him. She was grateful for the extra support as her knees began to feel weak and unsteady. If he hadn't been there, she felt she would melt right into the floor. A small sigh escaped as he deepened the kiss. A noise behind them made her jump away and Jordan rubbed the back of his neck, smiling like a guilty little boy. Lydia giggled when she realized the sound had only been from someone bumping the door closed all the way.

"I should go. No need to give those teenagers any fuel for gossip." His voice was so low, it was almost a whisper. They were still close enough for her to feel his breath on her face.

Lydia's eyes met his again, a darker blue than before in contrast to his flushed cheeks. "I'll see you soon." His smile in response made her heart feel as though it was trying to escape her chest.

"Absolutely."

Then the next noise really was someone entering the dance room. Her students began filing in for their class as Jordan slipped out, trying not to be noticed. Lydia quickly turned her back on the students to prepare the music. She couldn't stop smiling. Her fingers went to her lips, as if trying to preserve the feeling of their kiss.

Like most girls, Lydia imagined what her first kiss would feel like, but nothing had prepared her for what had just happened. It was beyond imagination. It was beyond description. It was simply something one had to experience for themselves to know how completely, perfectly, wonderful it was to be kissed.

Her hand rested on her cheek, which was warm from the flush that was most likely going to give everything away. She laughed softly under her breath. In all her imaginings she had never thought her first kiss would be in such an unromantic spot or that it would be rushed to avoid the eyes of her own students. And yet it was perfection. Now all she could think about was a repeat event.

~

Jordan practically stumbled out of the studio. He hadn't planned on kissing Lydia today. It wasn't as romantic as it would have been the night of their first date. But it hadn't been great timing then with the whole misunderstanding with Kathy and all.

Today, it was as if she was opening that door wide for him to walk right through. Her lips proved to be as soft and yielding as he'd thought they'd be. The way her green eyes deepened into an even darker mossy color made his stomach do flips all over again. He needed to tell her he loved her soon or he felt he'd burst.

Chapter Twenty-One

Lydia shivered, pulling her coat tighter and wrapping her scarf more securely around her neck. "The weather's been much colder than usual this week. Hopefully we won't get any snow before the performance."

"I don't think so. I keep watching the forecast closely and it's been clear so far." Kate wrapped her arm through Lydia's, as they entered their favorite antique shop, the bell above the door dinging. Already Lydia was feeling warmer, the heat on full blast in the small store.

"So, any ideas of what you're getting Steve this year?"

"Not really. I guess I'll know it when I see it." Just at that moment, an old record player caught Kate's eye and she gasped. "Oh! Steve would love this!" She gently brushed her hand over the beautiful, dark wood.

"It is gorgeous. And in perfect condition." Lydia inspected the doors in front. "Does he have records for it?"

"A whole heap of them! He's been collecting since he was a boy, and his current player has been on the fritz lately. I love that he can store them inside the cabinet!"

As Kate continued to caress the record player, Lydia continued to wander around. There were always such unique finds in this store. She was looking for something special…something meaningful to give Jordan for Christmas. Lydia stopped to look at some old photographs and cameras. It was amazing to her that someone would donate items with such intimate memories. Then a leather camera bag caught her eye.

"What's that?" Kate startled her.

"Don't sneak up on me like that!" Lydia playfully swatted Kate's shoulder as her friend giggled. "It's a camera bag. All the pockets are for storing various lenses and things. It's in perfect condition."

Kate flashed a teasing grin at Lydia. "I think I can guess who you'd be gifting that to."

"Well, Jordan's camera bag looked a little worn when I saw it."

"I think he'll love it. And, speaking of Jordan, there's this new glow to you when you talk about him. Did something happen?" Kate quirked an eyebrow.

Lydia tried to smother a smile, but she knew she wasn't fooling her best friend. "Maybe."

Kate's eyebrows flew up and her jaw dropped. "He kissed you, didn't he?! Oh, my gosh, finally!" She clapped her hands and bounced on her toes.

"Shhhh!" Lydia grabbed Kate's hands and pulled them down to still her excitement. "I don't want the whole world to know."

"Tell me! Where? When? Was it good?"

Lydia's cheeks suddenly felt like they were on fire. "He brought me a picnic at the studio yesterday between classes."

"He did it then? And you didn't tell me?"

"You'd left by the time I was finished with classes and cleaning."

"Mmhmm…" Kate pressed her lips together in playful annoyance. "Well, go on then. How was it?"

Lydia's smile said everything. "It was perfect. A little rushed, but perfect. I had a hard time focusing on the class and I couldn't stop smiling."

Kate squealed and wrapped her arm in Lydia's. "I see a sparkly ring in *your* future."

"You can't just hop from first kiss to engagement. We're definitely not there yet."

"Okay, okay. But it would be pretty cool to be engaged together, wouldn't it?" Kate wiggled her eyebrows.

Lydia laughed through her nose. "Did you decide on whether or not you wanted the record player?"

"Oh, I've already had the clerk put a sign on it so that nobody takes it while we walk around."

Lydia laughed, "There isn't anyone else here."

"It doesn't matter. I'm not losing that pristine player."

Once the friends had perused the entire store, checking a few people off their Christmas lists, they checked out. Kate would ask Trevor to come by and pick up the record player that afternoon in his truck. He was the only one that could hide it in his garage until Christmas day without Steve knowing.

"This was a really nice break in the busy week." Kate's nose was already pink from the chilly wind.

"I'm glad we could take the time to do this together. I'd offer to buy you some hot cocoa, but I have class in ten minutes." Lydia gave Kate a hug.

"Rain check." Kate waved as Lydia headed toward the studio.

One more evening of classes to go before the head teacher would be healthy enough to return. They only had a week and a half left before the big event. Lydia had already missed two rehearsals this week and would be missing another today. The stress was beginning to wear on her. *Lord, give me strength that will sustain me through this next week and a half. Grant me peace in releasing control of my performance to June. In Jesus's name, amen.*

Lydia took a deep breath, feeling the peace of God wash over her. Everything would be okay, even if it wasn't exactly perfect. Life was too short to be stressed over things you couldn't control anyway. At least that's what her mother constantly told her. She tried to believe it and apply it for herself but found it difficult, especially in times like these. But she took a deep breath anyway and focused on what she could control. As she walked into the studio, Lydia felt much lighter.

~

A sprained ankle. That was the best prognosis, but what if it was worse? What if it was a broken ankle? Her dance career would be over for sure. June's head was swirling in panic. She couldn't think straight. It was like it was happening all over again. Falling out of her fouettés and having her pointe shoe slip sideways, twisting her ankle. Hearing the damage as she fell to the floor in blinding pain. Her eyes burned as she watched the dancers gather around the one who'd fallen.

"Can you move it?" She heard one of the lead dancers ask.

The injured dancer hissed in pain as she tried to move her ankle. "Yeah, I think so. It's swelling up pretty bad though. I definitely can't walk on it."

"June!" The same lead dancer yelled angrily. "We need to get Emily back to the studio to ice her ankle. I told you someone was going to get hurt." Her eyes shot daggers at June, who stood mute.

She couldn't move. Couldn't speak. All she did was nod and watch as a couple of the men locked arms and made a seat for Emily to sit in and be carried back to the studio. June wasn't even angry at the dancer who'd just yelled at her. She was right. She'd been pushing all of them too hard. Even still, June couldn't allow the tears that threatened to fall to be released. Tears were a sign of weakness and she needed to stay strong in front of the dancers. Even if it was her fault all of this happened.

In an effort to take advantage of Lydia's absence, June had been scheduling too many back-to-back rehearsals. June could tell the dancers were getting tired, but she needed them to finish learning the changes before Lydia returned. Kate would be furious. She didn't even know how Lydia would respond. For some reason, thinking about Lydia's reaction made her gut clench. Seeing disappointment in Lydia's face would be a blow.

June had done her best at trying to keep the additional rehearsals on the down low, while Lydia was distracted. Kate had been distracted too with her engagement and organizing the budget and volunteers. Great friend she was to Lydia. She was supposed to be paying better attention to the schedule. But now Kate would definitely find out, and she'd tell Lydia as soon as she saw the dancers come into the studio.

Everything was quiet. All the dancers had followed each other back to the studio to make sure Emily was alright. June finally let the tears fall. She had to get away. She couldn't stay here. She couldn't face Lydia. There had to be a place that felt like home…normal. A place that didn't remind her of the pain and heartache of her crushed dreams.

~

"I can't believe I didn't pay closer attention to the rehearsal schedule." Kate chided herself. "I'm so sorry Lydia. I should have been paying better attention." She placed her face in her hands in defeat.

As soon as the mob of worried dancers had entered the studio, Kate knew something was seriously wrong. Trying not to panic, she handled the situation and made sure Emily was taken to the doctor to have her ankle X-rayed. Lydia was still teaching when it happened, but she had heard the commotion and something in her twisted with anxiety. It took everything in her to stay focused on finishing up her class.

"It's not your fault, Kate. I was the one who should've been paying closer attention. I'm just glad Emily seems to be doing okay." Lydia had the full story related to her once she dismissed her class and rushed to the lobby in search of Kate. Panic set in as she tried to figure out their next step.

"She might not even be able to dance the part." Kate was up and pacing the studio office. "Best case scenario is it's a simple sprain but even that would need to be rested without weight on it for who knows how long." Her hands clenched and unclenched as she spoke, trying to keep the anger and frustration at bay.

Lydia could feel angry tears surfacing but she forced herself to stay strong against them. Now wasn't the time to break down, it was a time that required action. "I'll have to dance it myself." The thought of adding one more thing to her plate made her even angrier. Like she needed more pressure and more stress.

Kate looked at her, surprised. "Are you serious?"

"What else am I supposed to do, Kate?" Lydia exploded, her hands going to her hips in frustration. "Emily obviously won't be able to do it. I don't have any backup dancers and even if I did, it would take weeks to get them ready. I already know most of the choreography if we get rid of whatever it is that June's been teaching." Her breathing was fast, and she tried to will herself to calm down. Lydia pinched the bridge of her nose, taking a full, deep breath and closing her eyes. "I'm sorry, Kate." Her voice caught.

Kate's hand rested on Lydia's shoulder. "Hey, I'm the last person to tell you to calm down. I'm kind of freaking out here myself."

"Yeah, but you don't deserve to be yelled at for something you didn't do." Lydia looked at her friend. Always there. Always supportive. She forced a small smile.

"If you think you can dance the part, I'll help with whatever I can to take some extra responsibilities off your plate."

"Thank you. I think what I need right now is a hot shower and some sleep so I can be ready to figure this out tomorrow morning with a clear mind."

"I think that's a great idea. And hey, Emily's injury may be nothing at all, right? Let's just wait to hear what's going on with her first before we make any final decisions, okay."

It felt like false hope, but it made Lydia smile. Her friend always had a way to calm her and speak hope into her life. Lydia nodded, not quite believing that Emily would be alright enough to dance.

Lydia gave Kate a hug before gathering her things and heading home. Indignation still bubbled below the surface as she got ready for the night. How could she trust June with the one thing that she put her all into every year? First, she had the distraction of Jordan, then the pressure of having Mr. Fairfax coming to town, and then having to fill in for her head teacher while she was sick for two weeks. Now she had to deal with an injured dancer who could quite possibly be out for the count.

She wanted to lash out at June for being so disrespectful to the dancers...to her. For going behind Lydia's back and scheduling additional rehearsals, knowing full well that Lydia was too distracted and busy to know until it was too late. But deep down, Lydia knew that getting angry and lashing out wouldn't solve anything. Hadn't she just prayed for peace and strength earlier that afternoon?

Father, now I need that strength more than ever. And patience. Ultimately, I just need direction. I'm so angry right now. Help me find peace again. In Jesus' name.

Chapter Twenty-Two

"You're kidding." Jordan couldn't believe his ears. Sarah had been completely serious when she had told him about the job offer and yet he still couldn't believe it.

"Not even a little." She remained straight-faced.

This was an opportunity that could change his whole photographic career. Having his art in the New York studio was easy. He'd also been planning to open his own studio and having his art in three different places gave him more traction. But, with an up-and-coming documentarian offering him a full salaried position as his photographer, traveling the world, meeting new people, trying new foods, seeing new sights. It was everything he'd ever dreamed of. Nothing was panning out the way he'd imagined.

"You okay?" Sarah was watching him closely. He knew his conflicting thoughts were probably painted all over his face.

Jordan cleared his throat and packed his doubts into a mental box to go through later. "Yeah, I'm fine. When did you say he wanted to get started?"

"The new year. He is taking off for Norway on January third."

"And how long would it be?" She'd already breezed through the details with him, but it hadn't really sunk in yet.

Sarah chuckled. "He said the itinerary right now takes you through Norway, then Iceland, Finland, and Sweden to start. It'll be about six to twelve months depending on the material and how long it takes to shoot."

Jordan nodded, taking it all in. Sarah handed him the packet of information she'd printed out with all the details the documentarian, Aaron, had sent over that morning. "Just read up on it and think about it. You don't have much time to decide though. He needs an answer the day after Christmas, otherwise he's going with his second choice." He nodded again, taking the papers from her.

"I better get back on the road. Looks like it might snow." He smiled at her and pulled her into a quick hug. "Thank you, Sarah. I'll let you know as soon as I've decided. Have a merry Christmas."

"You, too, Jordan." He turned to leave but she placed a hand on his arm to stop him. "Hey, I like Lydia…a lot. She's good for you. I've never seen you happier. But this is a dream job. This is an opportunity that could open so many doors for you. New York's great and all but this is huge! I don't want you to lose her, but I want you to be realistic with yourself. It's only a year…if that. There have been many instances where long-distance relationships have worked out. Just keep that in mind." Her face held some concern, but her mouth tilted up in a small smile.

"I will." Jordan patted her hand and he turned to leave.

What was he going to tell Lydia? Their relationship was still so fresh and new. He didn't want to jeopardize that, especially since he was pretty sure he wanted to spend the rest of his life with her. His heart soared at that realization.

Love was definitely on his mind when it came to Lydia, but he hadn't quite thought about the rest-of-your-life stuff. Her life was in Maple Ridge. He couldn't ask her to come with him without hurting her own career and dreams. Leaving her for that long would be hard, too. Jordan knew how hard it was on her to have people leave her. Having her dad gone so much throughout her childhood and teen years had been rough on her. The last thing he wanted to do was give her the impression he was abandoning her for something better.

Jordan exhaled a breath as he rubbed a hand through his hair. He didn't know what to do. This was terrible timing. Further down the road of their relationship, they could have been strong enough to be able to get by in a long-distance relationship. He'd been banking on having a permanent place in Maple Ridge. But now…The only thing he could do was tell her the truth and they could try and work out a solution together. His anxiety only multiplied as he thought of Lydia. He could see her disappointment clear as day. Another deep sigh escaped him. *Father, give me wisdom to know what to do.*

~

Lydia paced the studio office. It had not even been twenty-four hours, and she still hadn't heard from Emily. Kate came in and from the look on her face, Lydia could tell it wasn't good news.

It was a sprain.

Lydia's heart sank as Kate told her the news. The doctor had told Emily she couldn't dance for at least three weeks. Part of the ligament had torn pretty badly during her fall. The overuse had weakened the area but, thankfully it didn't require surgery. Not only was Emily's chance at auditioning for Boston Ballet out of the picture, but the performance couldn't go on without her. Never before had they dealt with something like this, this close to the performance.

As much as she wanted to freak out, she remained calm. Her mom had received the brunt of an outburst earlier that morning as Lydia struggled to reign in her emotions. Unable to stop anxiously trying to figure out a solution, she had tossed and turned the night before. Even Kate's hopeful belief that Emily would be fine didn't convince her. She felt horrible. All the stress of the situation and her dream job being on the line, not to mention the possibility of letting her dancers down when they had a shot at the Boston Ballet scholarships, was redoubled.

"What the heck are we going to do?!" Kate flopped into her desk chair and dropped her head into her hand.

"I don't know." Lydia sounded exhausted. She was sure there were dark circles under her eyes.

"What do we do about June?"

Lydia felt her anger resurfacing, "I don't know and honestly I don't care." She ground out, trying to keep herself controlled. Silence filled the office. What *were* they going to do? She was at a loss. *This is why theaters have understudies.* Lydia thought to herself. Maybe that wasn't such a bad idea for next year. Though she'd never had this problem before, it would be a good idea to be better prepared just in case. Then again, June had been at the center of all the issues so maybe not having involved her would fix things. "I should go."

Kate's head came up. She looked exhausted too. "Where are you going?"

"To go through the choreography myself." The thought made her nauseous.

"Lydia." Kate stood and grabbed Lydia's arm, turning her away from the door. "You're too overwhelmed and tired right now."

Lydia sighed deeply. "I don't have any other options. June ruined the performance and now I have to fix it." Her anger was getting the better of her again. Kate had to have known that she was right because she released Lydia's arm and nodded.

"Take care of yourself, okay. Take a nap or something so that you're not walking around like a zombie. We can't have you getting injured too."

Lydia let a light chuckle escape, releasing some of her frustration. "Okay."

The music wound down and Lydia hunched over, trying to catch her breath. Even with all the teaching she'd been doing, she still felt out of shape. *How in the world will I do this?* She took a sip of water. Kate was right, she needed a nap. The thought of filling in for Emily seemed like a good idea, but now she just wanted to collapse into bed and stay there forever.

"Hey!" Jordan's voice carried through the rehearsal room. He walked toward her in his socks.

She smiled. She loved the fact that he was so considerate. There had been many adults who thought that the "no street shoes in the rehearsal room" sign didn't apply to them. "Hey. I thought you were staying in the city for another night."

"I was, but I realized there wasn't a whole lot for me to accomplish there. I'd rather be here to help you out."

"I appreciate that."

Jordan's brows furrowed as he looked at her. "You look tired. Is everything okay?"

"One of our dancers got injured and I'm having to fill in for her."

"Oh, Lydia. I'm so sorry. Is she okay?"

"Yeah, she's fine, but she can't dance for a couple of weeks. It'll take her a while to heal and we can't wait for her to get better." A strange look came over Jordan as he looked at her. She didn't know what it meant but she felt her stomach clench as anxiety gripped her again. "Are you okay?"

In a blink, the strange look was gone, and Jordan's gaze softened as he took her hands in his. "I'm fine. Just a little tired, too, I guess."

Lydia wasn't convinced. There was something he wasn't telling her. Something that was clearly weighing on him. Why wasn't he telling her?

"Where's June?" The question was so sudden, and her nerves were so raw that Lydia flinched.

"I don't know. She disappeared yesterday." Lydia's voice sounded thick with anger and unshed tears. She needed a good, long cry.

Jordan pulled her into a hug, his chin resting lightly on her head. It felt good to be in his arms. Safe and warm. She closed her eyes and willed the tears to stay put. He absentmindedly rubbed small circles over her back. "How are you really doing, Lydia?" He asked her softly.

As if by magic, his words released the dam on her unshed, angry tears. She sniffed, trying to gain control but it seemed impossible. Jordan simply held her, allowing her to cry for a long while. When she felt that she had sufficiently cried out her frustration, Lydia pulled back to look him in the eyes. "Thank you."

He reached up and wiped her cheek with his thumb and smiled. "Seems like you needed that."

Lydia laughed softly, noticing the wet spot on his chest. She put her hand over it and rubbed it as if that would make it go away. "I'm sorry I got your sweater all wet."

Jordan looked down and shrugged, placing his hand over hers. "It's just a sweater. It'll dry." His face went serious again and he looked intently into her eyes. "Is there anything I can do to help?"

"Unless you can dance perfect ballet, I don't think so."

"Hmmm. Well, I wish I could, but I struggled with a simple waltz so I'm afraid I can't make that happen." Lydia laughed again. It felt good to laugh. "Was June responsible?"

She sighed, the anger and frustration from earlier had eased. Now she simply felt drained. "Inadvertently."

"I assume you haven't talked with her or anything?" Lydia shook her head. "Not that I want to make excuses for her because I've seen how difficult she is to work with. But I can imagine that this incident probably brought up a little PTSD for her." He must have noticed the confusion on Lydia's face. "I heard about her injury through Claire. She tells me everything. Even the things I'd rather not know." He laughed, making Lydia smile.

"I hadn't considered that."

"No wonder. You've been thrown into chaos." His thumb rubbed small circles on her arm as silence fell between them. When Lydia didn't respond, he continued, "She admires you, you know."

Lydia snorted. "She hates me."

"I'm sure it feels like that. But I saw how she watched you. She's bitter and angry about her failed dance career and envious of how well you're doing in yours. That doesn't mean that she hates you though. Below the surface, she does admire you. She just won't admit it to anyone. Not even herself I would imagine. Envy tends to do that to people."

Lydia looked down at the buttons by the neck of his sweater. She felt a tinge of guilt that she'd allowed herself to lash out at June, even if it wasn't to her face.

Jordan's voice was gentle and hushed, releasing all tension in her. "My guess is she feels like she can't move past the anger and hurt to make something of herself in a different way. Dance was what she knew and then it was suddenly gone. I can only imagine how hard it must be for her." He gently raised her chin so she would meet his eyes again. "I'm not discounting your frustrations. But I saw how hurt she was when she saw us together. I saw the longing when she looked at you when you worked with your dancers. I think she needs a friend right now."

He was right. Lydia had focused so much of her energy on the negatives of June's character and her actions, she'd forgotten about all the hurt she'd been through. She'd even forgotten about her conversation with her mom on allowing June to show who she really was. If she were truthful with herself, Lydia hadn't even given June a chance to be anything but bitter and secluded. "I should find her." Lydia spoke so quietly she was surprised he heard her, but he smiled in response. "I might actually have an idea of where she's gone."

"I love you." Jordan's eyes went wide, and his mouth stood agape, as if he hadn't intended on saying what he'd just said.

Lydia's heart started beating faster. She felt her face flush as her smile grew wider.

"I...uh..." Jordan coughed; his face flushed as well. "I mean...I didn't..." He stuttered and then rubbed his hands over his face. As he lowered his hands, his eyes met her again. Jordan grabbed one of Lydia's hands, the other hand gently cupping her cheek. "I love you." He repeated, this time with a surety that couldn't be denied. "I didn't intend on telling you now. In fact, I wanted it to be in a more romantic spot, but it seems like we can't find a moment outside of this rehearsal room." They both laughed.

Lydia felt as if she were soaring through the clouds. No, it wasn't the most romantic spot for someone to declare their love, and they had also been discussing June, which was far from being romantic. And yet, it was the most perfect time for him to announce it to her. There was only a slight pause after their laughter before Jordan pulled her close for a kiss.

If she ever thought that nothing could top their first kiss, she had been mistaken. Their first kiss had been soft, gentle, and rushed. But a kiss after a declaration of love. Lydia felt light-headed. Jordan's hand moved from her cheek to her nape, fingers entwining with her hair, as his other hand on her waist pulled her closer, deepening the kiss. She thought for sure she could feel his heartbeat beneath her hand on his chest, but then again, maybe it was hers and she could feel it down to her fingertips.

~

Jordan's skin prickled with awareness as Lydia's hand moved from his chest to entangle in the hair at his neck. He didn't want the moment to end. He didn't even care that she hadn't responded to his announcement. Well, he did care a little, but he hadn't exactly given her a lot of time to respond before pulling her in for the most passionate, delicious, knee-weakening kiss. A small moan escaped as he went in for another. Lydia's hair was so soft. He almost felt bad for messing up her perfect ballet hair. Almost.

After what felt like ages, he softened the kiss, dropping one final peck on her lips. Her eyes fluttered open, her face flushed, green eyes a deep, mossy color making him feel heady. Then, to add to his feelings of utter intoxication, he heard a breathy whisper. "I love you, too."

His pulse kicked up, "What?" He thought he'd heard her wrong.

Lydia smiled; her eyes sparkling. "I love you, too."

Jordan thought he'd soar right through the roof. "Really?"

Lydia laughed at him, linking her hands behind his neck. "Really." She initiated one final kiss that left him hungry for more. Then she left him to walk to the mirrored wall, fixing her mussed hair which made him smile with satisfaction.

"Can I take you to dinner?"

"I'd love that." Lydia hesitated, pushing a pin into her hair to secure the fly-aways. "But first, you're right, I need to find June. I need to make sure she's alright."

Jordan nodded. He was proud of her, even if it came between him and a date with the woman he loved. He didn't initially want to bring up June because he could tell that Lydia had been through so much already. But he could also see the anger welling up inside her. From what Claire had told him, as well as his own observations of June, Jordan could tell that she was lonely and broken.

"If I'm right about where she is, I won't be more than half-an-hour." She walked toward him again, keeping her distance but smiling flirtatiously.

"I'll text you in an hour then." Jordan closed the distance between them, wrapping his arms around her waist.

"I just fixed my hair." Lydia flashed a playfully irritated look at him. Even still, she brought her hands around his neck again.

"I won't mess it up again." Jordan winked, making Lydia giggle. Her laughter was like music to his ears. She was so beautiful. Suddenly a feeling of guilt pricked his conscience. How could he tell her about the job offer now? She trusted him to not leave her. But how could he turn the job down? Leaving her now felt like the most painful thing he could possibly do. Lydia noticed his growing pensiveness.

"What's wrong?"

Jordan took a deep breath, trying to quell the guilt, and forced a smile. "Nothing. I'm just a little overwhelmed." That was true. He was overwhelmed by Lydia and her love for him, and he was overwhelmed by this huge decision looming before him. But he should give Lydia credit because she didn't seem to fully accept that answer. Nonetheless, she didn't pursue the subject further.

"I'll see you in about an hour." Lydia kissed his cheek, lingering a bit to search his eyes. She was so perceptive, but now wasn't the time to share everything with her. She had enough to worry about without having the possibility of him leaving the country for a year hanging over her as well. He tried to shutter off those thoughts and leaned forward to kiss her nose as a distraction.

"I'll follow you out."

Chapter Twenty-Three

It was still fairly early, but the winter evening had grown dark by the time she and Jordan exited the studio. Lydia locked up, parting ways with him, and drove to the lake. Her thoughts kept swirling with so many emotions. Jordan loved her! That was the one that was most overpowering. But there had been something on his mind. The same thing that had caught her attention when he first came into the studio. Whatever it was, she hoped that he'd open up to her about it soon. Then again, it could simply be him feeling sad that his time in Maple Ridge was coming to an end.

Boston wasn't so far away. And if she ended up getting the job at the ballet, they'd see much more of each other. Her thoughts continued to go a million miles a minute as she pulled into the parking lot by the water.

At some point, in the past few years, June's mom had made a passing comment about how June had always sought solace at the harbor in Boston. The water calmed her, and it wasn't terribly crowded. It was unlikely that June had driven all the way to Boston, so Lydia thought she'd give the lake a try.

She didn't know what she was going to do or say. Jordan had been right. She knew that June was lonely and broken. But June hadn't exactly made it easy for them to get along or even for Lydia to be any sort of role model. She was just so…difficult! When Jordan talked about June and her possible PTSD, it clicked that maybe he was right about that too. Maybe June was suffering more emotional trauma from her previous injury than anyone realized.

Help me find her, Lord. And help me be patient with her. Give me the words to say. In Jesus' name. Amen.

Lydia parked and started walking to the water. The sun had set long ago, the bitter wind whipping at her face, making her skin feel raw. The only light was the bright, full moon and a few streetlamps. As she got closer, Lydia saw June, her dark hair pulled back into a slick bun. She was staring off into the distance and Lydia could tell her eyes were a little puffy from prolonged crying. The moment she saw Lydia, June angrily wiped away the tears that were trickling down her cheeks and crossed her arms over her chest.

"How did you find me?" Her voice sounded nasally.

Lydia calmly sat down next to her, maintaining some distance to make June feel more comfortable. "I remembered from a while ago that your mom said you used to visit the harbor often when you lived in Boston. I figured the lake was the closest thing to it." Silence filled the space between them for a while. "Are you okay, June?"

June glanced over at Lydia, likely surprised that she hadn't gone immediately to ridiculing her for what had happened. "I'm fine." She looked back at the water.

"June, I haven't known you for that long, but I've observed you the past few months. I know it's hard for you to connect with other people and I think that's because you don't want to get hurt again. I know how hard it is to move from a place that you love to a completely new town of total strangers." Lydia took a breath. "When I was ten, my dad enlisted, and we had to move to Maple Ridge. I had to leave all my friends, my dance studio, my childhood home. It was really hard."

Lydia looked over to see June's features softening just slightly in the moonlight. Fresh tears shone on her face. *Give me the words she needs to hear, Father.* She shifted a little closer to June and placed a tentative hand on her shoulder. "It's one of the hardest things in the world to have something you love taken away from you. When you invest your whole identity into something, losing it feels like you've lost a part of yourself." She knew she was treading on precarious ground, but June needed to hear this.

June turned to face Lydia, a pained look on her face. "You have no idea what it's like to hear that you can't ever do the one thing you love and are good at again! When I got injured, not only did the doctors say I couldn't do pointe, but my parents decided to take me out of my home and drag me to this stupid little town." The emotions warring inside her began to choke her as she turned away.

Lydia took a breath before answering. "You're right." June looked at her in surprise. "I don't know what that's like. I can't imagine how hard that must have been for you. But that doesn't mean that you can't find something else you're good at. You just might have a hidden talent that you haven't tapped into yet. I think finding people you can trust, believing that most of them only want the best for you is a good place to start."

June rolled her eyes. "Not everyone can be like you!"

"What do you mean?"

"You have the perfect job, the perfect friends, the perfect guy! You're perfect! You don't have to worry about failing or finding something new or..." Again, her emotions choked her, and she couldn't go on.

"June," Lydia was genuinely abashed, "I am far from being perfect. When I first moved to Maple Ridge, I isolated myself in dance and had a hard time making friends. I was lonely and shy and didn't know what I wanted to do with my life. I have people who love me but I..." Lydia hesitated. She was about to admit something to June that she hadn't even fully admitted to herself. She bit her lip and continued. "...with my dad leaving when I was young, I've always had a fear that I'd be left behind. That my friends would forget about me when they got involved in their own lives." Lydia's throat began to swell with her own emotions. June was facing her again and listening intently. "And that happened to some extent. Except for Kate, really." She cleared her throat. "I think that the both of us have been believing a lie for so long that it's become part of our identities." It was crazy, but a laugh bubbled out as she admitted her deepest insecurity. Even June's features seemed softer, more receptive. "June, these fears have been eating away at our confidence. But you know what? I think God placed us together so that we could help each other realize our fears and confront them. Together."

June took a deep breath and wiped her eyes. She was quiet for a while. The gentle slapping of the water against the shore made Lydia smile. It was no wonder June chose to be by the water for solace. It was calming.

"I'm sorry for what happened." June hiccupped.

Lydia's smile grew. "I forgive you. And I'd like to start fresh with you, if that's okay." June smiled back. "I know starting fresh can be difficult, so I'm here if you need anything. You know," Lydia remembered something an old friend had told her a few weeks ago, "I had a conversation with someone who has a friend that works in athletic rehabilitation. I believe that she works with athletes post-injury to help them get back into their sport. With the number of dancers that come through the studio on a regular basis, it might be nice to have someone with training in physical therapy to help them stay healthy and strong as well as rehabilitate any injuries."

June was thoughtful for a second. "I think I'd like that."

Lydia pulled her into a side hug. "I think everyone would be more than willing to give you a second chance. Just be yourself, because I have a feeling that you are a pretty wonderful person under all those layers." They both stood and Lydia shivered, pulling her coat tighter around her. "Now, I don't know how long you've been out here, so how about I treat you to some cocoa? You must be freezing."

"Thanks, but I'm okay. I think I'll head home. My parents are probably worried about where I ran off to."

Before Lydia could walk away, June pulled her into a hug. Her mom's words came back to her, *"You never know what a difference you are making just by being kind."* As always, she was right. June released her and cleared her throat, clearly a little embarrassed by her sudden outburst of emotion. To avoid embarrassing her further, Lydia said goodbye and headed toward her car.

God had given Lydia the words June needed the most. It hadn't felt like she did much, but June's hug at the end told her it was enough. Lydia hadn't expected to reveal her insecurities to June, especially since she hadn't fully realized them herself. She hadn't even talked to Kate about her fear of abandonment. Now that it was out in the open, it didn't seem as scary. There was even a bit of weight lifted off her shoulders, especially in regard to Jordan. She realized now that she'd been terrified of his departure. Him leaving, even if it was just to Boston, was generating a fear of abandonment. It wasn't fair of her to place that burden on him. Recognizing it was the first step, and now that she did, she could face it head on.

For so long, June had been living with this idea that she was the only one struggling. Now, Lydia had laid the foundation for comradery in their imperfections and similarities. Lydia hoped that one of these days, June would be open to a friendship that would allow them each to be accountable to the other. June would be a good partner if she could lay aside her personal doubts, fears, and preconceptions about Lydia.

As she got into the car and blasted the heat, Lydia smiled to herself. She was excited to see what would come out of her talk with June. She also couldn't wait to tell Jordan all about it at dinner.

Chapter Twenty-Four

Lydia struggled for two days before giving up. She didn't want to give up, but she found that she was too stressed to be able to retain the choreography. Kate wanted to help out but, unfortunately, there wasn't much she could do, other than be the supportive friend she always was.

"I just can't seem to remember anything!" Lydia huffed in frustration and plopped onto the dance floor, wiping her forehead with a towel she had brought.

Kate watched her sympathetically. It had occurred to her that there was another option, but she didn't want to bring it up in hopes that they wouldn't have to stoop so low. When Lydia announced that she'd be taking on the role, Kate didn't argue. But now, watching how discouraged Lydia was becoming, knowing there wasn't any way she could help, made her rethink her decision to keep their last resort a secret. She took a deep breath and sat down next to Lydia.

"There is another option we haven't considered." She cringed, realizing what she was about to say. Lydia looked at her, looking more tired than ever. "We could always have June fill in." Kate made a face that clearly showed how much she hated admitting that June would actually be of help.

Lydia's eyebrows went up in surprise and she let out an airy, sarcastic laugh. "You're kidding, right?"

"Believe me, I hate that I'm saying this. She ruined this performance, and she definitely doesn't deserve the right to be a part of it. But…" She couldn't continue so she just groaned instead. It might be their only option, but she didn't have to be happy about it.

Lydia was thoughtful for a moment. "She knows the choreography better than I do." Silence settled between them. "I can't do this, Kate." Lydia sounded defeated.

Kate wrapped her arm around her friend's shoulders and sighed. "I know."

"I don't think we have any other options at this point."

Kate bit the inside of her cheek. "I know." Silence again.

"I'll talk to her today." Lydia sounded more resolved. As if handing over this role suddenly gave her the energy back that she'd lost.

"Want me to come with you?" She didn't actually want to go, but offering to take part in the conversation seemed like part of her job description.

"No. I'll be fine. June and I have a bit of a repour now." Lydia looked over at Kate, a smirk on her face. "You're probably not the best person to be around June."

Lydia was right and she was grateful. Kate and June hadn't got along before the incident. Now, it wouldn't be easy for Kate to simply overlook the damage June had caused without a little animosity creeping in. Even after Lydia had talked to her about what had happened at the lake, Kate still wasn't convinced yet. It was best that she stay behind. "Really? Why do you say that?" They laughed together, the tension from earlier completely erased.

"At least try to forgive her. It wasn't intentional."

"I know. She's just so…"

"Stubborn?" Lydia offered.

"Sure." Kate smirked. Stubborn was a kinder word than the others she could conjure up.

"Sounds like someone I know." Lydia winked at Kate and nudged her shoulder.

"Bite your tongue, Lydia Foster! June and I are not alike."

"Hmmm." Lydia snickered as she stood up and started packing up her things.

Even as she protested, Kate knew there was some truth to Lydia's comparison. She and June *were* a little alike. They both had fiery tempers when they were challenged, both competitive, and they both *were* stubborn. Kate laughed through her nose. She couldn't believe that of all the people they relied on now to make the performance a roaring success, it was June. Kate rolled her eyes. *This will be interesting.*

~

After their talk by the lake a couple days ago, June had kept her distance from everyone on the *Magical Holiday Celebration* team, especially Kate. Lydia hadn't even reached out since then which didn't exactly surprise her. It was June's fault that they were down a dancer. That pain pricked at her heart. Then again, Lydia *had* forgiven her. Knowing that she had offered forgiveness freely was balm to her soul.

It was oddly exciting to think that her and Lydia could be friends. Even through all the bitterness and envy she'd felt toward Lydia, June still greatly admired her. Everything that Lydia did was so inspiring. Perhaps she was right. Perhaps June could find a new passion in life that included her love of dance. Having Lydia suggest working with dancers in a rehabilitative capacity gave her a thrill. Suddenly, June felt that a new door was being flung wide open for her, and she didn't exactly know what to do with it.

A knock on the front door brought June back to reality. Lydia stood on the doorstep, looking a little tired. When June opened it, Lydia smiled at her, not a single hint of animosity on her face. "Hi, June."

"Lydia." June greeted, not unkindly. She still wasn't sure how to be around Lydia.

"Can we talk for a minute?"

"Sure." June gestured to Lydia to follow her into the front room.

Lydia took a seat and fiddled with her purse before raising her eyes up to meet June's again. "So, I've filled in for Emily in the dance." June nodded. "The only problem is that I'm so overwhelmed with everything else that I'm having trouble retaining the choreography." She took a deep breath before continuing. "You know the choreography better than I do, since you've been handling the rehearsals lately. I'd like to talk about the possibility of you filling in for Emily instead."

June couldn't believe what she was hearing. Lydia was actually asking if she would fill in for the dancer, who was now injured because of her? When she didn't respond, Lydia bit her lip and gave her a pleading look. "June?"

"I...I can't." June shook her head. There was no way the dancers would allow her to just step in like that after how she'd treated them. She hadn't even built up the courage to apologize to Emily for what had happened.

Lydia reached over and placed her hand reassuringly on June's. "I know what you're thinking. I've already talked to the other dancers. They are okay with this decision."

"How? I was terrible to them." June couldn't meet Lydia's gaze. She felt ashamed of herself. Lydia might believe in her, but June still had a hard time believing in herself. She was afraid she'd fall into old patterns again.

"I know...and they know. But, like I said to you at the lake, they are ready to give you a second chance as long as you use it wisely. We all just want to see each other succeed. And this performance...everyone's put so much of themselves into it. Even you. It would be such a shame if it failed because of one incident." Lydia's smile brightened. "I've even decided to keep your changes to some of the choreography. It's actually really good."

June blew out a breath. One incident. It felt like much more than one simple incident. Forgiveness. Lydia offered forgiveness. It sounded like the dancers were offering the same. A second chance. June now needed to forgive herself. But how? "I don't know how to move past this."

Lydia's smile relaxed into a knowing look and nodded. "Can I pray with you, June?"

June had gone to church a lot as a kid, but as she got older, her parents allowed her to make her own choices. Church got in the way of extra rehearsal time, so she stopped going. She had always noticed Lydia and her family had this deep peacefulness about them. Maybe their faith had something to do with that. Lydia had never been shy of sharing her faith with those around her. June nodded and Lydia reached out to her. Placing her hands in Lydia's, June felt another wall of bitterness fall away.

"Father, I ask that you be with my friend June. Help her to realize her importance in your kingdom here on earth. Surround her with your peace and security. Most of all, I pray that you help her see how much you love her. And that no matter what, she can always come to you. That you offer forgiveness freely, with no strings attached. In Jesus' name, amen."

Lydia's prayer was the kindest thing anyone had ever done for her. June felt tears slowly trickle down her cheeks as she listened. She felt that forgiving herself might actually be possible now. The strength she felt from Lydia gave her confidence that all wasn't quite so lost. "Thank you." June felt lighter than she had felt in years. Like a giant weight had been lifted off her shoulders.

"If you ever need prayer or support in any way, I'm here for you." Lydia's eyes sparkled with the most beautiful inner light she'd ever seen. In that moment, June knew she wanted more of that for herself. "At least think about taking over Emily's role, okay. We can't do the dance without the role filled. We can't do it without you."

"I'll do it." She didn't have to think about it. The truth was, she wanted a second chance. She wanted to show everyone that she could be better. And maybe she even wanted to audition for a scholarship position as well. She no longer wanted to compete with Lydia for the choreographer position. She deserved it more than her. June made a mental note to cancel her interview with Mr. Fairfax. All she knew was that Lydia was offering that second chance and there was no way she'd turn it down.

"Great! I'm so glad! Then I'll see you at rehearsal tonight!" Lydia got up to leave and June followed to escort her out. Before they parted ways, Lydia hugged June. Never in her life did June believe that she'd be friends with Lydia. She also couldn't believe that she was actually considering going to church and learning more about God. For the first time in her life, June felt that nothing in life could be better than this very moment. At this moment, she was content.

Chapter Twenty-Five

Jordan had told Claire all about the job offer. She was thrilled for him, if not a little disappointed to see him thinking about living so far away. Travel photography was his dream, even if he gave it up for more stability and time with family. It had been the right choice at the time. Now he would be able to branch outside of his comfort zone in a way that kindled a sense of adventure. It was a one in a million opportunity. Still, he was hesitant to get too excited over the idea of accepting the job. His heart was being pulled in two different directions – his lifelong dream as an artist, and his love for Lydia Foster.

He'd wanted to tell Lydia right when he got back, but with the complications with June and the performance, Lydia had enough on her plate. That was clear when she'd broken down in the studio. The last thing Jordan wanted to do was cause her to believe he was abandoning her for something better.

No matter how many times he thought over the possibilities, he couldn't come up with a solution that would work for them both. He'd be far away in another country, possibly without service for long stretches of time, and she'd be here, or in Boston, living her own dream. Lydia had a real shot at getting the job at Boston Ballet. He believed in her. It had been an exciting prospect to think that perhaps they'd both be living in Boston together. But now…

"Earth to Jordan." Claire snapped her fingers a few times, pulling him back into the present. She was smiling down at him from the step ladder, where she was hanging some garland over the living room door frame. It was his job to hand up the little decorating picks she was sticking strategically through the evergreen. "Are you okay?"

He blinked up at her and let out a low chuckle that was a bit forced. "Yeah, I'm fine."

Claire's brows came together, and she pursed her lips in thought. "You're thinking about Lydia, aren't you?"

This time Jordan's chuckle was real. "How do you know exactly what I'm thinking all the time?"

"You're like my brother. I know everything about you. Even your facial expressions." She winked at him and held his hand as she climbed down off the ladder. Claire wiped her hands on her jeans and looked up, satisfied with her work.

"It looks beautiful, Claire."

"Thanks. Now don't change the subject." She led him to the couch and patted the cushion beside her for him to sit down. "Have you told her yet?"

Jordan sighed as he sat down. "No. She has so much on her plate already. When I saw her at the studio, she was so overwhelmed. I have been kind of...avoiding her since." He gave her a guilty look.

"What?!" Claire whacked his shoulder in annoyance. "Jordan Williams! You told her you loved her, kissed her, and now you've been avoiding her! What is wrong with you?"

Jordan blocked another assault. "I know, I know. I just haven't figured out how to tell her."

Claire raised her eyebrow, still annoyed with him. She stared at him for a bit and then softened, placing a hand on his shoulder. "I know she's busy, but if you wait too long, you might do more harm than good. If you accept the job, you'll be leaving soon. She deserves to know. You can't avoid your problems, Jordan. And she definitely doesn't deserve to be ignored after you've professed your love to her." The irritation returned.

He knew she was right. He hadn't been fair to Lydia the past couple days. More than anything he wanted to be there for her as she was preparing for such a huge event. But he couldn't look at her knowing that he had to tell her he might be leaving. Turning down the job seemed insane, but he also felt that he couldn't leave when their relationship was still so new. He and Lydia had barely had enough time to really get to know each other and now he might be ruining everything.

Jordan hadn't felt a connection like this with anyone. Even Kathy. That thought hadn't occurred to him until he had told Lydia he loved her. How on earth could they make a long-distance relationship work when being away from her, even for a day, made him feel that a huge part of him was missing?

"Hey. What are you thinking?" Claire's annoyance at him had completely gone, and in its place was genuine concern. She knew him so well.

Jordan forced a smile. "Just trying to figure out how this will work, I guess."

Claire sighed. "It's going to be difficult; I know. It was hard enough for me to deal with Kyle going through med school and now his residency. And he's only an hour away. But, if God wants the two of you together, He'll make it happen. You have to trust in that." Jordan nodded, the anxieties and fears slowly easing from his heart. "I know that's not a huge consolation, but God knows what you need better than you do." Claire smiled and patted his shoulder. "Well, I have to get lunch on." She gave him a pointed look as she rose from the couch. "Don't wait too long."

This time, Jordan's smile was genuine. "I won't. Promise." But how *would* he tell Lydia?

Father, please help me know the words to say to her. Give me direction. Help me to know where you're leading, even if it means turning this dream job down and staying here with Lydia. Jordan winced, not quite wanting to pray the next part. *Even if it means taking the job and saying goodbye to Lydia for a time.* It hurt to admit that leaving her might be where God was calling him, but Claire was right. If God had meant for them to be together, He'd make it happen. *I love her, Father. I just want what's best for the both of us according to your plan.*

Maybe Lydia was his new dream, and the job offer was just a way for him to realize that. There was still a battle going on in his heart. If she was his new dream, then why did he still feel the pull of the job offer? He needed to rely on God's guidance more than ever. Most of all, he needed to share his heart with Lydia before it was too late.

~

June had agreed to take Emily's place in the performance, and even showed up early to apologize to the dancers for her behavior and treatment of them. It was one of the hardest things she'd ever had to do. It wasn't like her to admit her wrongdoing, but there was something about Lydia's confidence in her that lit a fire of conviction in herself.

Even though it was painful, Lydia had been right about the dancers wanting to give her a second chance. During her first rehearsal dancing with them, June felt more welcome than she ever had. It wasn't long before they were chatting with her and bringing her into the fold of friendship. Her heart soared. For the first time in her life, June felt a part of a group that accepted her.

In all her years of performing and being a part of a group of dancers, she had never felt such camaraderie, such an absence of competition that everyone wanted to support each other. It was refreshing. No wonder they kept coming back year after year. Most of these dancers had known each other and worked with each other since Lydia first began the *Magical Holiday Celebration.* Finally, June felt accepted, not simply tolerated.

They had only one week left before the big day, and everyone was both nervous and excited. June had filled the position well, even if it was a little outside of her comfort zone.

She accustomed herself to the role quickly under Lydia's guidance. When she allowed herself to be led, she realized how good a choreographer and teacher Lydia really was. June had been so blind with envy and bitterness she hadn't seen Lydia for the wonderful person she was. She cared deeply about her work and the people she worked with. That was what drew others to Lydia. She simply…loved.

Kate, on the other hand, still kept her distance from June. She could tell that Kate had a newfound respect for her the past couple of weeks, but they still didn't quite get along. It didn't surprise her. They both had fiery personalities that tended to clash. Either way, June was finally enjoying herself and looking forward to the holiday season.

The *Magical Holiday Celebration* crew had only a couple more days to prepare for the performance. Spare time was a hot commodity. If the dancers weren't rehearsing, they were resting, helping finish up the final details of decorating, helping Ian in his large industrial kitchen, or pitching in at the studio to finish up regular dance classes before winter break. It was a time of togetherness and unity for the team. A time that each of them didn't take for granted. This was one of the parts of the performance that they each looked forward to the most simply because it brought them together. June loved being a part of it.

Lydia made sure that the crew had time set aside to spend with their families, so the holiday season didn't feel like it was all about work. The families of the dancers from out-of-town were given first dibs on hotel and bed and breakfast rooms for the holiday weekend. Maple Ridge was starting to fill with tourists, ready to celebrate Christmas. Shops, restaurants, and the local B&B were bustling with excitement and anticipation.

Emily was even staying in town with her family for the performance. There was no way she would miss such a big event, even if she wasn't able to be an integral part of it anymore. June had visited Emily and apologized for her part in the injury. That was yet another difficult hurdle to overcome. In the end, Emily had decided it was better to forgive June, than to hold onto the anger that had initially surfaced when June had arrived. They might not ever be friends, but at least June could rest easy knowing that she had made things right with Emily. It was the first step toward forgiving herself.

As more and more people came to town, it was getting more and more difficult to hide their rehearsals from curious eyes. Lydia had decided to move everything, except the large sets, to the studio until their final dress rehearsal. Costumes were completed, hair styles and makeup designs chosen, and fresh dance shoes purchased. Now all they had to do was make sure every detail of the choreography was perfected. Everything was coming together beautifully!

~

"Thank you so much Mr. Fairfax!" Lydia heard her heart pounding and she thought for sure everyone in the studio could hear it too. "See you soon. Bye." As she hung up the phone, Lydia took a deep breath and closed her eyes to calm her heart rate. She released her breath and bit her lip to contain her excitement, smiling so big, her cheeks were beginning to hurt.

Now wasn't the time to scream with joy. That would most certainly cause alarm among all the hard-working students in the other dance rooms. Their rehearsal had been going perfectly until she had to take the call from Boston Ballet. Now, as she stood in the hallway right outside the rehearsal room, Lydia felt like she was about to fly through the ceiling. She had to tell Kate…now.

Lydia popped her head into the room, barely able to contain herself. "June, can you handle rehearsal? I'll be right back." June nodded, clearly confused but before she could say anything in response, Lydia ran for the studio office.

"What in the world?!" Kate hopped up out of her seat in alarm as Lydia burst through the door. "What's wrong?" Her confused and frightened expression released a bubble of laughter from Lydia.

"Nothing is wrong." Lydia continued to laugh, the excitement she felt finding a release. "I got the job!"

Kate's eyes widened and she grabbed Lydia's hands. "You're kidding!" Lydia shook her head, joy radiating out of every pore. "Lydia! That's amazing!" Kate pulled her into a tight hug. "I knew you'd get it!" There was a pause and Kate looked at her, confused. "Wait. How did you get the job if he hasn't seen the performance yet?"

Lydia laughed again. "Okay, well, I didn't officially get the job. But Mr. Fairfax said I might as well count on having the job. He still wants to see the performance to be one hundred percent sure, but I guess his other candidate dropped out of the running for personal reasons."

"I hope it's nothing serious. But I am glad that you still have a strong chance."

"I just can't believe it. I guess I kind of felt the connection we made in Boston, but I wasn't sure he'd choose me with all the other, more qualified candidates in line."

"More qualified? Lydia, I've never known anyone more qualified than you for this position." Kate looked into her friend's eyes. "They would be lucky to have you as part of their team. I'm just sad to think of you being gone for a whole season."

"Boston's not that far away. I can visit. And you're welcome to come spend a weekend in the city with me." Lydia grinned. "It'll be so much fun!"

"Let's not get too excited until you are officially offered the job, okay." Kate raised her eyebrows at Lydia, unable to hide her enthusiasm.

They chatted a little longer about all the possibilities that could come out of Lydia being offered the job for real. Everything they had to rearrange and work out with the business. They even discussed the possibility of visiting a couture bridal shop in the city to look for Kate's wedding dress. That they could do even if she didn't have a job in Boston. Before she realized that the time had sped past, June stuck her head into the office.

"Everything okay?"

Lydia turned and glanced at the clock. "Oh, June, I'm sorry. I didn't realize what time it was." She got up and walked toward June. "Everything's fine. I was just discussing a phone call I had with Mr. Fairfax. He wanted to discuss a few things before coming." Lydia couldn't keep her excitement at bay. "He pretty much said I had the job but couldn't make it official until he saw the performance." She bit her lip to contain herself.

June's face brightened and she smiled. "That's great, Lydia! Congratulations!"

This new version of June made Lydia stand in awe of what God could do to change hearts. She seemed more content, more receptive to Lydia's words of encouragement. The fact that she was congratulating Lydia right now spoke volumes. "Thank you, June. And thank you for handling the rest of rehearsal. How did it go?"

"It went great. I think we're really ready for performance day."

"That's what I like to hear. Mr. Fairfax will be here in three days to audition everyone. He's looking forward to meeting you all."

A look of anxiety flashed across June's features. "Me too?"

"Only if you want. He's only auditioning dancers who want to try to get into the school. I would understand if you didn't want to start at the bottom again though."

Lydia could see that June was fighting a battle between her past and what she wanted to pursue for her future. She had connected June with the friend who worked as a Sports Physical Therapist. She didn't know how that was going, but since her first phone call, June seemed to be more confident.

Imagining the possibility of going back to Boston Ballet, a place where June had been severely injured and suffered pain deeper than physical pain, must have been a difficult concept to consider. Lydia placed a reassuring hand on June's shoulder.

"You don't have to make up your mind now. But it might be a way to face your fears, whether you make it or not. Besides, you could always say no if he does offer you a spot in the program." She smiled at June, and she felt the tension in her shoulders begin to relax.

"Thank you, Lydia. I'll think about it."

Lydia couldn't believe the gifts she'd been given this holiday season. She had a new, blossoming relationship with Jordan, and now that she would be moving to Boston, it made it easier for them to be together. June had slowly eased her way into friendship with Lydia and she could only see that friendship growing as the new year began. Her dad had even called to let Lydia and her mom know that he was coming home in time for the performance and would be staying through the new year. The cherry on top was that Lydia had a real chance at being offered a job that she'd dreamed about since she first started her choreographic career. God had abundantly blessed her.

Chapter Twenty-Six

To close out their final day of preparations, the entire crew gathered together at the amphitheater to put up the rest of the decorations and make sure the sets were in place and the paint touched up. Dress rehearsal would take place the next evening. Unfortunately, the weather hadn't held and the night before, Maple Ridge was covered in its first snow. An inch of powdery snow was still on the ground, half of it having melted during the day. Though it would most likely melt before performance day, they would have to come by early to make sure all the seats were dry.

Jordan had been a little distant lately, but Lydia hated to admit that she'd barely noticed. She'd been so busy that she hadn't had time to think about anything but her to-do list. He was present, but there was definitely something on his mind. As much as she wanted to know what it was, they hadn't had time to sit down and talk. Besides, nothing could possibly ruin such a perfect holiday. Whatever it was, he'd tell her when he was ready.

Lydia was holding the ladder for Kate as she hung the last piece of garland on the top of the amphitheater. Without warning, a snowball hit her on the leg, leaving a wet circle on her jeans. She turned to see Trevor, smiling a big, teasing smile, while he pressed together another snowball.

"Trevor! What are you doing?" Lydia laughed and brushed off her pants. Jordan straightened from his work on one of the sets and wiped his hands on his painting pants. Everyone's attention turned toward Trevor.

"We've been working like crazy the past few weeks." He made an exaggerated and comical face, "The past few months. I think it's about time we had a little fun. The decorations are all finished and anything else that needs to be done has to wait until the last minute anyway. What better way to let loose than a good, old-fashioned snowball fight?" He raised his brow in question, shaking the snowball in his hand. Before anyone could answer, he threw the snowball at Steve, hitting him in the shoulder.

A mischievous grin spread over Steve's face. "You're on!"

There were no teams, just everyone throwing handfuls of snow at whoever was the closest. Snow flew in every direction and shouts of laughter filled the air as each person tried to dodge and hide. Lydia was preparing to launch her snowball at Kate when she took a wrong step and slipped on a patch of ice. Before she could catch herself, Jordan caught her from behind. Losing his own balance, they toppled over together into a fit of laughter, as the cold snow seeped through their jeans.

When their legs began to go numb from the cold, Jordan helped Lydia up, his gaze holding hers, warming her from the inside. He broke the connection first, turning toward Trevor who'd sidled up to them, breathless. Lydia shook out her coat, trying to hide her flushed cheeks. Then she realized the cold probably made everyone's cheeks pink and stopped fidgeting.

"That was fun! I think we all needed that. Great idea, Trevor." Jordan clapped him on the shoulder. Since telling Jordan about her and Trevor's relationship, the both of them had spent some time together along with Steve. All three of them got along really well, and it warmed Lydia's heart to see Jordan building friendships with the people she loved so dearly.

"Thank you." Trevor bowed dramatically, making Lydia giggle.

Kate shivered and wiped some of her wet hair off her face. "It was fun, but now I'm freezing."

"How about some cocoa to warm up?" There was a resounding affirmative to Lydia's proposal, and she led her wet, tired crew to the coffee shop, cheeks and noses rosy. By the time they arrived at the coffee shop, everyone was shivering, except Lydia.

As they walked, Jordan had laced his fingers with hers. His closeness warmed her, despite their wet clothing. The connection they shared was so strong, it almost took her breath away. After they had all ordered their drinks, Jordan had been called away by the other guys on the team, and she felt his absence keenly.

Lydia took a seat, saving one beside her for when Jordan was finished talking. Only then did it occur to Lydia they hadn't had time to talk in almost a week. Hopefully, they could snatch some time to have a conversation before the town was thrust into a weekend of celebrating. She looked around at her friends. June was laughing and talking with some of the other dancers, her eyes sparkling with genuine joy. She looked happy for the first time since Lydia had known her.

Kate and Steve were cuddled up in a corner booth, warming up with cups of cocoa, and each other. Steve placed a dollop of whipped cream on Kate's nose. They laughed together as she touched her nose to his, moving in for a kiss.

Trevor was chatting animatedly with Ian, Jordan, and a couple of other guys about something that looked very interesting. Jordan looked so handsome. His hair was still damp from the snow and his sweater clung to him a bit. How on earth did she get so lucky?

For the first time in three weeks, Lydia felt like she could finally relax and breathe. Her crew had done such an amazing job. Now all she wanted was time to talk to Jordan.

"Hey, you!" Kate called out as she joined Lydia at her table by the fire.

"Hey." Lydia smiled up at her.

"What's up?"

"I was just thinking that this has been the best holiday season ever."

Kate nudged Lydia's elbow. "Is that really what you were thinking? I saw you staring."

Lydia flushed and tried to hide a smile. "Part of it was."

Kate laughed. "I can think of something that would make the season a lot better." She waggled her brows. "Maybe a kiss under the mistletoe and a dance at the party?"

"Maybe so." Lydia smirked, her gaze returning to Jordan.

"Speaking of, how is Jordan? He seems a little…distant."

"He seems to be doing okay. We haven't really had a chance to sit and talk lately."

"Hmm…well I'm sure the non-communication is due to you both being so busy."

Lydia nodded. Something told her there was more to Jordan's latest trip to Boston than simply dropping off pieces of art. A flutter of anxiety made its way into her heart.

"How's preparation going for your dad's arrival?" Kate changed the subject.

"Mom's been cleaning the house from top to bottom." Lydia laughed. "It's been so long. It will be great to have him home again."

"I'm so glad you will have that time with him. He's retiring soon, right?"

"Yeah, next year. He should be home for good by the end of summer."

"That's wonderful!"

Lydia sighed. "I just wish summer wasn't so far away."

Kate wrapped her arm around Lydia and pulled her into a side hug. "I'll be praying for you and your mom. You are two of the strongest women I know."

"Thank you, Kate."

Lydia watched, as Jordan separated himself from the group of guys. Their eyes immediately connected, and he smiled, making her insides flutter like a million butterflies were caught there. Kate must have noticed his approach because she began to leave, whispering in Lydia's ear, "I'll leave you two alone."

"Hi." Jordan took the seat Kate had just vacated, his eyes never breaking contact with Lydia's.

"Hi." Lydia instinctively shifted closer to him.

"It's been a great day." He reached over and took her hand, lacing his fingers with hers. She didn't think she'd ever get used to how perfectly their hands fit together.

"I couldn't have made it this far without these guys." Lydia briefly broke eye contact and glanced around the room, a contented smile on her face. "Especially you." The heat from the fire was nothing compared to the heat in Jordan's eyes as he looked straight to her heart.

He smiled, that delicious dimple making its appearance, and chuckled under his breath. "It has been my pleasure. I'm just glad I was nosey enough to enter an area closed to the public."

Lydia laughed then, "I probably looked like a crazy person, pushing you out like I did. A complete stranger."

"Maybe a little." He gently nudged her shoulder with his. "But that just made me more intrigued by you." His eyes were glued to hers again, and it looked like he was going to kiss her. Before he did, however, Lydia changed the subject.

"My dad's coming for Christmas. I'd really like to introduce you to him."

Jordan's eyes widened slightly as if he was taken off guard, but he smiled. "I'd like that."

Lydia laid her head on his shoulder as he pulled her closer to his side. They watched the fire leap in the fireplace, sounds of laughter filling the coffee shop. The snow outside, glittering as the lights from the stores and streetlights shone down on it. This day *had* been pretty great. She took a deep breath and smiled, as Jordan gently rubbed circles over her hand with his thumb.

Meeting Jordan, and falling for him, had made everything even more perfect. Having him meet her dad was a huge step. But despite the twinges of anxiety that still pulled at her heart since Jordan's return from the city, Lydia didn't feel nervous about the introduction.

As much as she wanted him to kiss her earlier, she wanted to wait until everything between them was resolved first. And as much as she wanted to resolve it all now, she was too content sitting by his side in silence to ruin the moment. They'd have another moment to talk. Now she simply wanted to enjoy the peace that came from knowing they were that much closer to the big event.

Chapter Twenty-Seven

Lydia woke up the next morning, feeling a combination of excitement and anxiety. She'd be heading to the studio today to make sure it was clean and ready for Mr. Fairfax to conduct the auditions and interviews for the dancers. As she walked down the stairs, she noticed a suitcase and duffle bag propped up against the staircase. She squealed with delight and ran into the kitchen, finding her father seated next to her mom, eating breakfast.

"There you are sleepy head." His deep, familiar voice filled the kitchen. He got up and opened his arms, ready for a hug from his daughter.

Lydia leapt into his arms and squeezed tight, taking in the familiar scent of his cologne. Tears welled up in her eyes as she finally released him. She wiped them away as he held her out at arm's length to look at her.

"You are just as beautiful as when I last saw you. Just like your mother." He wiped away a stray tear from her cheek and placed a kiss in its place.

"I missed you so much, Dad." Lydia sat next to him at the table, not letting go of his hand.

"I missed you both more than you know." He reached over to clasp Allison's hand with his free one. She wiped away her own tears but smiled through them. "I can't wait to see your performance, Lydia. I want to hear all about it."

Lydia spent the morning with her parents, catching her dad up on everything that had happened the past few months. She told him about June and the drastic change that had come over her after their heart-to-heart. She told him about Steve's proposal to Kate and their collective excitement over the upcoming wedding. She even told him about Jordan, their date in Boston, and how their relationship had progressed since then, resulting in a declaration of love.

"When do I get to meet this, Jordan?" Lydia's dad smiled at her good-naturedly, a teasing sparkle in his eyes.

She blushed slightly. "I was hoping to meet him for lunch this afternoon. We can meet in town together."

"That sounds perfect." Her dad squeezed her hand and smiled. "I look forward to putting the face to the name. From what you've been telling me over the phone, and from what I've heard now, he sounds like a great young man. I'm very proud of you, Lydia. You've handled yourself wonderfully through all the obstacles. I can't wait to be here to watch you and be a part of your life more often when I retire." Before more tears could fall, he smiled and stood to give Allison a kiss on the forehead. "I should go unpack."

"Are you ready for tomorrow?" Allison asked when he was gone.

"Mostly. I'm going to go by the studio to make sure it's clean and ready for the auditions with Mr. Fairfax tomorrow."

"Remember to be calm today. Why don't you go do something with Kate? Something fun and completely unrelated to the event."

Lydia chuckled. "That's not a bad idea. I'll see what she's doing." Allison knew that Lydia tended to overthink during times of anticipation, and it made her more anxious. Kate was always the perfect person to go to for a distraction.

"Well, you go to the studio, and we'll meet you for lunch around one."

Lydia nodded. "That sounds perfect. Thanks mom."

Introducing Jordan to her dad was a huge step in their relationship. She'd prepared Jordan about the possibility of meeting her dad last night, but she hadn't expected that he'd be showing up today. They had expected him tomorrow. Lydia hoped that Jordan wouldn't mind the last-minute suggestion of lunch with her parents. At least it would be a casual way for him to get to know her dad.

As she headed to the studio, Lydia tried to take deep breaths, praying that Jordan and her dad would hit it off. It meant so much to her that the two men she loved most would get along. But as she prayed, a quiet voice told her to be calm. God had everything under control. She simply had to trust in Him.

"I can't believe that tomorrow is the performance!" Lydia was rushing around the dance studio, making sure everything was clean and tidy. Mr. Fairfax would be arriving the next morning. Kate followed her around, trying to help out as much as possible, while also trying to calm Lydia.

The peace and calm she felt about Jordan visiting her parents didn't quell the anxiety she felt about the next two days. The whole studio staff had been so busy lately that there was a layer of dust on everything – the shelves, mirrors, sound systems. Only the floors were squeaky clean.

"Lydia, you pretty much have the job. I understand that you want the studio clean, but why does it have to be spotless? He's here to hire you based on your choreography skills, not the cleanliness of your workplace."

"He's the artistic director for one of the best dance companies in the United States. I want him to see the studio at its best." Lydia wiped down the final mirror and stood back with her hands on her hips. "Besides, the studio hasn't had a good cleaning like this in almost a year."

Kate laughed and helped Lydia gather up the cleaning supplies and they headed for the lobby.

"Hey ladies." Jordan entered the studio, an unsure smile on his face. Lydia's heart sunk slightly at his expression. Something was wrong. Suddenly the anxious feelings that had been swirling around in her stomach about his distant behavior shattered all peace she had felt about him earlier.

"Hey, Jordan. I was just…going to put these in the closet in the back." Kate sensed the tension and made her exit as quickly as she could, with her arms and hands full of cleaning supplies. Lydia normally would have laughed at the spectacle, but her mind was focused on Jordan's uneasy expression.

He flashed a grateful smile in Kate's direction before looking back at Lydia. "Lydia, can we talk?"

Lydia felt like her feet were lead. Why did he look so uncomfortable and nervous? Her anxiety levels shot through the roof as he led her to the back office. She needed to get her emotions under control and have a clear head for what was to come. A deep breath helped calm her thumping heart, at least a little.

It took Jordan some time to start talking. He paced the office for a few minutes, trying to find the words to say what he needed. Lydia couldn't take the silence any longer. "Jordan. I can't take this anymore. What's going on?"

He stood still, a pained look in his eyes. "I…" he paused, his brows furrowed, "Sarah had an interview lined up for me when I was in Boston. One of the guys I met when you and I visited is a well-known documentarian and is currently hiring a photographer to join him on his upcoming project." He paused again and rubbed a hand over his face. "I guess he specifically requested me, and Sarah agreed to a face-to-face meeting. I figured I'd go and see what he had to offer and most likely turn it down, but then I started talking with him…"

Jordan sat down. Lydia just stared, not exactly knowing where this conversation was leading, but it didn't sound good. "This job is a huge opportunity. I wouldn't just be taking photos like I normally do with travel photography gigs; he wants me to film content and be his production assistant. The project is based on Vikings and their exploits, so we'd be traveling to all the places where Vikings plundered and lived."

Lydia, her palms sweating, heart racing, thoughts swirling, didn't know how to respond. She could see the sparkle of excitement in his eyes as he spoke. The Vikings weren't in Boston, that was for sure. The realization took hold and she felt she couldn't breathe. All she could focus on was the fact that Jordan was telling her he might leave. His eyes searched hers for some sort of answer. When she didn't verbally respond, he stood up and held her hands in his.

"Lydia, I'm not saying I'm leaving but I wanted you to know what was going on."

"This is a huge opportunity for you." Her voice was quiet and forced.

Jordan nodded slowly and his jaw twitched. "It is."

"But you want to turn it down?" Lydia frowned. She was conflicted. She wanted to be with him. Her new job in Boston, should she get it, was supposed to bring them closer together. But she also didn't want him to turn something down that he was clearly passionate about. He loved travel photography, and this was a type of job offer that didn't come around often.

"I honestly don't know. I want to stay here, but…" he sighed and rubbed a hand over his face again, breaking eye contact and dropping her hands.

Lydia wanted to be supportive. To smile at him and say that everything would be alright, but she couldn't. She could barely take a full breath let alone say anything. Tears stung her eyes, as she felt her head swirl with various responses to what he'd just told her. Jordan looked at her again, his eyes filled with concern.

"Lydia? Talk to me, please."

She tried to clear her throat, but the tears had made it thick. Her voice was squeezed with emotion. "How long would you be gone?"

The look in his eyes told her everything she needed to know. If he took the job, he would be gone for a long time. She blinked and two tears trickled down her cheek as she looked down at the floor.

Jordan's finger crooked under her chin and brought her eyes back up to his. "Lydia, I'm sorry I didn't tell you sooner, but I didn't want to ruin things for you right before your big night." She nodded and tried to smile. "I'd be gone for six to twelve months. I couldn't come back home often…maybe a few major holidays, but even then, I couldn't promise that." He pressed his mouth into a tight line. She could tell he didn't want to say the next words. "We might not see each other that often."

Lydia forced herself to take a deep breath. It was shaky, but her heartbeat seemed to relax a little at Jordan's calm tone and the sincerity in his eyes. He was hurting as much as she was, that was clear to her. He didn't want to leave her. She could see the battle going on inside his heart. This was a big deal for him. Deep down, Lydia knew that if she told him no, he'd give it up for her.

Father, give me strength. She closed her eyes as she prayed her silent prayer, taking another shaky, deep breath. She placed a hand on his arm and smiled, her mind clear. "Jordan, this is a huge opportunity for you. It'll advance your career." She sniffed and worked to gain control of her emotions. "It's not a permanent job, right? You can add to your resume while you continue to figure out your permanent career path." They could handle long-distance. As long as he wasn't gone forever. She'd done it with her dad. Besides, she'd probably be so busy in Boston that at least three months would pass by quickly.

He returned her smile but, there was still a look in his eyes that didn't quite relieve all her fears. "No, it wouldn't be permanent." She searched his eyes for more. He seemed to be holding back on her. But before she could analyze his heart further, his features softened, and he released her hand to cup her face. "We can make it work."

"We could make the time you are home even more special." She felt a little more at ease, his thumb wiping away the stray tears.

"You're amazing, you know that?" Jordan looked at her with deep admiration and love. Her cheeks felt warm under his gaze. "I want to make this work between us."

"Me too."

"I'll pray on it, okay. God knows what's best for the both of us." His confidence strengthened her. If he believed they could make it, so would she. Jordan hugged her for a long time. She enjoyed the feel of being in his arms. She felt safe. How could she go a full year without that feeling? Her heart ached at the thought of not having him nearby. He pulled back and kissed her forehead. "I ran into your mom." Lydia's eyes met his, and she could see merriment in them. "Apparently, we're meeting your parents for lunch."

Lydia laughed softly, her breathing steadier than it had been since entering the office. "Yeah, I was supposed to tell you. I forgot."

Jordan's features became serious again. "Lydia, I want you to know that I'd give anything to be with you."

"I know." Tears threatened to fall again.

"I love you." He rested his forehead on hers.

Those three simple words made Lydia's fears fall away. If Jordan loved her, they'd make it work. "I love you enough to know that you need to make the right decision for you." He raised his head and looked at her, a little surprised. Lydia rested her hand on his chest before he could say anything. "I know you're going to pray about it. But if God's telling you to go, then you go. Okay?"

His eyes glistened slightly with tears of his own. Jordan nodded. They stood close to each other for a few moments. "We should probably get going." Lydia whispered. Jordan's emotions were under control again, so Lydia decided to infuse some humor into her voice. "My dad's a real stickler for time management."

A quiet chuckle came from Jordan. "Hmmm. Well then, let's get going." Jordan wrapped his arm around her shoulders and led her to the lobby. "Anything I should know about your dad before I meet him?" Jordan feigned nervousness and made Lydia giggle. It felt good to laugh. She loved how he could make her laugh.

"He might be a little tough on you at first, but he's a marshmallow. Don't worry, dad will love you."

~

Jordan hadn't told Lydia the whole truth. How could he? He needed to be extra sure that this was what he wanted, that this was what God was calling him to before he told her when he'd have to leave. Claire would say he was being a coward, and maybe she'd be right. If he and Lydia only had a couple more weeks left together, he wanted to savor each moment.

As far as this job not being permanent, that had been true. Besides, there wasn't any guarantee that this job would lead to another. But something that Aaron, the documentarian, had told him was that this project could lead to another. He was planning on submitting it to a film festival and if this documentary won awards, he wanted to make more. Jordan's heart soared at the idea of combining two things he loved into one – photography and travel. Especially when he thought that door had been closed long ago.

Having Lydia beside him was impossible. She couldn't leave her studio and her home. He wouldn't ask that of her. But if this job did become permanent, how could they make something like that work? The only way to know was by taking things one day at a time.

Accepting this job didn't guarantee the acceptance of the job that *might* come next. Besides, he still had plans for his own studio in the back of his mind. Thinking ahead into the future only added to fear and doubt. If God was calling him to be a part of this project, Jordan would accept the offer. They'd make their relationship work through it. Anything after that was something only God knew.

"Hey dad!" Lydia waved at her parents as they walked toward them. Jordan's palms began to sweat as they walked closer, his thoughts returning from the future to the present. He hadn't been worried about meeting Lydia's dad, but now that the moment had come, he was more nervous than he thought he'd be.

Lydia squeezed his hand which gave him a little boost of confidence. "Jordan, this is my dad. Dad, Jordan."

Jordan stuck his hand out to Mr. Foster. "Nice to meet you, sir." His handshake was firm and the smile on Mr. Foster's face reminded him of Lydia's own smile.

"Likewise. I look forward to getting to know you better. My daughter has told me a lot about you already."

Conversation flowed easily between the four of them, as they walked to the restaurant and were led to their table. Jordan felt integrated into their family already. The nervousness from earlier melted away as they ordered their meals. Lydia's dad was very amiable and genuine. He chuckled to himself about Lydia's comment about him being a marshmallow. She wasn't wrong.

Even though her dad hadn't been exactly tough on him, Jordan could tell that he was very protective of Lydia. They were so much alike. He caught the glances that Mr. Foster directed at Lydia, his look of adoration apparent. Lydia was his only daughter, his only child, so Jordan could only imagine how hard it must be for her dad to watch her grow up and move on.

When discussing Jordan's career, the new job opportunity came up. Mr. Foster was supportive of Jordan's decision to take time to pray over it and make sure it was the right thing for him. Overall, Jordan felt he had the stamp of approval from Lydia's dad to date her. Before they parted ways after lunch, Allison had pulled him into a hug and her dad heartily shook his hand.

"It was wonderful getting to know you, Jordan."

"You as well, Mr. Foster."

"I look forward to seeing your handiwork at the performance. Lydia won't even let me see anything before the big night."

Lydia laughed and hugged her dad.

"It was my pleasure to be able to help her out."

Mr. Foster winked at Jordan, "I can see that."

Jordan felt his face flush slightly, but he smiled through it. He placed his hand at Lydia's back as they bid her parents goodbye. Lydia had wanted to head back to the studio to finish getting it ready for tomorrow, so he decided to accompany her. He let out a deep breath. "That went well."

"Did you expect it to go badly?" Lydia laughed as she linked her arm through his.

"No, I just was a little nervous about meeting your dad."

"Lucky for you, my Dad's pretty laid back. There was definitely nothing to be worried about. He wasn't even tough on you at all. You got to see his marshmallow-y side right up front." Her golden laughter rang through the air.

"I guess the thought of him being in the army made me think he was going to be a little more...intense. That and your comment about him being tough on me. And the time management quip." He nudged her slightly as he chuckled.

"Yeah, sorry about that. I needed to lighten the mood." Lydia hugged his arm tighter as they continued to walk. Entering the studio, they found all the crew, musicians, singers, and dancers gathered in the lobby. Kate ran up to Lydia the moment they entered. "What's going on?" Lydia giggled.

"We wanted to surprise you and give you these before the craziness of the next two days sets in." Steve came up behind Kate with a bouquet of roses. He winked at Jordan as Kate discreetly handed him something. Lydia's quick eyes caught the exchange, and she spun around to face him.

"You were in on this?"

"I was." Jordan grinned at her and brought his own bouquet from behind his back.

Lydia gasped as she took the flowers and took a deep breath of their scent. "These are beautiful!"

"I would have given them to you after the performance, but I knew you'd be busy with Mr. Fairfax and your students. Besides, there's more that you might want to use right away."

"More?"

Steve chimed in, handing Lydia the bouquet he was holding. "You've worked so hard to put together the *Magical Holiday Celebration*, so as a thank you for all your hard work and dedication, Jordan and I pitched in to give you two this." He took an envelope out of his pocket and handed it to Lydia. Lydia exchanged a glance with Kate.

"I only knew about the flowers." Kate's hands went up in a shrug.

Lydia opened the envelope and out slid two vouchers for the local spa thirty minutes out of town. Her eyes widened and she looked back up at Steve.

"Those are for you and Kate to pamper yourselves this evening in preparation for this weekend. You both deserve it." Steve had barely finished talking before Kate flung herself into his arms. They all laughed as he lowered her feet back to the floor.

"You guys!" Lydia's eyes glistened. "This is so thoughtful! I should be the one giving you flowers. I couldn't have done any of this without you. Thank you so much for these. They are beautiful. And thank you for the spa vouchers. I can't wait!" She gave Jordan a lingering glance that went straight to his heart.

"Me either." Kate snatched her voucher and looked it over.

Lydia laughed at her friend, as she pulled roses out one-by-one and handed them to her crew members. Her bouquet was almost gone by the time she was finished.

"Now, you two should get going. There's nothing else for you to do until tomorrow. Go relax." Jordan kissed Lydia on the cheek. "And have fun." Lydia deserved to be pampered and taken care of. She'd put her heart and soul into her team. When he and Steve had discussed how they were going to spoil her and Kate, they'd settled on the spa, knowing that their anxiety levels had been high all month long. Seeing their excitement was worth every penny.

Kate grabbed her coat and wrapped her arm through Lydia's. "Let's go!" Lydia giggled as she handed over her bouquets to Jordan, his arms ready for them.

"I'll take care of these." He called after her.

Jordan was proud of Lydia. He had watched her as she dealt with June, eventually seeing her soften into contentment after the conflict of her bitterness. He saw how much Lydia loved and truly cared about every single person on her team and in her classes. Everyone who entered her studio could feel the love radiating off her. And then he felt her strength as they discussed his future plans even through her fear. She was one of the most incredible women he'd ever known. He never wanted to lose her.

Chapter Twenty-Eight

The dancers were gathered at the studio early the next morning, preparing themselves to meet and audition with Mr. Fairfax, the artistic director at Boston Ballet. They knew that his arrival brought a future with the company for only a few of them. The air in the studio was thick with anticipation and just a touch of fear. Lydia tried her best to keep everyone calm as they patiently waited.

"Mr. Fairfax. It's great to see you again." Lydia greeted the man in the lobby. "Thank you for coming to meet the dancers today. They're all ready for you in the rehearsal room."

"Thank you for having me. This town of yours is very quaint. I look forward to seeing more of it while I'm here. I'm also looking forward to seeing what your dancers have to offer." His kind smile removed any tension Lydia had allowed to build up during the waiting period.

Lydia led him to the rehearsal room, where the dancers were all gathered, chatting nervously and in hushed tones. He slowly looked around the room at each of them and gave a firm, single nod of his head. Mr. Fairfax set his briefcase down by the audition table and clasped his hands in front of him. There was no need to clap his hands or raise his voice to call attention as all eyes were on him the moment he entered the room.

"I want to thank you all for coming to audition today. I look forward to seeing you perform tomorrow, but I wanted to be able to see you individually and get to know you a little better before I decide who I might consider for Boston Ballet's scholarship program. As you all know, this scholarship is for our school, which could eventually lead to a company position down the road. Today, during our interviews, I would like to know why you think you should be a part of the program and how you believe you would fit in with the company. I also want to see your individuality in your auditions. There are only a couple of spots open so you must be able to prove to me why you're better than the rest." He smiled warmly at them.

Lydia's heart beat faster at his closing words. The heavy competition for the scholarships would pit them all against each other. Nonetheless, she knew that Anthony Fairfax was kind, though incredibly firm and direct, and wouldn't allow rejection to dampen their confidence as dancers. At least she hoped her assessment of him was correct.

He had allowed Lydia to remain in the rehearsal room to watch the auditions. Mr. Fairfax was definitely a harsh critic, making comments very rarely, but his face showed everything he was thinking. She could tell when a dancer wasn't impressing him. He scribbled on his notepad, writing meticulous notes about each dancer.

Kate had lent her office for the interviews once the individual auditions were completed. Each dancer was invited in for about five minutes. As the interviews continued, the dancers left in the studio grew more and more anxious for their turn. Nervous half-whispers echoed through the room as well as occasional laughter from those trying to keep themselves relaxed.

Lydia noticed that June was sitting alone in a corner, clearly nervous as she twisted a strand of hair that had strayed from her tight ballet bun. June had decided, almost at the last minute, to be a part of the process. Her dancing was beautiful! Lydia couldn't help but feel proud watching her. As she approached, June tried to hide her anxiety with a small smile.

"How are you doing, June?" Lydia took a seat next to her on the floor.

"I...I don't know. I want to dance for Boston Ballet again even if I'm not on pointe, but..." She sighed deeply and smoothed the loose strand of hair back, tucking it into her bun. "I'm just not sure if that's possible."

Lydia placed a reassuring hand on June's shoulder. "Hey, you were beautiful!" June gave her a look that said she was unsure. "Really. And even if you're not chosen, you did it. You conquered the fear of auditioning."

"And if I do? Make it." The doubt rang clear as day in her voice.

"If you do, you have a choice. You can either accept it and return to the company with your head held high and dance your heart out. Or you can turn it down and see if God has something else for you. Either way, I'll be praying that you will know what to do when the time comes." Lydia was always open about her faith with her students, but with June it didn't always come so easily. Now that they were beginning to become friends, Lydia felt that June needed the assurances that only God could provide.

"Thanks, Lydia."

"Absolutely! And you know, you can always pray too. God can hear your voice just as well as He can hear mine." Lydia gave her a quick side hug. June nodded, not quite convinced, but at least she was more open to the conversation of prayer. They both stood as Mr. Fairfax called June's name. "Good luck!" Lydia reached out and gave June's hand a quick squeeze. "You'll do great!" June flashed a nervous smile as she headed out of the rehearsal room.

~

June was trying her best to keep her knees from buckling under her as she took her seat in the office. Mr. Fairfax flipped through his notebook and poised his pen above the page, ready to take notes on their conversation. Her stomach suddenly clenched, and she felt the desire to run...run far, far away.

Instead, she clasped her hands together and willed herself to stay put.

"So, June." His voice was clear and crisp, but his eyes were kind and gentle. "I'm aware of your previous involvement with Boston Ballet. You have an impressive resume for someone so young."

"Thank you." Her mouth was so dry she was surprised the words came out clearly. She tried to smile.

"Don't be nervous." He smiled at her, his face softening, calming her nerves. "You are aware that if you do end up securing a scholarship, it would bring you back to ground zero and not company level?"

"I do."

He nodded. "I'm also aware that you left because of an injury to your ankle that could prevent you from doing pointe again. However, in spite of this, I have been considering giving you another chance at returning. You are a very talented dancer, that is apparent." He paused and looked down at his notes. June shifted in her seat. "There are some concerns I have, especially since you wouldn't be able to progress in the company if you weren't able to perform on pointe. Have you since been reevaluated to see if it's a possibility?"

June swallowed. *You're facing a fear. Be honest.* She cleared her throat. "I haven't. When my doctor told me I couldn't do pointe again, I pretty much gave up trying."

"Hmmm. Well, if you're willing to be reevaluated by a doctor that specializes in sports medicine, that could be a huge factor in my final decision."

"Of course!" The words just jumped out before she could think. "I'd be happy to meet with someone about it."

Mr. Fairfax chuckled slightly under his breath. "If you end up scheduling an appointment, please relate to me the doctor's findings as soon as you know. I know it will be difficult with the holiday season and all, but I would need a definite answer before the new year." June nodded. "Okay, so now we get to the big question. I know how you would fit in with the company, but why do you believe you deserve the scholarship?"

June felt her fear tighten around her heart, but she was determined to push through. Lydia believed she could do this, and that confidence gave her strength. "When I was a part of the company before, I was lost." She saw his eyebrow quirk upward slightly. She cleared her throat. "I didn't have any particular vision for my life, only the desire to be the best dancer. When my injury happened, I felt like my whole world had come crashing down around me. Since being here, and working with Lydia, I've discovered that I don't have to be the best or perfect all the time for people to accept me." June fought against the emotion that was threatening to interrupt her speech. "I love dancing. It's been such a huge part of who I am for so long. I know I have a lot of things to work on personally, but I believe that, should I be given the opportunity to dance with the company again, I wouldn't take it for granted. I want to be a part of a team that supports one another and encourages each other in the art form. More than that, I believe that, with Lydia at the helm, your spring season could be the best ever. I'd love nothing more than to be a part of that."

Mr. Fairfax's expression didn't change during the entire speech. Now that she was finished, she realized that she might have just insulted him with her last statement and bit her lip. Finally, a small smile touched his lips, and he leaned back in his chair, bringing his hands together in front of him.

"I'm sorry. I didn't mean that Lydia...I mean..." June searched for the right words.

He raised his hand to her. "No, no. I understand what you're saying. I, too, believe Lydia will make a huge difference in our spring season. I'm not offended at all. It's why I chose her as a candidate for the position." He looked more amused than annoyed, and June felt her heart slow its pace again. "I appreciate your honesty, June."

She didn't know if she should thank him or not. June opted for a silent nod. With a small grunt, Mr. Fairfax stood and walked over to June.

"It's been a pleasure speaking with you. I look forward to hearing what the doctor says and seeing you perform tomorrow night."

June stood and shook his hand. He escorted her out without another word, her head swirling with questions. What had just happened? Did he approve of her answer? Was he still considering her, or was he just being nice? He hadn't even mentioned the fact that she'd decided against being interviewed for the choreographer position. As she took a seat in the lobby to gather her thoughts, June felt like she was going to be sick with all the pent-up anxiety still swirling in her stomach.

Then she remembered Lydia's words. It didn't matter if he did or didn't offer her a spot with the company school. She had just faced a huge, nearly insurmountable fear. That was reason enough to be proud of herself. Never, since she'd moved to Maple Ridge, did June believe she'd be able to return to the company she'd left behind so many years ago as a dancer. As she continued to breathe deeply, June felt herself relax. Her heart returned to its regular pace, and she no longer felt sick. She felt…proud.

Chapter Twenty-Nine

Today was the day!

Lydia stared at the ceiling, taking deep breaths. *Father, help today be a day of peace. Help us all do the best we can and not worry about the rest. Most of all, help us all enjoy every single moment. In Jesus' name, amen.*

A smile came to her face as she got ready for the day and stayed there as she headed to the amphitheater. They were having an early rehearsal so that the performers could have time in the afternoon to spend with their families and prepare for the big night ahead.

When she arrived, everyone was there, warming up. Steve had turned on the stage heaters that would keep the dancers and musicians warm for the time it took to get through the entire show. Thankfully, it was a sunny morning and the snow had completely melted. A few of her crew members would come by and make sure all the seats were dry closer to the performance.

Jordan was chatting with Trevor and Kate, his blue-green eyes sparkling with amusement at something Trevor had said. Trevor always had a knack for making people laugh. That's probably why he and Lydia were such great friends. She didn't often consider it but if he hadn't been dating when her family had first moved to Maple Ridge, she'd probably have considered dating him. It was funny to think about now. As she stood and watched, Lydia was struck again with the disbelief that God had brought Jordan into her life. She'd prayed about meeting a man like him, and now here he was. It was as if she were living in a dream.

As if he could sense her presence, Jordan turned and looked straight at her, their gazes locking. Lydia's breath caught as she felt the warmth of his smile, directed only at her. She took a deep breath of the cool, crisp air to calm the fluttering in her stomach and clapped her hands to get everyone's attention.

"Okay everyone! If you're all warmed up, take your places and we'll get started." The dancers shed their extra layers and took their places. "Now, even though you are all very ready for tonight, this rehearsal will hopefully work out any kinks in the lighting."

Lydia had moved to the front with the rest of her friends, and she found that Jordan had moved to stand beside her. Her awareness of his presence was kindled immediately but she tried to focus on the matter at hand. Not an easy feat. She cleared her throat and smiled at her dancers.

"I don't want to tire you out too much, so I'd like to only run through this once so let's make it the best yet. Or at least your second best. Save your best for tonight. Pressure's on you, Steve." Lydia flashed a teasing smile his way and he saluted.

"And don't forget that tonight, before the performance, we'll be getting pictures done at the studio, so you'll need to be there around five with costumes on and makeup and hair done. Deb will be there for any last-minute adjustments." Kate announced.

With that, Lydia pointed to Ellie and Peter, ready to begin. As she watched, all aspects of the performance coming together as one, Lydia felt tears in her eyes. All the hard work everyone had put in, all the dedication through the frustration and Emily's injury, even the ability to forgive June and incorporate her into the performance had led up to this. Lydia no longer hoped that Mr. Fairfax would love their performance, she *knew* he would.

~

"Ta-da!" Lydia smiled triumphantly as she checked off the very last item on the countdown calendar.

"We did it!" Kate pulled Lydia into a tight hug, tears stinging her eyes. "I feel like this year has been the craziest and yet the most satisfying year yet." She wiped a stray tear that had fallen.

"I couldn't have done any of it without you." Lydia also wiped away a tear that had slipped.

Kate laughed. "Why are we crying?"

"I think, at this point, it's simply a release of all the tension we've been holding the past few months." They laughed together and sniffed.

"Maybe you're right." Kate took a deep breath. It had certainly been a long four months. "I'm glad it's almost over if I'm being honest."

"Honestly…me too."

"Really?"

"I just can't get thoughts of Ian's menu out of my head." They laughed again and Kate wrapped her arm around Lydia's shoulders as they headed to the studio lobby. They had both stopped by to make sure everything was ready for the night. After they locked up, Lydia placed her arm through Kate's, and they headed toward their cars. "I promised my mom I wouldn't stress over anything today. I'm taking the day slowly, resting and getting my hair and makeup done."

Kate loved Allison. Since moving out of the city, she hadn't seen her own mom in some time. They'd never had the best relationship, but it was still difficult to be away from her. Allison filled that motherhood role for Kate so easily that she felt part of the Foster family. Her advice was always the best.

"Sounds like a great idea. Steve is taking me to lunch and then I'm going home to do the same." Kate glanced over at Lydia. "What's Jordan up to today?"

She noticed a slight change come over Lydia's face that was a mixture of both excitement and anxiety, but a smile lifted the corners of her mouth. Any time she mentioned Jordan's name,

Lydia was bound to smile. It was great to see she still had that reaction even after the news of his job offer. Lydia had told Kate all about it after the auditions were over yesterday. Her heart ached for her friend and the difficult decision Jordan had to make.

"He's meeting up with me at the theater. He had a few things to take care of at Claire's today."

"He'll love your dress." Kate had gone dress shopping with Lydia and her mom a few weeks ago to find the perfect dress. Lydia always made a quick presentation on stage before and after the performances, so they had made a tradition of finding a new Christmas gown every year. Kate had always joked with her that at the rate they were going, Lydia would have to get a whole new closet to keep all her holiday dresses. So, Lydia decided to end the tradition after this year, reusing her old gowns for the coming years. But this year was special. She had an artistic director, and a new boyfriend to impress.

Lydia blushed but didn't respond. Only the smile remained. Kate was so happy to see her friend falling in love. She remembered back to the time when she and Steve had started dating and spending more time together. It was like a dream. She still felt like she was living in a dream. At a time when she felt like she'd be alone forever, Steve had entered her life, adorable, funny, and strong.

When she met Steve, Kate's faith had been very new, but God had used him to help her grow deeper in her faith. To search out God's love for her. Lydia was the first to help her recognize God's love, but Steve helped her see how deep that love really was. He showed her every day what real love was. And now she'd have the privilege to be able to spend the rest of her life with him.

Sometimes she could barely grasp the concept. She'd glance down at her hand and see the sparkling ring he'd given her, and her breath would catch at the reality of it all. Now, to see her friend walking a similar journey of love, life felt perfect and complete. Kate uttered a silent prayer as they walked in silence. *Father, thank you so much for your great love. Thank you for the reminders you give us every day of how deeply you love us.*

"Would you like to stop by after your lunch and get ready with me?" Lydia broke the silence as they stopped at their cars.

"That sounds perfect!"

"You'll help me stay calm." Lydia laughed softly.

Kate loved how their friendship balanced them both out. Lydia was one of the dearest friends in the world to her. "I have a feeling there will be absolutely nothing to worry about. This year will be the best yet." Kate winked at her friend.

She had said something similar every previous year, but she had a feeling about this year. Everything about this year felt different. Lydia was falling in love, even if Jordan might take a job in another country. Kate was engaged and planning a wedding to the man she loved with her whole heart. And even Lydia's dad was close to retirement and here on leave for the holidays. What could possibly make this season any better?

Chapter Thirty

Steve and Trevor had removed the barrier blocking the amphitheater. Almost immediately, tourists and locals began to gather to take a closer look at the sets and decorations, all based on the *12 Days of Christmas*. They marveled at everything they saw. Children pointed to various ornaments and glittering objects while whispering to their parents.

The whole amphitheater had been transformed into a magical, Christmas wonderland. Closer to the performance time, Peter led the musicians through some classic Christmas songs as everyone found their seats. Meanwhile, Lydia was helping Kate with getting pictures taken and preparing the dancers at the studio. Lydia checked her watch. Only thirty minutes until the performance! Her heart felt like it would escape through the boning of her dress. She took a deep breath to try and calm herself.

"Kate, it's time to go!" Lydia called down the hall of the studio.

Kate's voice came from all the way in the back. "I'll gather everyone, you go."

Lydia grabbed her coat. *Stay calm. Stay calm.* She tried to remind herself to breathe. Lydia closed her eyes and took a deep, calming breath as she started her car and headed for the amphitheater. "Here we go!" Lydia said aloud, a smile growing on her face.

~

Jordan had spotted her immediately and he felt like he couldn't catch his breath. How could he miss her? How did everyone in their seats not turn to see her? Lydia was an absolute vision.

There she was, the woman of his dreams. He couldn't tear his eyes away from her. Lydia was the woman who had shared her greatest fear with him, the woman who had trusted him and joked with him and smiled at him in that special way of hers. The woman who had undeniably stolen his heart in a way that he felt he could only breathe correctly with her right by his side. He loved her. Loved her more than he ever thought was possible.

Seeing her standing there in that gorgeous evergreen dress, so confident and calm, he felt blessed beyond measure that she loved him back. As he watched her greet people, slowly making her way down the steps toward where he was standing, Jordan smiled to himself. *Thank you, Lord, for bringing Lydia into my life. And thank you for bringing me to Maple Ridge.*

Her eyes met his for a brief, heavenly moment and she smiled at him in a way that made his insides melt. His mouth went dry and suddenly he didn't feel the bite of the crisp, winter air anymore. Jordan drew an unsteady breath to calm himself.

"What a night, huh?" Steve came up and clapped Jordan on the shoulder, only barely dragging his attention away from Lydia.

Jordan cleared his throat and swallowed. "Yeah, beautiful." He couldn't seem to say much more. Steve winked at him and chuckled.

"You and I will have to work extra hard at focusing on the performance tonight and not the stunning dates we have with us." Jordan chuckled and rubbed the back of his neck to hide the flush that had most assuredly crept into his neck and cheeks. Steve looked past him and smiled even brighter. "I'll catch up with you later." Jordan looked to see that Kate had shown up and was wearing a beautiful, sparkly red dress. Already, Steve was bounding up the steps toward her. Yes, they'd both have trouble focusing all right.

A light touch settled on his arm, his heart beating so hard he thought for sure everyone could hear it too. Jordan turned and there were those beautiful green eyes, looking up at him. He felt he would melt into a puddle at her feet. Lydia blushed under his gaze but didn't look away. The pink of her cheeks made her eyes look even greener.

"You look incredible." He managed to force himself to say but it was barely above a whisper.

Her eyelashes fluttered to her cheeks in a moment of shyness before her eyes were locked on his again. "Thank you." Her voice was quiet as they shared the moment, just the two of them, everything else fading into the background.

"Lydia!" A voice called, probably her mom's, he couldn't tell, but Lydia immediately broke eye contact to find whoever it was that had called her. He found himself missing the connection they'd shared.

Lydia smiled and waved, but before she left him, she took his hand, slipping her fingers between his. "Let's go find a seat."

It had been her mom who'd called and as they approached, he could see that Lydia's parents had saved seats for them.

"You look beautiful sweetheart!" Allison pulled Lydia into a hug and then her dad hugged her, looking her up and down and twirling her. "Most beautiful girl here." Her dad's smile was full of so much love and admiration.

Allison turned to Jordan, "Jordan, we've saved you the best seats in the whole place." He nodded, hoping his smile was enough of a response as words seemed to fail him as long as Lydia's hand was on his arm.

As he took his seat, Lydia waved at the three of them, casting a lingering glance in his direction as she headed for Steve, who'd returned to the sound system. After her introduction on stage, she'd sit next to Jordan. He couldn't wait to have her back, snuggling into him for warmth.

~

Lydia brushed a hand down her stomach, smoothing her dress and trying to calm the butterflies fighting in her stomach. The thought of Jordan's gaze as she came down the steps of the amphitheater still warmed her from the inside out. The look in his eyes the moment he saw her was a moment she'd remember forever. It was like nobody else existed in the world but them. She loved him. Truly loved him, with her whole heart. All the nervousness she was feeling about going on stage and having Mr. Fairfax in the audience couldn't dim the smile on her face.

"You're up!" Steve handed her the wireless microphone. "Knock 'em dead! Obviously not really, but you know." He made a face and Lydia giggled. She walked up to the stage, her long skirt swishing and sparkling in the spotlight. The music went silent, and a hush came over the audience. *Breathe.*

"I want to welcome you all to Maple Ridge's fourth annual *Magical Holiday Celebration!*" She paused as light applause made its way through the amphitheater. "Thank you so much for being here and taking the time to be a part of one of our favorite Christmas traditions that celebrates the arts. If this is your first time here, we are so excited to welcome you to the Maple Ridge family. Be sure to stay for the Christmas Eve party tomorrow night for delicious food, dancing, and a guest appearance by Santa himself. Before we get started, I just wanted to quickly thank everyone who was involved in making this performance a reality, including our generous vendors and patrons. Without you, we wouldn't be able to get this event off the ground. Now without further ado, it is my great honor to present to you the *12 Days of Christmas.*"

The spotlight on her immediately went dark as loud applause erupted. Lydia carefully found her seat next to Jordan, trying not to bump into anyone or anything on her way. A quiet shuffling on the stage told her that the dancers had taken their places. Jordan reached for her hand and laced his fingers between hers. This was it! The night they had all been waiting for was finally here!

Chapter Thirty-One

Lydia held her breath, her heart pounding as Peter tapped his music stand. As the music filled the air, Jordan gave her hand a reassuring squeeze and her breathing calmed. She glanced over at Mr. Fairfax, who had taken a seat toward the front on the opposite side of the theater.

"He'll love it." Jordan whispered. Somehow, he knew exactly what she needed to hear at that moment. She took a deep breath for the millionth time that evening and forced herself to relax.

"On the first day of Christmas, my true love gave to me..." The singers began their chorus. Fairy lights flickered on the pear tree and a spotlight shone on the partridge in her perch. Her gold, feathery costume glittered in the light as she delicately wrapped her legs around the hoop and hung in arabesque. Her dance was simple but absolutely elegant, just like a bird.

The next verse welcomed the second gift, as lights shone from the base of the set for the two calling birds. The pas de deux that Lydia and June had argued over so often came to life. Suspended silks allowed them to "fly" through the air, their feathered costumes floating as they spun and performed intricate lifts.

The French hens made the audience laugh at their quirky pas de trois, and June stole the show for sure. Lydia could tell she was having fun with her role. She had been hesitant at first, knowing that the French hens would be more comedic than delicate, but June had adapted beautifully. Lydia was so proud of her.

An upbeat jazz began to play as the calling birds performed in a cage adorned with purple flowers. As the music fluctuated to represent each gift uniquely, Lydia could hear the audience "ooh" and "aah" around her.

She glanced over at Mr. Fairfax and noticed a small smile on his face, eyes glued to the stage. She let out a breath she'd clearly been holding and turned her eyes back to the stage just in time for the grand introduction of the five golden rings. A brief applause broke out as the glittery ring box slowly opened to reveal five dancers in golden flapper costumes performing the Charleston.

"On the sixth day of Christmas, my true love gave to me..." Six beautiful dancers in black and white tutus danced in a makeshift nest, next were seven "swans" floating gracefully around a set decorated as a pond in a snow globe. The "water" glittered as the light hit it. Steve had rigged a small fan that would lightly blow their costumes while they danced as well as stir up some small pieces of fake snow to add to the snow globe effect. It was perfect!

One of Lydia's favorite sets was the one for the eight maids a milking. Trevor had made a cow that the dancers would perform a lively folk dance around. She heard occasional giggles from some of the children, making her giggle herself. The dancer's milkmaid outfits fit perfectly with the folk dance, and they even carried small buckets in their hands.

As the singers began the next line in the chorus, a spotlight shone on a brightly colored music box. It opened to reveal nine dancers dressed as dolls, their faces painted and their costumes just as colorful as the box they'd just emerged from. The audience clapped in time as the dancers began a Viennese polka.

The tenth day of Christmas was even livelier, with many leaps high in the air and some Scottish-style dancing. Finally, the last two gifts in the song brought more colorfully designed toy boxes in which were elegantly clothed toy soldiers with their drums and pipes.

Children pointed eagerly at the soldiers as they tapped to the beat of the music. Everyone went silent as all the lights came up at once and the music reached a crescendo and the dancers began their finale. Each group performed a condensed rendition of their previous choreography.

When the music finally hit its final note and the dancers struck their poses, the audience exploded into enthusiastic applause. Hoots and whistles were heard from every corner of the amphitheater, as everyone stood as one. Lydia wiped away a few stray tears and glanced over at Kate doing the same.

As the dancers, musicians, and singers took their bows, Lydia once again took the stage to close out the evening. The audience regained composure and quieted down, as Lydia accepted the microphone from Steve. He gave her two thumbs up as he backed away.

"Thank you again for coming out tonight! I hope you were thoroughly entertained this evening by our performance," more applause and whistles sounded, "We hope that you will choose to join us again next year as we continue this tradition. Have a wonderful Christmas!" More applause as Lydia exited the stage and ran to her family. Her dad scooped her up into a tight hug.

"That was even more beautiful than I could have ever imagined! I'm glad you didn't give me any spoilers." Lydia laughed as he placed her feet back on the ground.

"That was incredible!" Lydia turned to see Sarah standing beside Jordan.

"Sarah! You made it!" Lydia pulled her into a hug.

"I'm glad I did! You are an amazing choreographer, Lydia. Now I see why Jordan was so enamored by you. You're truly, very talented."

Lydia laughed, "thank you."

"Well, was I right, or was I right? That was the perfect theme." Kate joined them and everyone laughed together, joy filling the air around them. Lydia hugged her friend.

"You were totally right. Genius."

"Thank you! Now how to top it for next year?" Kate showed mock concern and made a show of scratching her head.

"The pressure's on now!" Lydia laughed at Kate.

Once all the congratulations and hugs were given and photos were taken, Lydia noticed that Mr. Fairfax was standing by the stage, patiently waiting his turn to speak with her. She excused herself and walked over to him with a huge smile on her face.

"Lydia." He greeted her. "You did a marvelous job! I was captivated from beginning to end. You know, I'm very impressed with what you have accomplished in your small town. I was surprised when I heard about how popular your annual performance was. Now I see why people love it so much."

"Thank you so much, Mr. Fairfax. I'm so glad you enjoyed it."

"Anthony, please." His smile gave her the feeling he had more to tell her. "You'll have to start calling me by my first name if we're going to work together this spring. I look forward to all the wonderful ways you can add to our company. That is, if you accept the offer."

"Of course! I'd like nothing better." Lydia couldn't believe her ears. She got it! She got the job!

"Wonderful!" He shook her hand, and they discussed the next steps that would make her position official once Christmas was over. Anthony checked his watch. "I have to leave early in the morning. I wish I could stay longer to enjoy the party, but my wife is waiting for me. Have a very merry Christmas Lydia."

"You, too!" She waved as he disappeared into the crowd still gathered, chatting animatedly about the performance. The moment felt surreal somehow. The adrenaline was still coursing through her veins, energizing her. How could they ever top this next year?

~

The feeling was euphoric. Dancing again and being a part of a performance this big was like putting a piece of her life back in place. June's heart raced with adrenaline and the thrill of performing, as she took her last bow. Going back to normal life again seemed impossible after a night like this.

Suddenly, June was very aware that she desperately wanted to be a part of the Boston Ballet company again. Even if she had to take a scholarship to their school and start from the ground up. She *had* to dance. The moment she was able to separate herself from the adoring public, June found Mr. Fairfax. She had to speak to him before he left.

"Mr. Fairfax!" June called to him as he slowly headed toward the back of the amphitheater. He didn't hear her. She pushed her way through the crowd and called again. Finally, he turned and smiled at her.

"June. You did a beautiful job."

"Thank you." She tried to catch her breath. The rush of emotions made it hard to breathe properly. "I wanted to discuss something with you."

His eyebrow quirked but the smile never faded. "Okay, I'm all ears."

June took a deep breath and swallowed. "I know that you wanted me to let you know when I met with a doctor to check the progress of my injury, but I couldn't get an appointment scheduled until after the new year. I also know that you'll be making your final selections on scholarship recipients before that time." June breathed deep again to calm her racing pulse. "Sir, I need to dance. I love it. Even if that means taking a scholarship and starting from scratch again or never being promoted within the company. I have to dance again."

Mr. Fairfax listened with interest, his face not revealing his thoughts. After a few moments of silence, he rubbed his chin and his smile widened. "June, I never intended on presenting you with a scholarship." He paused and she felt her heart sink. Then he laughed as though her disappointment was the funniest thing. "My dear, I was going to invite you to return to the company. Your performance tonight confirmed that decision."

June's eyes widened in surprise. She couldn't believe what she'd just heard. "Really?"

"Yes." He still chuckled. "You are a very talented and dedicated dancer. It would be an honor to have you return to the company. But I would still like to know what the doctor says before we make any solid decisions." He grew more serious.

June felt as if she were floating on air. This was beyond anything she could have ever imagined. "Absolutely! I'll contact you as soon as I have more information."

"Wonderful! I hope for the best."

"Me too!" June turned, giddy with excitement. She had to tell Lydia. Then she remembered, she hadn't said goodbye. "Merry Christmas, Mr. Fairfax!"

He turned and chuckled again. "Merry Christmas, June."

She ran for Lydia. "Lydia!" She pushed through the crowd surrounding the dance teacher, congratulating her, and taking photos with her. No wonder. She was the star in that gorgeous dress! But June wasn't envious anymore. She was beginning to see Lydia as everyone else did now. Someone who cared deeply for others and wanted the best for everyone. "Lydia!" June called again and Lydia waved, a smile on her face.

Lydia gave her a hug. "June! You did an amazing job tonight!"

"Thank you." She still couldn't believe that her and Lydia were actually friends now. Well, beginning to be friends, but still. "I wanted to tell you before anyone else heard." She paused, catching her breath. "Mr. Fairfax wants me to return to the company."

"June! That's wonderful!" Lydia grabbed June's hands and bounced on her toes in her excitement.

June laughed and shrugged her shoulder. "Provided I can produce a doctor's note stating that I'm able to dance on pointe again."

Lydia's features softened into a calmer expression. "Well, I'll be praying, then."

Normally, Lydia's proclamations of faith would irritate June, but she was touched that she cared enough to pray for her. Tears threatened to fall, and June swallowed the lump forming in her throat. "Thank you."

"I got the job by the way. Mr. Fairfax gave me the assistant choreographer job. So, if you're coming to the company, we'll be there together!"

"That's amazing! Congratulations!"

She gave Lydia one more hug before running off to find her parents. She'd spotted them toward the middle during the performance. They looked so proud, and it made the tears she'd just swallowed form again. She'd never expected to admit that their choice to move to Maple Ridge might have been one of the best decisions they had ever made, but it was true.

Chapter Thirty-Two

The only two thoughts occupying Jordan's mind were – what type of gift he should get Lydia for Christmas and how he would tell her about when he'd have to leave, if he accepted the documentary job. Between getting ready for the performance and the chaos of cleanup afterward, he hadn't had time to discuss that last thought with her. Besides, he wanted to leave that until she had fully enjoyed her success.

As for the gift, he couldn't think of anything worthy of her. He wanted to give her something special and unique. Reluctantly, he decided to confide in Claire, his matchmaking, meddlesome cousin. He smiled to himself as he descended the stairs, finding Claire curled up on the couch, reading a book.

"Hey, you." He sat down next to her, as she closed her book and smiled at him.

"Hey." Her brow arched, and her smile became a smirk. "What's up?"

"I need your opinion on something."

Both brows went up then, a teasing playfulness in her eyes. "Oookaaay." She drew the word out and he chuckled softly. She knew him too well.

"I want to give Lydia a Christmas gift, but I'm not sure what. I was hoping you'd have some ideas."

An exasperated look replaced the playfulness, her smile fading into a disapproving frown. "It's Christmas Eve, Jordan. You're just thinking about this now?"

"I know. I've just been a little…busy."

Claire shook her head at him, squinting her eyes in disappointment. "Do you have any ideas?" Jordan winced and gave her a guilty look.

She whacked his shoulder and shook her head. "Jordan!" He blocked another assault, and finally she giggled at him.

"So, you'll help?" He smiled his most charming smile and gave her puppy eyes.

Claire laughed and launched herself at him, almost knocking him flat on the couch, clinging to him in a tight hug. He couldn't help but laugh at her. "Of course I'll help!"

"Yeah, well, let's not get too crazy about it, okay." He smiled, shaking his head in amusement.

She pulled back, her hands on his shoulders. "How could I not make a big deal of it? This is the first Christmas gift you'll be giving her as her true love. If you'd asked me twelve days ago, I'd have told you to do exactly what the song says." She shrugged her shoulders and Jordan rolled his eyes. Her expression sobered. Her sudden seriousness made him chuckle again. "Since we're working from scratch, I guess we have some work to do."

Claire rubbed her hands together ready to put her skills to use. Except that this time, Jordan encouraged her and approved of how she was going to utilize them.

~

Lydia hadn't gone to bed until late the previous night. No matter what she tried, she couldn't sleep. The thrill of the performance, and the idea that she'd be working at Boston Ballet in the spring, were two things she had to fully process before her mind could relax enough for sleep. Finally, however, sleep did come, and she awoke late the next morning.

With her work for the holiday event completed, Lydia chose to spend the day resting at home. Kate had decided, at the last minute, to come by and do some wedding planning. It was an odd request, but Lydia thought it would be a fun distraction from the sadness that it was all over.

"I almost can't believe it's over." Lydia was curled up under a blanket, fabric swatches laid out on her legs.

"I know. I'm glad I have wedding planning to do or else I'd not know what to do with my time." Kate laughed. "Oooh, what do you think of this one?" They were looking at bridesmaid's dresses and deciding on colors. She pointed to a beautiful, deep garnet dress in the catalogue she was flipping through.

"It's beautiful!" Kate had decided on a late summer, early autumn wedding using her favorite, deep reds and oranges in the color scheme. Lydia secretly thanked God that she looked good in both colors her friend chose. Not that it was her day, but Kate had picked out some really…interesting colors and styles, that initially made Lydia nervous. "Looking forward to the food tonight?"

Kate dropped the catalogue and closed her eyes. "I've been dreaming about it." They laughed together. "I'm definitely hiring Ian to do the food at the wedding."

"What's Steve doing today?"

Kate picked up a couple of the fabric swatches and suspiciously avoided Lydia's eyes. "He's…taking care of some stuff before the party. We're meeting up there."

Lydia's brows came together in confusion. "What stuff?"

"Christmas stuff. You know."

"Hmmm." Kate still hadn't met her eyes, but a smile played on her lips. Clearly Steve was up to something. "Okay. Well, speaking of Christmas stuff, are all your gifts wrapped?"

"They are! I stayed up late last night getting it all done. Trevor even dropped off the record player this morning at my place since we'll be spending Christmas over at Steve's. You?"

"Yup."

Kate nodded. A flutter of excitement stirred in Lydia's stomach. Clearly her friends were planning something. Something that Lydia wasn't allowed to know about. Maybe that something involved Jordan, considering he'd made an excuse this morning as well. Lydia bit her lip to hold in the thrill she felt.

With only a few minutes until the party was open to the public, Ian and his crew were working hard to finish setting up the food and drinks. Ian had created one hundred of each of the twelve hors d'oeuvres and desserts. It was a huge undertaking, but he had accomplished it with time to spare. He was determined to serve the best food the visitors of Maple Ridge had ever tasted.

There were twinkling lights and garland hanging on the walls and counter. The tables were decorated with white tablecloths and some of the fresh flowers that had been used on the sets. Ian's food looked beautiful among all the other decorations.

Lydia and Kate arrived early to see if he needed any extra help. "Wow! Ian, the place looks amazing!" Lydia looked around in awe.

Ian brushed his hands on his apron and joined the ladies. "Thanks. It was a lot of work making this much food, but it turned out pretty well. Let's just hope that these people are hungry, otherwise, I'll have lots of leftovers to store." He chuckled to himself.

"If they aren't, I'll eat the leftovers." Kate laughed.

Lydia checked the time. "Well, it looks like people will start arriving in about fifteen minutes. Trevor should be here in his Santa suit around five thirty."

"I guess I should clean up and get ready." Ian eased his apron over his head and disappeared into his industrial kitchen.

"I'll help clean up." Kate helped carry the empty food storage containers to the kitchen with the rest of his crew.

Jordan walked through the door just as Lydia started removing her coat. Their eyes met and he smiled, as he walked up to help her out. "Where have you been all day?" Lydia questioned.

"Oh…just hanging around town." Jordan hung up her coat and returned to her, placing his hands at her waist, and pulling her closer.

"You and Kate are being very secretive today." She wrapped her arms around his neck and smiled flirtatiously. Jordan was smiling mischievously. "What's going on with you two?"

"You'll know soon." He said with an amused sparkle in his eye. He touched his nose to hers. "I can't spoil your present." Lydia wanted him to kiss her with every breath. He was so close she could feel his breath on her cheek. Guests were beginning to arrive, Christmas music playing in the background. A kiss right now wouldn't be ideal, especially in the middle of the room. Instead, Jordan smiled again and kissed her nose before backing away to a safe distance.

As the party progressed, Ian's food slowly disappeared. He had placed a few of his regular crew members at the table to ensure that each guest received only one of each item. Everyone raved about the food, which made Ian smile proudly at each satisfied guest that left the table. He was happy that his hard work had paid off.

Lydia had hoped that she and Jordan would have some time together, but there were so many people who wanted to talk with her, congratulate her, and ask her all about her plans for next year. Jordan had wandered off to give her time, flashing his adorable, dimpled smile her way. Even though it was nice to chat with the guests, she missed Jordan's presence.

"Ho-ho-ho!" Trevor burst through the front door in his Santa suit, carrying a large sack of gifts. Some of the local businesses had donated small gifts for the event. Children of all ages cheered and ran up to him, eager to see what he had in his sack. "I heard that there were many good little girls and boys here celebrating Christmas together. Would you like to see what I have in my bag?"

The children all cheered in the affirmative. His voice was lower than usual, but the rosy cheeks and sparkling eyes were all Trevor's. Lydia laughed, watching him take on the character. This was his first year being Santa, and he was doing a fantastic job.

"Well, well, well. Let's see then." Trevor made a show of digging through his sack of gifts and pulled out small packages one-by-one and began handing them out. Once all the children had a special gift from Santa, he posed for pictures. Lydia watched as each child excitedly told Santa their secret Christmas wishes.

She looked around for Jordan. The people wanting to talk with her had gone to their separate tables when Trevor had entered. Now all she wanted was to spend the last couple hours of the party with Jordan.

"Santa has a little surprise for you as well." Lydia turned to see Trevor holding out a present for her.

"What's this?"

"Kate mentioned that you might want to give it to Jordan tonight." Trevor winked at her and smirked.

Lydia hugged him and took the present. "Thanks Trevor."

Trevor held a finger to his lips. "Shhhh. I'm Santa, remember." He winked again and laughed in another round of ho-ho-hos before turning to go change in the back room, waving goodbye to all the children. Lydia giggled as she watched him go.

Lydia noticed that Jordan was grabbing his coat, and she immediately thought he was leaving without saying goodbye. "Where are you going?" He held her coat out to her.

"*We* are going to see your gift." He helped her on with her coat.

"Really?" Her tone was flirty to match his.

"Mmhmm." He noticed the gift she was holding. "What's this?"

She quickly tucked in behind her back and gave an innocent look. "Nothing."

He looked as if he was prepared to wrap his arms around her to grab the package. The thought seemed to cross his mind, a small smile on his face. Instead, he slipped his hand around her waist and leaned in close. "I guess we both have surprises." He whispered. His breath on her cheek made her shiver.

"I guess so."

Jordan led her outside, the cold air hitting her face so hard it made her teeth chatter, her breath lingering in the air, like a thick fog. He must have noticed, because he wrapped his arm around her as they walked to his car, his warmth seeping through her coat.

"We have to drive there?"

"Yes. But I'll have you back at the party before it's over." He opened the passenger door for her and handed her in.

This must be quite the big surprise.

Chapter Thirty-Three

Claire had been brilliant! Her idea of the perfect gift for Lydia was more than he could have ever imagined himself. She had suggested giving Lydia an experience rather than a tangible item. It was an excellent idea. More than that, it was the perfect way to share his final decisions about his future. As Lydia sat there beside him, silently waiting for what lay ahead, Jordan could barely catch his breath out of excitement. He pulled up in the parking lot and handed her out, watching the confusion on her face.

"Where are we going?" Lydia's brow was furrowed.

He reached out and laced his fingers in hers, leading her toward the amphitheater. "You'll see." As they walked closer, Lydia looked over at him even more confused. "Close your eyes." She crinkled her nose, and giggled as she closed her eyes. In a matter of seconds, the amphitheater was lit up with so many twinkling lights; he was convinced everyone back at Ian's place could see them. "Okay…open them."

Lydia gasped, taking in the view. Jordan had brought some of his favorite pieces from the new collection he'd been secretly working on the past two months. These were pieces he hadn't even told Sarah about. They were hung in various places around the sets that had been left on stage until after the holidays. Each print and painting were rimmed with fairy lights to highlight the details. There were photos and paintings of Lydia smiling, dancing, teaching, and even her walking by the water in Boston. Most were from their photo shoot in the park, but some were from moments he'd captured in his heart and didn't want to forget.

But his favorite painting, the impressionist one of her Jordan had shown her at the showcase, was right in the center. She slowly made her way around the stage, looking at each piece with a smile on her face. This time, Jordan didn't feel nervous or shy as she looked at them. When she finally settled in front of his showcase piece, Jordan joined her.

"That one is my favorite."

"Mine too." She didn't take her eyes off the painting.

"These will be going in my future studio. The studio I hope to one day open here in Maple Ridge." She turned to him, her eyes glistening. "This one, I wanted to keep as the star of my new collection." He gently rubbed his hands up and down her arms. "It reminds me of the fact that you are my new inspiration." A single tear slipped down her cheek as she looked at him. "Merry Christmas." Jordan brought his forehead to rest on hers and whispered the words.

"I can't believe you did all this." Lydia laughed, sniffing.

"You said you wanted new prints for your studio, so I figured I'd give you first pick." He winked.

He moved back and looked at her with all the love he felt. "I wanted to show you how much you inspire me. How much you inspire others. You are the most beautiful woman I've ever known. Not just because of your outward beauty. But because of the inner beauty that can only come from God." Another couple tears fell on her cheeks, and he reached up to gently wipe them away with his thumb. "I love you, Lydia." Her face lit up with the most radiant joy he'd ever seen in her.

"I love you, too."

Jordan drew her closer and her arms wrapped around his waist. They stood there in silence, enjoying each other's company for a few moments. "Oh, I almost forgot." Jordan took his phone out of his pocket and tapped on a playlist he'd made earlier that day. Romantic Christmas music played from a small speaker. Claire had helped him with the choices. He held his hand out to her, "Dance with me?" Her hand slipped into his, and he pulled her into a relaxed, waltz stance, swaying side to side.

"Hmmm. You're a pretty good dancer. Who taught you?" Lydia smirked at him. She'd never looked more beautiful.

Jordan twirled her away from him and pulled her back in, holding her close. Her head came to rest on his shoulder. "I had an incredibly beautiful and amazing local dance teacher show me how it's done."

"She must be pretty special."

"Oh yeah. I'm pretty sure she's the love of my life." Lydia looked up at him, her eyes full of love and hope. Jordan cupped her cheek, leaning down to touch his lips to hers. He kissed her with all the love in him. When he reluctantly pulled back, they were both out of breath. They stood, their foreheads resting together, eyes closed simply drinking in the moment. She was perfect. This moment was perfect. Everything he ever dreamed.

Finally, after years of wondering if he'd ever find a real, lasting love, he had found Lydia. God had brought him to Maple Ridge, that was a certainty. But more than that, God had given him purpose again. In Lydia, Jordan saw the depth of love and kindness that could only come from the Father above, and it made him yearn to be a man worthy of her love.

The past month, as he'd worked to figure out his true feelings for her and the direction God was calling him in, Jordan had prayed like never before that God would help him to be the man he was meant to be. To give him a passion for life and a place to belong. Jordan knew that God had a plan for him and Lydia. With God, all things were possible, and that was something Jordan believed now more than ever before. However, the happiness he felt was shadowed by the fact that he hadn't told her about when he was to leave.

"Oh!" Lydia shattered his thoughts and brought him back to reality. "I completely forgot about your gift. Although all this kind of puts my gift for you to shame." Before he could protest that anything she gave him would be better than any other gift he'd ever received, she turned and picked up the package she'd been holding earlier. "Merry Christmas." Her green eyes under all the lights made his heart flutter, and he wanted to kiss her again.

"This is amazing!"

"I found it at my favorite store in town. I figured yours looked a little worn and this is real leather." He turned the camera bag over and looked into each pocket. It was an amazing and thoughtful gift. "Perfect for your new job." Lydia's smile held no fears of him leaving, only enthusiastic support and confidence.

"About the job." He had to tell her. Her questioning look made him feel guilty. *Out with it Jordan! Just tell her!* "If I accept the job, I'll have to leave right after New Years."

Lydia's smile faltered and her brows came together slightly. "That soon?"

"Unfortunately, yes."

She was biting her lip, clearly thinking things over. She looked so unbelievably adorable when deep in thought. "You should do it."

"What? You really want me to take it?"

"I really think you should. I don't know. I feel like you're already leaning toward accepting it, and I feel a peacefulness about it. We can make things work. You can open your studio when you get back. I'll be here." She smiled again.

Her confidence sparked his own. How they'd make their relationship work for that long, he had no idea. But hadn't his thoughts from a few moments ago been about how God could make anything possible? She knew him about as well as Claire did. It was like she could read his heart. He *had* felt like accepting the job was right for him. Now he just wondered why on earth he had waited so long to tell her.

"Okay. I'll call the director and tell him I'm on board."

"Good." Lydia's forced seriousness made him laugh. Her hands came to wrap around his neck. "Thank you for this. It's the best gift I've ever received."

"The first one of Christmas." Jordan winked at her, and they both dissolved into a fit of giggles.

Chapter Thirty-Four

Hand-in-hand, Jordan and Lydia returned to the party, practically glowing. Kate and Steve immediately spotted them and waved them over to where they were seated. Lydia couldn't believe how happy she was. Jordan had given her the best gift she could possibly have asked for. The gift of his love. In all the years of praying for her future husband, Lydia couldn't have imagined a more perfect way to meet and fall in love than the story that had unfolded over the past few months. Even though they had a long road to haul, she knew God had brought them together for a reason. She could see a future with Jordan.

"So, how'd it go?" Kate asked, her eyebrow raised and a smirk on her face.

Jordan laughed. "It was perfect. Thanks for the help, guys."

Steve clapped Jordan on the shoulder, "Anything for our friends."

"You guys are terrible liars." Lydia flashed a teasing smile. "But I didn't expect that big of a surprise."

Claire ran up and wrapped Jordan in a hug from behind. "How was it?" She came around to sit next to him.

"It was perfect, Claire. Thanks for the idea."

"I guess it's time to hang up my matchmaking career." Claire sighed in feigned disappointment.

"I didn't realize you'd been a part of it too." Lydia chimed in.

"It was more than a pleasure, Lydia." Claire beamed at her. "Jordan needed some serious help." She laughed as Jordan shoved her shoulder playfully. "I've been wanting to help bring you two together since the beginning though. I guess this was my contribution. I can't take credit for introducing the two of you personally, but I *can* take credit for introducing Jordan to the idea of you."

Lydia shared a confused expression with Kate. "What do you mean?"

Claire laughed and Jordan groaned playfully. "You're never going to let me live this down, are you?"

"Probably not!" Claire laughed heartily. "I've set Jordan up on a few dates in the past, so when I mentioned that he should meet you, he put his walls up immediately." She flashed him a teasing smile and nudged him with her shoulder. "He basically told me to back off."

"I'm just glad I changed my mind about meeting Lydia." Jordan wrapped his arm around Lydia's shoulders.

"You guysss!" Kate gushed.

Party guests danced around them, filling the room with holiday cheer. Jordan had told them about his plan to accept the documentary job. It was a scary decision for the both of them to make, but their friends were supportive and ready to help whenever they could. Lydia couldn't feel prouder of him following his dreams. Sure, she'd have a hard time saying goodbye to him for such a long time, but he was truly passionate about this project, and she wanted him to follow the path God had laid for him. They'd cross the bridge of long-distance and visiting times when they came to it. For now, they would enjoy the time they had together for Christmas and New Year.

"Well, I see a lot of double dates in our future." Kate winked at Jordan. "When you get back, of course."

"That sounds like a great plan." Jordan smiled.

"Oooo…I love this song!" Kate clasped her hands together.

"Milady." Steve hopped up and offered his hand. Together they joined the other couples in the middle of the room, swaying to the music.

Kyle even came up and snatched Claire away to join the other dancing couples.

"Shall we?" Jordan held his hand out to Lydia. They joined their friends on the floor. It felt wonderful to be held in his arms. Lydia couldn't imagine life without him. *Thank you, God, for an amazing Christmas.* Lydia smiled as she rested her head on Jordan's shoulder. She could have stayed that way forever. Gently swaying with the music, feeling like nothing in the world could destroy what they had in each other. Then Jordan moved back and, holding her hand in his, led her away from the crowd.

"What are we doing?" Lydia asked.

"This night has been so perfect already. But it just wouldn't feel like Christmas if we didn't follow in this tradition." He looked up and she followed his gaze to the ball of mistletoe hanging just above them.

Lydia laughed and looked straight into his beautiful blue eyes. Before she could say a word, he took her breath away with a kiss that could have melted the snow that had begun to fall outside. And as the party continued to wind down around them, the two of them only thought of how this year had been the best that they could remember. Life had many adventures in store for them. Her in Boston and him all the way on the other side of the world. They had people to inspire and their faith to grow. It was exciting to see where they were headed. They were each ready to chase their dreams with God, and each other, by their sides. With all that, nothing else in the world seemed to matter, except the love they shared.

Amanda is an NCSF-certified Personal Fitness Trainer & Health Specialist, choreographer, dance teacher, and owner of La Belle Vie Dance Company. Her love of dance has made itself apparent in her writing as she writes both informational health & fitness books as well as novels. She loves writing about topics that reflect her own life as well as inspire her readers to cherish family, friendships, and love. Most of all, Amanda's faith is the most important part of who she is and her greatest goal in life is to spread the Word and love of God to those who are searching. You can find out more about her other works as well as any upcoming author events at www.myhyggetime.com.